Another Life

Owen W Knight

Burton Mayers Books

Copyright © 2020 Owen W Knight

Content compiled for publication by Richard Mayers of Burton
Mayers Books. Cover artwork designed by Richard Mayers,
based on photographs by Owen W Knight.

First published by Burton Mayers Books 2020.

A CIP catalogue record for this book is available from the
British Library

10 9 8 7 6 5 4 3

ISBN-13: 978-1916212626

Typeset in Garamond

www.BurtonMayersBooks.com

For My Children

Also By Owen W Knight:

The Invisible College Trilogy

Book 1 *They Do Things Differently Here*

Book 2 *Dust And Shadows*

Book 3 *A Perilous Journey*

ANOTHER LIFE

CONTENTS

I dream of you, to wake: would that I might
Dream of you and not wake but slumber on;
Nor find with dreams the dear companion gone,
As, Summer ended, Summer birds take flight.
In happy dreams I hold you full in night.
I blush again who waking look so wan;
Brighter than sunniest day that ever shone,
In happy dreams your smile makes day of night.
Thus only in a dream we are at one.

(from *Monna Innominata: A Sonnet of Sonnets*, Christina
Rossetti)

Part 1: Two Mysteries

I HAVE DREAMS

I know they are dreams, yet I see nothing outside of them. I live in a black hole with no contact with the world. This must be like what it would be to wake up blind: to open your eyes and expect to see something. You see nothing; everything is inside your head. You have forgotten what to do to see and try to remember what it is you are not doing.

There is a light above me that changes. I can see it with my eyes closed. Is this part of the dream? It's like looking out from a spaceship to the surface of a planet whose gaseous clouds swirl slowly, continuously; marbling the surface below.

I see a woman, a beautiful woman. She bears a resemblance to my daughter, but she is not my daughter. She is beckoning. I want to follow her. I know that it will be a one-way journey.

I am afraid.

Ever since I can remember, I have been blessed (or cursed) with the ability to imagine objects and places that I have never seen or visited. When conditions are ideal (I shall explain this later) a comprehensive image will lodge itself at the centre of my brain's consciousness: three-dimensional, in colour and alive.

In times of stress, my gift has provided me with solace and distraction from a hostile world. A world lacking in empathy, where everything is going in the wrong direction, working against me, making progress impossible. I am able to immerse myself in a kingdom of my own creation and insulate myself from harm, no more so than at night, when the terrors of what we believe to be real life threaten to overwhelm.

I reason that if I can create a landscape in my own mind then it must exist, as an entity in itself or as an amalgam of places I've been to, or am aware of from books, magazines, or other sources. When I look through the photographs I took in my teens and early twenties, there are a notable number - not many, but more than a few - recording a solitary tree in a field, taken from the mid-distance. Trees of various species, always deciduous, in many locations and in all seasons. Something stable in the landscape, enduring, changing, weathering all around.

In better times my gift has endowed me with the means to create and provide comfort and inspiration to strangers. It has allowed me to envision alternative ways of looking at their worlds and to share my imagined viewpoint with them. There can be no greater pleasure in life than to help improve the lives of others in ways they will consider to be of their own making.

Happiness is a condition that eludes me and I don't know why. When I look at the lives of people who believe they are happy, or working towards creating conditions of happiness, I feel the sadness of living an illusion, that contentment is a mirage beyond my reach, if not theirs. I want other people to enjoy happiness, more so than for myself, yet I fear I am projecting my view of the world onto others and draining the joy from their existence.

*

I am drifting. I see a village of mellow stone cottages, nestling in a crucible of undulating farmland, encircled by wooded hills, away from the gaze and trajectory of those journeying past the timeless landscape. I am floating through the streets and lanes of this hidden community. It's as though I am drifting in a calm, flowing river, steered by the current, surrounded by silence, in a place unknown; a lost domain. Did I dream it, or was I there? The knowledge that I dreamed it and could see and describe it in detail, in colour, and to remember the smells and sounds, must surely confirm its existence.

I have to go back, to return to where it all began.

My name is Oliver Merryweather…

TO THE VILLAGE

On a spring morning, many years ago, I set off from my home in Essex to visit a friend who had moved to a village close to Stratford-upon-Avon. I had left before dawn and had chosen not to take the direct route. My plan was to visit some Cotswold villages to take photographs. Even as a child, I had a fondness for vernacular architecture, although of course, I would not have described it as such at the time.

I had another mission: to buy some books. I intended to visit a small independent printing company, the Walnut Tree Press. It was a new venture, founded two years earlier, and had quickly built a reputation for its small print runs of hand-printed books and its poetry imprint. Many of the books on their list were illustrated with engravings, by new and established artists, and had already become collectors' editions. Some people bought them for their investment potential. I admired them both for their content and as well-crafted artefacts, as objects of beauty that combined interest and quality with appealing design.

I had spent hours browsing their catalogue. It was difficult to make a final decision on which to buy. Once I had produced a shortlist, I could have placed an order, either by post or telephone (this was in the days before the Internet). I was hesitant to do so; I wanted to hold them in my hands and to turn the pages, feeling the quality of the paper, to touch and smell them before confirming my purchase. They were expensive, understandably, although would no doubt hold their value, in the unlikely event I should ever need to sell.

The press was located in a small village. I had not telephoned to ask whether it would be open. Such was my indecision as to whether to spend what was to me at that time a large sum of money on inessential items. By leaving it to chance, the acquisition, or otherwise, would be resolved by destiny. I was, after all, just passing through on my journey to another place.

The village was not as I thought it would be. The single main street was narrow, with half a dozen lanes leading from either side. There were no shops and, unusually for a village in those days, no inn. Many of the cottages were of a similar design. Some were empty and falling towards dereliction. I had the impression that they formed all or part of a collection of workers' cottages, from an estate that was in the process of being sold or dissolved, its owners' dynasty at an end.

I parked my car and began to look for the press, taking time to look discreetly through the windows of some of the houses. Through my inquisitiveness, I was able to confirm that many were unoccupied and had probably been so for some while. Even those houses that were lived in or, I should say, had furniture and curtains visible, showed no other signs of life. Perhaps the owners were still asleep. I had arrived at the village far too early. It was only eight o'clock.

There was no sign of the press on the main street. I did not have the full address, only the name of the village. I wandered down a side lane and back and then down another, admiring the lush, overgrown cottage gardens, evidently self-seeding and now battling against weeds. I stopped; my attention drawn to an open door to a small single-story thatched stone building that may once have been a barn.

I knocked at the half-open door. There was no response. I eased the door fully open and walked in quietly, so as not to startle or disturb anyone who might be inside. At the centre of the room stood a manual printing press. Against one wall, wide cabinets with many drawers, some open, housed sectioned trays of movable woodblock type, in old-fashioned faces. There were tables, with piles of books, posters and a selection of what appeared to be test prints, some smudged, torn or scribbled upon. There were watercolour drawings, brushes and water pots, and a variety of papers, inks and unidentifiable printers' tools, some looking more like instruments of medieval torture.

'Can I help you?'

I turned to look the smiling woman in the eye. She seemed in no way disturbed by an uninvited visitor in her workspace.

'No, no, thank you…I mean yes, you can, probably!'

She laughed. I felt embarrassed, despite my honest intentions.

'I've read about you… the press and its books. I wanted to see them for myself. I'm sorry, I should have telephoned in advance, or written.'

'It's not a problem. Feel free to look around and please do ask questions. Have you travelled far? Would you like a cup of tea?' My name's Miriam, by the way.'

'Oliver Merryweather. Delighted to meet you.'

Miriam filled the kettle from a sink in the corner of the room. She explained the process of book design and production, from conception to printing and demonstrated the smooth operation of the printing press. She talked about bookbinding and showed me some examples of her own books, including two that I was thinking of buying, and works by other writers and illustrators.

She described the engraving process and the tools employed. What strange names they had: spitsticker, scorper, graver, bullsticker… The vocabulary of the craft hinted at membership of a secret society, a cabal. She showed me the sharpening stone and emphasised the importance of maintaining the engraving tools in a constant state of immaculate readiness to work with the woods: boxwood and lemonwood, specimens of which lay on a leather sandbag which, she added, was used to support the material at the best angle of cut. I am sure she could have spoken for an hour or more on the characteristics of the weights, textures and other qualities of the papers that would bear the reverse image from the finished block.

By now the tea was cold and irrelevant. I was so fortunate to have arrived at the right time on the right day to meet an author and illustrator in person. She did not have copies for sale there, at the press. I would need to visit the farmhouse where the owner and his partner lived, just a few miles away, on the other side of the main road.

She gave me directions and handed me a copy of an engraving I had admired, on rough, handmade, deckle-edged paper. I asked her how much she wanted for it. She refused to take any money.

'I'd like you to take it as a souvenir of your visit, and in any case, it's imperfect and there is a tear at one edge.'

I thanked her for her kindness and for the time she had taken to describe her work and returned to my car. I followed her directions to the farmhouse, where the owners, John and Rose, and their dogs welcomed me. To describe it as a farmhouse does not do it justice. I was led into their great hall of a living room, which, they explained, dated back to medieval times. I would have loved to have been able to visit in winter when the enormous stone fireplace would have been lit.

I was curious as to how a young couple, in their thirties, came to be running a niche business in a rural area, with the good fortune to live in such a characterful home. They explained that they had both been successful in mainstream publishing and now wanted the freedom to follow their own passions and interests. They had bought the farmhouse at auction and, yes, it was in a sound structural condition, albeit in need of constant care and restoration. The roof was expected to last another five years, allowing them time to establish their new enterprise, an enviable coming together of business and pleasure.

More tea was offered, and accepted, before they showed me to a room with heavy oak tables piled with many copies of their publications. It was a joy to hold them and to stroke the covers and to smell the pages. They were so finely produced that I felt I should be wearing white gloves.

I was enjoying myself, although conscious of outstaying my welcome. I decided to buy copies of two of Miriam's books. I could come back another time to buy more. They wrapped the books in tissue paper and placed them in a paper carrier bag bearing the name of the press and its walnut tree logo.

As I was preparing to leave, I noticed a display cabinet in the corner of the room. It was the sort you would find in museums: table height, with four legs, a sloping glass top and a keyhole at the front. It was partially covered with a white sheet, presumably to protect the contents from the light.

'May I ask what's in here?'

'By all means,' said John, lifting the sheet. 'These are a few of our first editions. A copy of every one of the books we produced in our first year.'

Seven books were arranged in two rows. Three were poetry collections, two books of illustrated essays and a book of farmhouse recipes. While they all looked attractive and well designed, it was the title of the seventh, in the bottom right-hand corner that caught my attention: 'An Illustrated Account of the Old Religion, its Beliefs and Practices, by a Believer'.

'What an unusual title - how mysterious.'

'Indeed it is. There's a tale attached to that one,' said

John.

'Really? I'd love to hear it, but I've already taken too much of your time.'

'Don't worry. I'm in no hurry.'

'It sounds as though it's a reprint of an older work, seventeenth century, perhaps. The title sounds suggestive of the time of Matthew Hopkins, the Witchfinder General. I know he operated in a different part of the country, but there were others like him.'

'It's definitely modern,' said John. 'The "Old Religion" is a fairly modern term. Something invented about fifty or sixty years ago, in the nineteen-twenties or thirties, along with Wicca and the like.'

'New Age stuff, you mean. Constructing a quasi-religion based on scraps of pagan beliefs.'

'I wouldn't put it that way. There's quite a bit of interest in the subject around here. All a bit secret squirrel. It's not something they like to talk about though. They don't want people to know. It would attract the wrong sort - bring strangers here,' said John.

'And the authorities,' said Rose.

'So how did you come to produce it?'

John looked at Rose, raising his eyebrows.

'Go on. Tell him,' she said.

'We were approached by someone, out of the blue. He knocked on the door one day and claimed he had a wonderful idea for a book that would suit our press. We were still quite new then, trying to get the business on its feet. We believed we should be open to new concepts. He showed us his ideas and his drawings, which were indeed very seventeenth century in their style, although he claimed they were his own. As the title suggests, it describes a belief system, based on practices and rituals dating back to pre-history, as recounted by an adherent.'

'We assumed it was a hoax, something he'd invented. A complete work of fiction,' added Rose. 'He spoke very calmly, insisting that it was factual and a tradition handed down orally, for generations, centuries, in rural communities close to here. It's worth remembering that since time immemorial this has been border country, in the space between England and Wales. Right here, where we're standing, we're in the landscape occupied by the Celtic Dobunni tribe. The Dobunni, together with the Cornovii to the north, controlled all of the area adjacent to what was to become Wales, at the time of the Roman invasion of Britain.

'The Romans weren't very interested in Britannia Secunda, as they called Wales, but they wanted to maintain control over it and at the same time to spread Christianity. It's said that the Dobunni were also known as the "tribe of witches". A load of nonsense, or so you'd think, but you have to remember that, although there were frequent uprisings of the Celtic tribes against the Romans, on the whole it was better to co-exist, to go along with things, including religion. So you have a mixture of pagan beliefs, completely undocumented, and later conversion to Christianity overlapping. It was natural that elements of a merger, or assimilation, of some aspects of each other's religion would occur. It's like a little Bermuda Triangle here. Even apparently harmless images, such as the Green Man, which goes back to pagan times, were accepted by the Church. Indeed, the history of the Green Man can be traced back through Europe and as far back as Ancient Egypt. I could see where our visitor was coming from, with his book: - making a connection between local beliefs and the wider context.'

'He was very convincing, this writer,' said Rose. 'Our business had not been going all that long. We were hoping to break into the American collectors' market. We thought this would be a good starting point, what with their interest in British history and their own Salem witch trials. He was very secretive, though. I'm not convinced we ever knew his real name. He made us swear to keep the project secret. I thought this was just to add a little mystery to the process, to encourage us and make us feel special.'

'We were happy to go along with it,' said John. 'There's no point in telling everyone about a new venture until it's ready, in case someone tries to copy your idea and get there before you. We spent a long time with him: setting up the book, making minor changes and sounding out the Americans to sign up as many pre-orders as we could. You can imagine how much these books cost to produce and we didn't want to take too big a risk. We decided on an initial print run of five hundred, which was large for us at the time. As the publication date approached, we were beginning to feel more and more confident that we could have a success on our hands. We actually got as far as printing and binding the books!'

'So what happened?' I asked.

'We had an enquiry,' said Rose. 'Someone else contacted us and said he had an interesting proposition. He said he was a collector and that he wanted to meet us to discuss. Well, we thought Christmas had come! We invited him down here and he made us an incredible offer. He wanted to buy the complete run of the five hundred books.'

'We weren't sure at first,' said John. 'As I said, we saw this as our way in to the American market, with rich collectors who would buy other books and spread the word. We explained our position, which was that we wanted to get them out quickly to be able to gauge whether to go into another run. We asked him if he would be prepared to take fifty, or a hundred, with more to follow later. He was insistent on buying the whole lot, and then he spelled out what he wanted in detail. He would buy the complete set for four times what we were asking, on two conditions. Firstly, we were not to print any further copies, either then, or at any time in the future and, secondly, we were not to discuss the deal, or the content of the books, with anyone.'

'We had no choice,' said Rose. 'The money would give

us the opportunity to grow. There would be other books. The amazing thing was that he had brought the money with him. He counted out the cash from his briefcase. Just like in the films!'

'He must have been confident we'd agree,' said John. 'We had an idea that the book was likely to upset a few people and that we might even be asked to withdraw it from sale, but to have someone willing to buy the whole set was totally unforeseen.'

'But you held one back. You still have a copy, right here,' I said.

John and Rose looked at each other, unsure of what to say.

'It's a proof copy, produced before the full print run, said John. 'It doesn't count as part of the deal.'

I was tempted to ask John whether he thought it was right to retain a copy when the purchaser's clear intention was to withdraw them from circulation. I held back. There was nothing to gain from such a question and a lot to lose. And as yet they had not discussed the contents of the book with me.

'It sounds fascinating. The sort of thing I could be interested in buying.'

This wasn't entirely true. It being the single surviving proof, John and Rose would expect a premium price, possibly into thousands of pounds, especially if signed by the author or printers.

'I'm afraid that won't be possible,' said Rose. 'We've mislaid the key and, as I say, it's the only copy.'

With such a rarity in their possession, and the interest in suppressing it, I was surprised that it was not hidden in a safe or a bank vault.

'That's a shame. Is the author local?'

'He was. Dead now. At least we assume he is. He disappeared without trace just after the print run.' said John. 'We wrote to him, to offer his agreed royalties on the sale of the books - the inflated price, that is. It was quite a tidy sum, as you can imagine. We never received a reply.'

It was time to leave. I thanked them both for their hospitality, before resuming my journey, declining the offer of another cup of tea.

In those days we did not have Satnav and were reliant on paper maps and road signs. I located the farmhouse and memorised the general north-easterly direction of the route I intended to take.

I must have been driving for over half an hour when it occurred to me that I hadn't seen a sign to a significant town for several miles, only fingerposts pointing to villages whose names were unfamiliar; nor had I reached or crossed a main road. I had been following my instincts, thinking that I was travelling in the right direction. I now realised that I couldn't be sure, owing to the overcast sky and the strange light.

Rural villages across the country are generally between five and seven miles apart. They grew from hamlets at a time when farmers needed to be able to walk to market, and labourers to their work in the fields. An hour's walk, twice in a day, dictated the maximum distance between villages.

It took no more than a few minutes to arrive at Durncot. The name of the village conjured up images of trees. It did not disappoint. I parked the car and checked the map for the general area I must have reached. I could not find the name, either on the map or in the index.

It was still quite early, not yet ten o'clock. The village was belatedly coming to life on this new day, although there was a noticeable absence of cars and birdsong. I decided to take another break in my journey, to take a stroll and savour the atmosphere.

Durncot was a community built almost entirely of seventeenth and eighteenth-century stone cottages. Unusually, there appeared to be none of the expected nineteen-fifties bungalows and council houses (as we knew them in those days) spreading to the perimeter, nor were there modern housing estates eating into farmland or filling the gaps between. Towns and villages evolve over the centuries, the style of the buildings and their later extensions embossing a date-stamp on the landscape. Durncot's development appeared to have stopped two hundred years ago.

Several cottages were notable for their topiary, with yew trees and hedges fashioned into arches framing old wooden or iron garden gates, or the open porches, while other gardens featured layered geometric and animal shapes. In times when a car can travel between most parts of the country in a day, such homes seemed symbolic of a refuge from modern life. Within the porch of one such cottage, beside the front door, a solid wooden fruit crate (unlike the cardboard of today) contained a bowl of fresh eggs and a handwritten note inviting passers-by to help themselves in return for a donation of their choice. A handful of silver coins lay in the box.

I passed the village school, where two men were erecting a maypole, supervised by a woman, presumably a teacher, who was waiting to attach coloured ribbons and bunting from a box at her feet.

I took photographs of the scene, with their permission, from several viewpoints. This was in the days before digital photography. I was aware of the need not to spend too much time here, especially as I was unsure of my precise location. It had been a long, unintentional detour from my planned route for a single image. I decided that I could afford to spend a little more time; after all, there may well be other subjects of interest.

I walked down the street from the cottage to the edge of the village, where the narrow lane met a broader one in a T-junction. Opposite the junction, a tarmacked path and a roughly cut grass verge bordered a chest-high garden wall, built using the local honey-coloured stone, tinted by age with cream and grey separating the cottage garden from the lane.

I crossed the road and looked across a low gate, set into the wall. I admired the way the stonemason had crafted the opening where the gateposts stood to give the appearance of being uniformly vertical, while composed of individual irregular-shaped stones. One of the stones bore an etched geometric design that seemed familiar, though I don't know why. Its shape resembled a skein of wool. I made a sketch in my pocket notebook.

The wall defined the longest edge of a cottage garden, stretching the whole of its length, towards the former privy by the back door. The garden was laid out like an allotment: well-tended ridges and furrows of rich, fertile soil, moist and almost black. It was half bare, but neat and tidy; half full of rows of spring vegetables, burgeoning towards harvest and flowers, colourful and bright. I remember thinking how still it was: the silence emphasised by the lack of wind and birdsong.

I walked down to the mid-point of the garden and leant on the wall, enjoying the warmth of the early sunshine, both on my back and from the stones. From where I stood, the garden sloped away, in a continuation of the valley from the lane I had just descended. The house was one of a terrace of three, running at right angles to the slope and bordering a narrow, surfaced track. Being the end house, the roof was a little higher than that of its neighbours. In earlier centuries the three may well have been a single farmhouse, with the farmer's accommodation in the two higher-level buildings; the animals stabled in the lower third.

The upstairs windows were not the original wood. They had been replaced with nineteen-fifties style metal frames, revealed beneath the several layers of peeling white paint. Even in a traditional cottage this no longer seemed out of place. It was just another date-stamp on the passport of a building that had changed organically through the decades and centuries while retaining an overall integrity of rural style. I wondered whether, perhaps many years in the future, this might form part of a listing status, a testimony to the changing fabric.

At first glance, the house looked empty - not surprising at this time of morning. The village remained quiet. Unusual for an English village - you would expect a steady flow of routine, unhurried activity.

Inside the furthest upstairs window, I could make out the shapes of ornaments arranged on the sill. In the darkness at the back of the room, a figure bustled back and forth. Although I could not yet see her features clearly, I could tell from the changes of height and spring in her movement that this was a woman, a young woman.

I turned sideways to face the house, still resting on the wall. I crossed my legs. As I did so, the woman opened the window wide, placed her elbows on the sill and leant forward. She looked slowly to her left and right without looking down, taking in her surroundings with all her senses, stroking the external stone sill with her fingertips. It was as though she were confirming her relationship to the familiar things around her, in which she was an integral, harmonious part.

She looked radiant in a natural, unaffected way and displayed an absence of self-consciousness. This I deduced from the way she gently shook her long brown hair from side to side, not caring if anyone was watching.

I dared not move. I felt I was invisible, and that the spell would be broken should I do so. I had not intended to stare; I could not have known she would appear at the window. Even once I had acknowledged the figure in the room, a female figure, I could not have predicted the effect her appearance would have and the emotions she would draw upon, not only then, but in years to come.

Without thinking, I stood up straight and took my hands from the wall. She had noticed me and gave a friendly wave of her palm. I noticed what appeared to be a mark on the inside of her right arm, above her wrist. From where I was standing, I couldn't tell whether it was a birthmark, a skin blemish or possibly a tattoo, which would have been unusual in those days. She cocked her head and offered a gentle smile, then turned slowly into the room and disappeared from sight.

I felt a flush of embarrassment; she had seen me staring. It was as if I had been caught naked in a crowded place. It was too late to give a polite acknowledgement or to return the wave. She was gone. I briefly considered knocking at the door to apologise, before dismissing my foolish thought.

I turned to walk back to the car. As I did, something caught my eye, something I hadn't previously noticed. Embedded in the wall was a stone face, an image of the Green Man. It was remarkable, as I must have had my chest placed against it while leaning on the wall. True, it was not immediately obvious as such; the stone was worn and the detail faded. Once I was aware of it, it was impossible to ignore. I was familiar with the Green Man from my interest in history and folklore. I knew that it comes in many forms and variations, and that it is found across Europe and Asia and is alleged to have originated in Ancient Egypt.

I leaned down to inspect the face. I peered inside the open mouth, from which sculpted leaves and branches spouted profusely, I could make out something loose, placed inside. It looked like a piece of folded paper. The opening was too small to put my hand in. With some difficulty, I used my first and second fingers to draw a corner towards me, and then to pinch it and slide it between the stone branches. The paper was old and thick, almost like parchment, with watery stains at the edges. I opened it. Written in an archaic copperplate script were the words:

'We have been waiting for you. Your destiny is here.'

My first thought was that some children must have put it there as part of a game, or playing a trick, keen to create a mystery. This was not the handwriting of a child, even a practised child after spending hours imitating the form.

Perhaps it was part of a long-forgotten treasure hunt, what these days we would call geocaching. I thought to put it in my pocket, before deciding to replace it where I had found it. The next finder would surely be equally puzzled and amused.

It was time to continue my journey. I checked my position in my road atlas, or had intended to. With the passing of an hour, I had forgotten that I had been unable to locate either the name of the village, or any of the nearby villages I had driven through, on the map. This was impossible. I was confident of my approximate location from the distance and direction I had taken from the printing press. Durncot was a small but not insignificant village in size and must surely be recorded. There was no obvious reason for this. My road atlas was large scale and had been reprinted the previous year. There were several unnamed hamlets of a few houses shown, although these were much too small to be Durncot.

There was nothing to be done. I had no idea of the direction to take, other than to continue north-eastwards. How could it be that I found myself in the centre of a cartographical black hole? I drove on, still thinking of the beautiful woman. I turned right from the lane onto a larger road, or so I intended.

Deep in my thoughts, in a remote village with little traffic, I had failed to take the basic precaution of a second glance to my left. I braked hard and instinctively as a large blue tractor crossed in front of me at a speed I would not have expected from a farm vehicle. I had no idea where it had appeared from, as I had definitely looked in that direction, down the straight road, just a second or two earlier and had seen nothing. I was shaking and felt sick. The tractor sped away, towing an uncovered trailer from which its dusty contents blew as it bounced over bumps and holes in the road.

Although shocked, I could see that here was an

opportunity to escape to the mapped world, to follow another vehicle that was driving with a purpose, albeit far too fast within the confines of a village.

I put my foot down on the accelerator, feeling guilty that I, too, should not be driving so fast. It was not long before the tractor, with me in its wake, had left the village. It continued to drive at speed, along lanes whose route alternated between narrow and winding passages and then straight stretches through barren fields. The driver paid scant regard to forks in the road and to junctions. The tractor drove erratically, though with continuing purpose. The weather had been dry. As its rear wheels grazed the verge, clouds of dust flew up from both the tyres and the trailer, forcing me to concentrate on remaining at a safe distance behind. I did not have time to read the occasional signposts to see whether I recognised any of the names. After about what must have been half an hour, though it could equally have been an hour, the tractor slowed and turned off-road onto a track leading to a pair of large metal gates at the entrance to a wooded enclosure.

There was no point in following it further but, if I could ask the driver for directions… I pulled over and stopped the car, half on the verge. I took care to look in the mirror before opening the door and stepping out.

I turned to walk down the track but there was no longer any sign of the tractor. I could not understand how, in the time it had taken me to stop and get out of the car, the driver could have reached the gates, stopped and unlocked them, driven through and then locked them before disappearing into the woodland beyond. I walked to the gates, where I could see nothing beyond the curving track.

Perplexed, I returned to my car and continued straight on. It took another ten minutes to reach a junction with a main road. I turned right, this time paying careful attention to the traffic. Soon I was at a roundabout with signs to familiar towns, which indicated I was heading the wrong way. I drove around the roundabout and returned in the opposite direction, the way I had come. I looked out for the turning from which I had emerged, but did not spot it. At least I was no longer lost.

I recall little of my visit to Stratford-upon-Avon, other than having passed a pleasant few days in good company. I do remember that, as I started on my journey home, I considered whether to return to Durncot. I had not been sufficiently bold. I should have made contact with the mysterious woman. I should have made the effort to communicate with her and had the courage to knock on the door. She had, after all, waved and smiled in a friendly, albeit causal and detached, way. I could have explained to her why I had returned - to look at the garden, to take photographs that I regretted not taking the first day...

I could not think of a convincing reason, a justification, and so decided against retracing my journey. I was not sure that I could find the village again, let alone the house and garden, especially as I had been unable to locate the village on the map, or others close by.

No, I would return home to savour the moment and to think and dream of the pleasant and positive thoughts it had stirred within me. Within a day or two, the fantasy had faded into minor significance.

And although I thoroughly enjoyed the books I bought, which I still have today, I did not return to the Walnut Tree Press, nor did I place more orders, until one day, thirty years later ...

Part 2: The Persistence of Memory

I am tired now. I spend the greater part of each day inside my own head. I find this to be the safest place to be, for most of the time.

THE MESSAGE

A strange thing happened today; two things, in fact.

I was out shopping, early in the morning in the town close to my home village. A woman approached me in the street; someone I had never seen before. She gave me some information. It's difficult to describe what she told me: the words made sense, individually, but the sentences they formed were nonsense. I took it all in - the information - or so I thought at the time. It was only later, having reflected on the conversation while walking back to the car park, that I realised I had not understood what she had told me. All that I could recall was the idea that she was telling me I had to do something, to go somewhere.

The encounter became more peculiar when by chance I bumped into a friend. I told him what had happened and was amazed to discover that he had met the same woman, according to his description. He had had a similar conversation with her, which had made as little sense as mine.

We decided to return to the spot where she had accosted us individually, in the hope that we might see her again.

We did not find her.

When I say that I was none the wiser for the conversation, it continued to play on my mind. That evening I went over it, again and again, both in my mind and on paper. I made notes of individual words and sketched out, in the rough form of a mental map, the few connections I was able to assign to what she had told me.

It was no use. It still made little sense other than to implant the thought that I had to undertake a journey to an unknown location for a purpose equally mysterious.

The second strange thing happened later that same day. I had to go back into town to purchase a few small items I had forgotten to buy earlier. I felt irritated by this. It would mean wasting the afternoon on something that wasn't going to take my life forward in any way.

I could have bought these things locally and would have done so that morning, had I not forgotten, and now, after prevaricating for far too long, I decided to drive to Cambridge and make a decent half-day out of it. Cambridge would offer various attractive diversions: the Fitzwilliam, the Botanic Gardens, Jesus Green, the river: options that would bubble around in my subconscious and prioritise themselves for when I was ready to choose, according to my prevailing frame of mind.

I have established routines for most things. The template for a visit to Cambridge begins with an hour's leisurely drive to the Trumpington Park and Ride, taking the bus to John Lewis's, where I will have a coffee. There have been days where I have not travelled further than John Lewis; this would not be one of them.

I completed my purchases quickly, having steeled myself against unnecessary distractions. I walked out from the Grand Arcade, through Lion Yard and turned right on Petty Cury. I instinctively turned left onto Sidney Street. As I did so, I glanced towards the Lloyds Bank building, considering whether to walk in to withdraw some cash. It's a pleasure to do so there, inside a good old-fashioned and spacious banking hall.

I stopped, still staring at the building, to my right…
and then the shock occurred.

It was as though I had brushed against an electric
fence. A large hand, the bones visible through its thin
green skin, clutched my right shoulder. The sensation
lasted for less than a second. I turned, hearing giggles of
childish, juvenile and adult laughter from twenty or so
amused onlookers, to see a tall figure, painted and dressed
in green foliage, with flowing curls of green hair, standing
on a green box, grinning furiously - yes, furiously - as he
leaned over my face, his head turning from side to side.

I should have been alert to this. So often I have seen
students, as I assume most of them are, dressed as robots,
knights, axemen, or comic book characters, performing
mechanical routines in automaton-like styles, sometimes
smooth and graceful, others in a jerky, clockwork manner,
to attract coins to a hat for their support or for charity.

I felt foolish, not that it mattered in what was not my
home town, in front of strangers, who laughed without
malice at the unexpected reaction of an equal stranger to
this demonic mischief. The best policy was to go along
with the trick. I bowed to the Green Man in a theatrical
fashion, doffing an imaginary cap in a sweeping gesture.
The onlookers applauded; a few cheered, perhaps relieved
that someone else was the subject of attention.

The Green Man, covered in foliage, swayed gently from
side to side, mimicking a tree in a gentle breeze, silent
other than for the rustle of the foliage that covered all but
a small part of his face and his hands. I mirrored his
gestures as best I could while staring at his face, which was
fixed in an exaggerated wide-eyed smile, the whites of his
eyes accentuating the metallic green of the skin paint.

I considered a couple of minutes of our improvised
dance to be enough to allow me to continue on my way
with recaptured dignity. I dropped a few coins into the
upturned hat, not bothering to read the handwritten sign
placed against it.

It's strange how the mind makes connections between unrelated events. That evening, as I played over the events of the day, I realised that the Green Man automaton reminded me of something I thought I had forgotten: the figure in the wall of the woman's cottage in Durncot thirty years ago.

THE BEST OF TIMES

There can be few greater pleasures than to cradle your newborn child in your arms and breathe its sweet scent, other than to enjoy the experience more than once, as your family grows. Each new delivery is more satisfying than the previous, as I discovered with our second and third children. However much you look forward to the first, and however well you are prepared for the firstborn, there is the underlying anxiety that not all will be well, a fear that diminishes with familiarity. And so it was with the arrival of Freya, Alex and Adam.

My common feeling with all three was both of love and the sense of additional responsibility, the recognition that this new human is totally reliant on his or her parents for all of their physical needs. These decline as their social and emotional development grows over many years, before stabilising at a mutually satisfying level.

Well, that's the theory.

Each birth was the start of a new adventure, a consolidation of the growing family and a small step towards detachment from one's own selfish needs.

Stephanie and I would ideally have liked to have had a larger family. We were fortunate enough to have been able to afford to bring them up comfortably and there was no shortage of love. We agreed that for practical reasons that we should restrict ourselves to three.

How I now wish that we hadn't.

Some of our friends and family said it was too young an age: that a child should not be taught to read before the age of four. I strongly disagreed, as did Stephanie.

All parents will know how curious young children are and how excited they are to learn new things or, rather, to find that they can do something they previously couldn't, through a process of discovery, with the acquisition of knowledge or skills that are suddenly opened up to them.

When you read to a child daily, nightly, they naturally look at the illustrations. As time goes by, they can be introduced to individual words, starting with the names of characters, which they quickly remember and learn to recognise on the page. They can then be encouraged to learn other nouns and verbs and to point them out in the story. From here, the sounds of individual letters provide the breakthrough towards reading sentences, some of which will initially be read, in part at least, by predicting or recalling the story from memory. The shape of the words on the page, together with gradual memorisation of the letter sounds, builds towards the complete skill.

The reward, to both parent and child, is when the first book is read unaided, unprompted, from cover to cover. This is what happened with our eldest child, Freya. At the age of two years and five months, she read The Little Red Hen from start to finish without assistance.

Reading, after language acquisition, is perhaps the most important intellectual skill a child will learn. He or she acquires the means to become independent. From that point on, it is possible to assimilate more knowledge, without the need for assistance from adults or other elders, provided the child has access to books and technology. The rate of learning can now increase exponentially.

The box was now open and could never be closed again. It was as though a creature had grown to a size where it now needed continuous feeding to avoid starvation. We had to take action. In those days there were no state nursery schools to feed our daughter's hungry mind. It would be another two years before she would start state school.

We were both working. I commuted to the office, while Stephanie worked from home. We had a nanny who came to the house each weekday. Stephanie validated the candidates for the position. She insisted that the successful applicant should be formally trained and to possess a recognised childcare qualification. Laura was reliable and enthusiastic and was loved by our daughter, and later our sons, but she was not qualified to teach and did not have the level of education to fill this role. It would have been unfair to expect this much from her.

We were against the idea of private education in principle, both of us believing it to be elitist. It was fundamentally wrong to buy a start in life, to use money to provide an advantage that many could not afford. Our friends did not necessarily agree and pointed out that if others could purchase an early start for their children, legally, then there was nothing to gain from not doing so, and that we would be doing a disservice to our daughter if we held her back, did not allow her to fulfil her potential in this way.

It was not an easy decision. I, in particular, felt guilty that we were able to take advantage of our two incomes, both of our careers attracting an above-average salary. On the other hand, if the state could not provide what our daughter needed, why should we put her at a disadvantage?

After a couple of weeks of debate, we agreed on a compromise, albeit a fairly weak one. We would send Freya, and later Alex, to the local private school, from nursery through to the end of primary, at which point she would go to a state school. We recognised that attending a state school in their teens would provide our children with a more balanced social environment, where they would mix with others from a full spectrum of backgrounds. There were several corollaries to this decision, one of which was that we would have to treat all of our children (we only had two at that time) in the same way.

I would not deny that we used all manner of invented justifications as excuses for our short-term choice. It was possible that the quality of nursery teaching would not be good enough although, with two private schools within a mile of each other, parents had the option to change. Pupils at the school would be of mixed ability; if our daughter were to prove to be exceptional, she would be in the company of others with a whole range of talents. No doubt the school would have a strategy for catering for both the more and the less gifted or able. This would, or should, be the case at any school and reflects the real world in which the more fortunate have a responsibility towards the less able.

This was not a decision to be taken in isolation. Alex had been born the year after Freya. Adam, the baby of the family, arrived three and a half years later. Our children were to be treated equally.

And so, at the start of the term in which she would attain the age of three, Freya started school.

I clearly remember her first day; she looked so tiny in her uniform. The top of her head, even with her hat on, barely reached the height of the kitchen worktops. She was bemused by the fuss we made, yet was looking forward to making new friends and doing new things.

We had prepared her well, to be left with new people in the playground. She understood that all of the other children, on this day reserved for the new intake, were sharing a common experience.

I stood with her for several minutes, until the bell rang, as an act of reassurance, to make it seem an ordinary event.

She asked why other children were crying and clinging to their parents. I explained that perhaps they not been separated from their parents during the daytime before and that those parents may not have explained in detail the order in which things would happen and how interesting and enjoyable it would be. I assured her once more that once she went into the school, I would go off to work and that Laura would collect her at lunchtime to take her home.

Our summer holidays were spent abroad. In the early years, we travelled to several regions of France by car, staying in gîtes, eating out or cooking in, visiting local attractions and occasionally the beach. The children adapted well to new surroundings and learned to deal with the pleasures that some excursions brought, contrasting with others that were less successful. Our holidays provided memorable experiences that we relived and recounted with joy to friends. I will come back to one of these later.

Whenever we returned home we made a point of discussing the holiday with the family, to establish and consolidate our memories for all time. I remember in particular one such conversation.

It was a Sunday. The summer holidays were drawing to an end. The children would return to school on Tuesday.

'Have you had a good time over the summer?' I asked them at the dinner table.

'Yes, it's been lovely!' said Freya.

'We've done so much,' added Alex.

We asked what they had liked best and why. Freya and Alex competed with their answers, each shouting joyfully above the other.

Adam was quiet. Not unhappily so, he smiled and fidgeted on his chair. He was frequently the listener of the three, taking everything in, assessing the conversation, before adding his own comments later.

'What about you, Adam? What did you enjoy most?'

He frowned, and then looked up at me.

'The seaside,' he replied, and then added, 'What is there to look forward to, daddy?'

I smiled at him and stroked his hair.

'The rest of your life.'

THIRTY YEARS ON

The two odd encounters I described occurred thirty years after Durncot, I was living through one of those periods in my life when things were not going well. In my worst moments, I felt that whatever I touched went wrong or, at best, did not go in the planned or desired direction.

I kept thinking that there must be a better way, that there was something I could change to create better outcomes. No matter how hard I tried, I was lost for ideas, so lost that I lapsed into an old habit of wondering how different life would have been had I made decisions to take other directions at significant moments in the past.

A long time ago I had resolved to reject this method of thinking. It was unproductive. I kept telling myself that I could not change the past, yet I could influence the future, that my present mood was an indulgent moment, which I would surely regret later as being a waste of time and creative energy.

I had to leave the past in its place and I would have succeeded, had I not had a dream.

I dreamed of Durncot.

I saw the girl at the window. At first, I thought she was waving to me, to acknowledge my presence, or in recognition. And then I saw that she was beckoning to me, inviting me to join her, as though reeling me in. I was drawn to her, with a feeling of submission that only exists in dreams, that never lasts. I remember floating upwards towards her, closer and closer, as she stood at the bedroom window. I could feel sleep deserting me. I woke reluctantly, desperate to remain in a better world, with hope and the promise of release from worldly cares. Though the dream was long, within seconds I could recall only what I am telling you.

I hadn't given a thought to Durncot for years. I have no idea why it came back to me on that spring night. Perhaps it was the photograph I had seen in the newspaper, of a topiary hedge behind the stone wall of a Cotswold cottage. Perhaps it was just a random thought thrown up by my wandering, unfocussed mind. What made it even stranger was that it was the day after my dream that I met the woman in the street who had told me I was to make a journey.

I decided the best strategy was to devote twenty minutes of concentrated thought to the woman at the window and to consider the possibility of trying to find Durncot again. In this way I half hoped to purge the idea of her from my mind, to 'put her away', as it were, rather than allow her to interrupt, invade and dominate my thoughts at will.

It was no use. I had been bitten by an irrational urge to explore the mystery of the woman and the hidden village. I had to return to Durncot, wherever it was, to find her, and to carry out the instruction, if that was what it was, given to me by the woman in the street. I had made a connection between two events, one real, one imagined, dreamed, that more rational people would have dismissed.

Over the next few weeks, I planned my trip - not in any great detail, after all, I had had no idea how I had found myself in Durncot all those years ago, or how I had found my way back to my intended route.

Fortunately, we now have the Internet. I Googled

Durncot. Not a single hit! I would have thought that there would be something, even if the village name could not be found. I did not feel discouraged by this; it only reinforced my determination to find it.

I decided that a good starting point would be to revisit the Walnut Tree Press and to take it from there. Their catalogue of books, while expensive, was so appealing. I would be spoilt for choice. I quickly confirmed that the press still existed. I clicked on the website and spent a good hour browsing through their publications and events. If only I had been prompted by the dream a few weeks earlier, I could have attended their annual Open Day, organised by the 'Friends of the Press'. It would have been a good opportunity to meet other collectors and possibly some of the authors and illustrators.

I was surprised to discover that Miriam was still there, after all these years. She was definitely the Miriam I had met: it's not a common name now, neither was it then. The website included photographs of her, both recent and from her youth. This puzzled me a little, as my recollection from meeting her was that she was several years older than me. I was convinced that she was the same woman, yet I am not sure I would have recognised her from the photographs.

The website made no mention of being open to the public. The address was the same... Well, it was located in the same village. I decided to telephone a few days in advance, to say I was interested in buying a book, although I would like to see it first, along with their other current publications.

My call was answered by a man whom I imagined to be in his late fifties or older. He had a quiet voice and a confident manner. He listened to my request patiently before asking which book interested me. I gave him the title and he confirmed it was in stock.

'We can post it to you if you give us your credit or

debit card details. It would save you a journey.'

'I'd prefer to collect it if I may. I need to come that way, and there are a couple more I might be interested in buying.'

I should have thought beforehand that if I mentioned only one book, it may be unavailable and that would have invited the response that there was no point in coming.

He asked when I would like to visit.

'That's good timing,' he said. 'We will have finished a print run the day before and will have some time available to talk to you. Can you get here for 10 a.m.? To the press?'

'Yes, that would be fine. Thank you.'

'May I take your name please?'

'Oliver Merryweather.'

'And do you need directions, Oliver?'

'No thank you. I've been there before - many years ago. I bought two books by Miriam.'

He asked me which books. I told him and said I had met him and Rose at the farmhouse.

'Well, well. I think I vaguely remember. It'll be a pleasure to meet one of our first customers again.'

'Me too. I look forward to seeing you.'

I arranged to take a few days off work. I packed an overnight bag, to allow myself time to search for Durncot. If I were to make interesting discoveries, I could choose to extend my trip. After all, if I was travelling all that way…

To think that was thirty years ago. It was a ridiculous idea to try to find it again! I wondered how different it would be. Would the house still be standing? Would the garden still be there? Surely the streets would now be filled with parked cars, apart from outside the few large houses with former stables attached.

But first to the Walnut Tree Press.

I arrived at the village early. I parked the car and set off for a stroll around the village.

It hadn't changed as much as I had expected. A pair of old cottages that I remembered as derelict had been renovated in a tasteful manner, avoiding over-gentrification. Their gardens were mature and abundant. I imagined that the owners had moved here to enjoy the tranquillity of a village that remained without a shop or a pub.

As I had arrived too early for my appointment, I decided to seek out the printing press, to confirm its location and in the hope of reawakening further memories. The geography of the village felt familiar, as if I were returning to a childhood home.

The lane! Now, where was the lane where I had stumbled across the press? Why hadn't I Googled it before I set out? This was not really a problem in such a small place. I was certain that it was off to the right of the main street and soon found it, its opening partially obscured by leaves of the overhanging branches of a house on the corner. Evidently, no cars ventured down here. I quickly located the building. Its structure was more or less as I remembered; it was now in a better condition and looked much tidier.

The door was closed. I couldn't see much through the high windows. I was too excited to wait until the agreed time of my appointment to see inside. As soon as I touched the handle, the door was opened in a brisk motion.

'You must be Oliver.' An outstretched hand greeted me, followed by a brief hug and slaps on my shoulders. I had expected John or Rose to answer.

'Miriam?' I was unsure. Although I remembered her as looking just a few years older than me, I would not have recognised her from the website photograph.

'I am indeed. Come on in. John told me you would be coming. He'll be here shortly. Let me show you around. It's been a long, long time!'

'Really? You remember me?'

'Of course I do. Visitors to the press were rare in those days, especially those who bought my books.'

It was a pleasure to be shown around again, to admire the presses, to browse the selection of recently published books and to handle the hardwood blocks.

Posters and sample pages were pinned to the walls, together with a selection of photographs of the press taken over its thirty and more years' history. Several were of gatherings of people, which Miriam confirmed were taken at the annual Open Day, held in the orchard behind the building.

'It certainly looks a merry affair.'

'It's very popular. We lay on a buffet and wine, a little music and give talks and demonstrations. The orchard becomes a garden of earthly delights for a day. Most of the guests are customers. We also invite a few journalists and other people in the trade, as well as anyone else who asks for an invitation. In fact, we started the event in response to customer requests, oh, about ten years ago. Some fly in from the United States and the Gulf. We've even had one from New Zealand. Many of them see our work both as the continuance of traditional processes and as a link with the past. They often buy the books out of nostalgia for "the old country". I expect you know that we publish books illustrating poetry, traditional buildings and the farming seasons... The countryside, in its many forms, is a major theme. If you're interested, I can show you our photograph albums. We have one for every year. They're over here.'

'I'd be delighted.'

I started with the most recent and worked backwards. Each contained a collection of small posters, flyers, cards, and of course photographs. Several faces appeared in more than one year. One of these was a woman whom I paid little attention to at first. Something about her stuck in my mind: something familiar yet at the same time strange. Almost subconsciously I found it nagging at me, a cumulative irritation, until I realised she was wearing the same clothes at each event and, although in none of the photos was her face fully visible, she did not appear to age; she remained a young woman, year after year.

I checked back to make sure I wasn't imagining it. Now curious, I skipped through the pages of the oldest albums, looking for her, my interest growing. She appeared in every one, dressed identically.

And then I noticed the mark…

'Tell me. Miriam. Who is this woman? She's in every year's photos and is always dressed in the same way.'

As I spoke, the door opened. A man in his sixties, dressed like a gentleman farmer, filling his fraying tweed jacket, walked into the room and offered his hand. In his other hand, he carried a small bag of books.

'Ah, John, our guest is here.'

'Good morning and welcome back. Rose sends her apologies. She's a little under the weather. Nothing serious, just a heavy cold. Did you have a good journey?'

'Yes thank you. It was made shorter by looking forward to the treasures to be discovered.'

'Oliver has been asking after our "mysterious friend" at the Open Days.' Miriam made a gesture to signify the quotation marks.

'Oh her,' said John. 'Nobody knows who the hell she is. It's the only time we ever see her. We don't even know how she gets here.'

'On a broomstick probably,' said Miriam, with a hint of a giggle. 'We call her Bella. We've no idea if that's her real name.'

'Do you have any idea why she comes here?'

'No idea why,' said John. 'Never buys anything, or takes much interest in the workings of the press.'

'Well, that's a little unfair,' said Miriam. 'She would buy a book, but the one she asks for every year is no longer available.'

'And you don't mind her coming along to every

event?'

'Not really. There is one odd thing though,' John paused for a few seconds, stroking his chin and looking up towards the ceiling.

'What's that?'

'Oh, I don't know. Just something people have said. It seems nonsense…'

I wanted to ask questions, but did not want to risk losing the goodwill shown by John and Miriam. After all, this in a way was what I was here for, even though I would not have been able to articulate it in that way before I arrived.

'Oh, you tell him, Miriam,' John waved his arm and grimaced, more in apparent embarrassment than annoyance.

'Well,' Miriam took a deep breath. 'She asks people if they've seen someone, a man. It's as if she's lost someone, years ago and is revisiting places where she thinks he might turn up. The trouble is she doesn't have a name for him, only a vague description. We think she's a bit doolally: not all there. If it weren't for that we would probably bar her from the event. In truth, we feel sorry for her.

'She does no harm, other than to irritate some of the guests. Most of them are gracious about it and understand. You see, it's mostly the same people who attend each year: the regular customers the friends of the press, and others with a shared interest in the manual technology and traditional book production. It's as much an annual party and reunion as a commercial event, probably more so.'

I picked up the album from the recent Open Day and held it open at one of the photos of her.

'Do you have any idea what this is? The mark on her wrist. It looks like a tattoo of an unusual shape.'

'It's a Solomon's Knot,' said John. 'It's found in a number of cultures, Roman, Islamic, Central Asian. In this country, it often occurs in mediaeval graffiti. They're mainly found on church buildings: on the walls and on the carpentry. They're most common in East Anglia, but there are a few around here, including on old houses and cottages.'

I knew I had seen it somewhere before. It was the same symbol I had seen inscribed on the gatepost of the cottage in Durncot. I had made a sketch of it at the time. I wondered whether I still had the notebook.

'Does it have any significance?' I asked.

'Yes. It's regarded as a symbol of eternity and immortality. Paradoxically, it's also considered to be the most powerful device for subduing demons,' said John.

'It's the latter that gives it the popularity around here, I suspect,' said Miriam.

'Years ago, when I came here before, you told me about the Celtic tribes and the persistence of pagan beliefs.'

'The Dobunni, and the Cornovii. Yes, nothing much has changed, superstition-wise,' said John.

'So although you joke about Bella arriving on a broomstick, she's wearing a tattoo designed to ward off evil.'

They both laughed.

'I'd reserve judgement on that,' said Miriam. 'If you'd met her you'd understand.'

'May I ask what book it is that she asks for every year?'

'Yes, it's one we discontinued after the first print run, a couple of years after we opened,' said John. 'The title is "An Illustrated Account of the Old Religion, its Beliefs and Practices, by a Believer".'

'Ah yes, I can remember you telling me about that too, when I came to the farmhouse to buy the books. How a mystery buyer had purchased the complete print run on condition that you didn't reprint it. You had a copy in a covered display case, but you had mislaid the key so you couldn't show it to me. I don't suppose...'

'Oh yes, I remember now,' said John, interrupting. 'I

know what you're going to ask. Trouble is, we don't have it any more. It was stolen some years ago. A very strange affair altogether. And we never did find out what happened to all those copies. We half expected them to turn up on the open market - for someone, a dealer perhaps, to offer them back to us, but no, we never saw them again. We can only think they must have been destroyed, for whatever reason.'

'I wouldn't be surprised if that's why Bella asks for it every year: to check up on whether we have stuck to the bargain. Perhaps she knows the buyer of the print run. Another reason to keep her sweet. You can never be sure of people's allegiances,' said Miriam.

'I sometimes wonder... No, I can't say it.'

'Go on, John, what are you thinking?' I looked back and forth to John and Miriam. Would either of them respond?

'Oh, it's unfair really. I sometimes wonder whether she was connected in some way to the theft. The funny thing is that I call it a theft, but there was no sign of a break-in and nothing else was missing. It was more of a disappearance. All of a sudden it had just gone. The cabinet was still locked - no damage to it - and we never have found the key. The display cabinet's not something we look at every day, so we had no idea of when it happened. It wasn't worth reporting it to the police. There was no evidence and the police are few and far between around here.'

'Is it possible the key was stolen, rather than lost?' I asked. 'That someone took the key, then came back later, removed the book and relocked the cabinet?'

'I've thought about that from time to time,' said John. 'If someone took the key from inside the house, they might as well have taken the book there and then, if they knew what it was for. We never leave visitors unattended in the house and we never go away. It's a complete mystery.'

The conversation returned to the press and its publications, its successes and the few failures, and John and Rose's plans for the future. I had kept an eye on the time; I did not wish to outstay my welcome. John had brought the three books I had discussed with him on the telephone. And two more that he thought might interest me.

One of these was a book of poetry, 'Dreamscapes of Memory', described on the website, he said, as 'nostalgic but not unduly sentimental'. I remembered reading the description. The listing had included one of the poems, although there was 'no image available'. Now that it was in my hands, the engraving on the front cover looked familiar. The style was reminiscent of Miriam's engravings, yet lighter, more delicate. And then I realised it was an image from the village - from Durncot. I read the author's and artist's names.

'Poems by Quercus with engravings by D.W.'

For some reason, they wished to remain anonymous.

'Do you know these people?' I asked John.

'We know the author of the poems, but not the engraver. It was the poet who brought the work to us. We felt the poems were good, although not exceptional. They convey a certain timelessness, in a soporific, backwatery sort of way. It was the engravings that sold us on it.'

I turned the front cover open, with care. I was keen to see more of the engravings inside, but at the same time felt apprehensive, anxious almost, as to what I would find. I concentrated on appearing calm. I was resolved not to show any reaction to whatever surprise lay within. The words were not my prime interest. I wanted to see the engravings.

'It's the last remaining copy,' said John. 'It's sold well, but we won't be reprinting.'

'Why is that?' I asked.

John laughed.

'You won't believe this. We are unable to trace either

the author or the artist. Just like with the Old Religion book. Neither did we have their bank account details, so we're holding a tidy sum of money on their behalf, hoping they'll get in touch. We'll give it a couple more years, then we'll think about whether there's some way we can give it to a charity.'

I continued to leaf through the book. I recognised several of the locations as Durncot. Perhaps they all were; after all, I hadn't walked around the entire village. The school, the cottage with the yew tree topiary, even what looked like the wall of the cottage, where I had leaned... I scanned the words quickly, searching without success for the village name.

There was no doubting the skill of the engraver. He or she had used as few lines as possible to describe features to suggest dream landscapes. The delicate, economic lines and the use of space defined perspective by what was left out, leaving the observer to construct three-dimensional scenes.

I had to have this book. The sublime illustrations would reinforce my memories of Durncot and may well inspire more to surface.

'Yes, I'd like to buy this one please and this one, the one we spoke about on the phone.'

'Would you like to buy all three, as you're here,' said John, in an encouraging way, without implying pressure.

I said I was undecided on the third and may well come back again or order it online.

'You are very welcome to come back whenever you like,' said John, handing me my change and placing the books in a canvas bag. The bag bore a simple logo, designed in the style of a sixteenth-century engraving, with the name of the press above the image of a walnut tree, beneath which stood a woman holding a basket, with leaves and walnuts at her feet.

'It's a pleasure to meet you again after all these years. We'll have to invite you to the Open Day next year.'

'Thank you so much. That's very kind.'

Again I thought, if only I had had the idea a couple of months ago, I might have been invited to this year's Open Day, and have met Bella.

'I must be off. Thank you so much for your time, both of you. Please give Rose my best wishes.'

John and Miriam followed me to the door. I shook John's hand and gave Miriam a kiss on both cheeks.

'Are you off back home now?' asked John.

'No, I'm off to Durncot,' I explained that I was retracing a route I had taken when I last visited the press. 'I don't suppose you can give me directions. I can't find it on the map. I discovered it after the last time I came here, by accident. It's about an hour to the north-east. I'm not sure I can find it again.'

John and Miriam looked at each other, shaking their heads.

'Oh, Durncot,' Miriam chuckled.

'I don't understand. What's amusing about Durncot?'

'Well, you are the second person to mention it, said Miriam.

'Really? Who was the other person?'

'You won't believe this,' said Miriam. 'Our mysterious friend Bella. She talks about Durncot as though everyone knows of it, that it's just a short distance away. The thing is, that no one else has heard of it, or knows where it is. You can't find it on any maps.'

'Yes, I know.'

I was unsure of what to say.

'Perhaps it's a local name, a variant used only by residents. As I say, I passed through by accident the last time I came here, over thirty years ago. I thought it was an interesting place. I'd like to go back to see how much it had changed.'

I didn't mention that I recognised some of the engravings in the book I had just bought as being of locations there. Miriam looked me in the eye, in a polite but enquiring way, as if waiting for me to volunteer more information, as if inviting me to prove my sanity.

'I can guess what you're thinking. Believe me when I say that I saw the sign at the entrance to the village. It was only later that I, too, discovered that it didn't appear on maps, which is why I assume it must be a local name. I'm hoping to recreate my journey. It sounds a bit strange, I know.'

'Well, we must wish you luck then. But beware of Bella!'

They both laughed again, without a hint of mockery.

'If you find it, you must let us know,' said Miriam.

'I certainly will. Thank you once more. I hope to see you again soon.'

I returned to my car and sat quietly. Returning to the press had been a success, a good idea. I had purchased two books and re-established some links with the past, which had made it worthwhile. And a new mystery was unfolding.

Could the woman in the photographs possibly be the woman I had seen at the bedroom window or was this my mind playing tricks to satisfy my need to explain an enigma? At least she now had a name. Whether it was accurate or not I didn't know and didn't care. What evidence did I have that she was the answer to my question? Both women had a mark on their wrists. Was it a coincidence that the design of Bella's tattoo was in the same form as the mark on the gatepost at Durncot? I had not been close enough to make out the detail on the wrist of the woman I had seen there.

At Durncot I had been acknowledged with a wave and had found the message hidden in the wall: 'We have been waiting for you. Your destiny is here'. There was no reason to suppose it had been written and placed there for me. Bella was searching for a man, but was unwilling or unable to provide a name or an accurate description. John had described the whole area as steeped in pagan beliefs beneath a veneer of Christianity, though I had yet to see any sign of the latter.

Despite the scant evidence, in my mind, the woman at the window and Bella had become the same person. I was beginning to feel a connection. I would use my time here well. I would seek out the buried world.

But first I had to find Durncot.

CELEBRATIONS

Christmas: the giant pile of gifts stacked in front of the fireplace, contrived to look as though it had been emptied from a sack, convincing enough to a child, if not to an adult. We were so fortunate to be able to afford a comfortable, spacious home and to be able to lavish treats on our children. We took care, too much perhaps, to select items we considered to be in good taste and offering both a play and educational value. It sounds terribly middle class, and I suppose it was.

We were very aware of the misfortunes of others, whose lives were a terrible injustice, an unfortunate consequence of the time and place in which they were born and lived. Sometimes we discussed inviting a guest or guests to Christmas lunch: a homeless person, refugees or a poor family, a brother and sister in care. We never did.

It was my fault that it didn't happen. It would have been a good thing to have done, to have given pleasure, warmth and comfort to strangers in need. It also felt self-indulgent, as if I was trying to make myself feel less guilty of the plight of other people. In no way did I consciously regard it in this way. It didn't seem right to take unfortunates from their accustomed deprivation for a single day, and then to return them to their normal life. It would have been like teasing them with a glimpse of a lifestyle beyond their reach, a way of living that they might never experience for themselves.

We agreed that a better course of action would be to offer some relief in their daily surroundings. We wrapped and donated gifts, suitably labelled with an age range, for a local children's care home, enclosing a note to the carers of the exact contents so that they could pair the gift with the most appropriate child. We bought gifts similar, and sometimes identical, to those our own children would receive.

One Christmas, we deferred our traditional lunch until the evening. We decided by the toss of a coin which of us would volunteer to serve lunches at a shelter for homeless people. Stephanie won; she thoroughly enjoyed the experience. I stayed at home to prepare the dinner and to enjoy the domestic pleasures of managing the children's expectations.

Throughout the remainder of the year, we gave occasional discreet donations to carefully selected charities, mainly those supporting poor communities in developing countries, both in the hope that we might make a small difference and to assuage our guilt and our embarrassment of good fortune.

None of this would inhibit us from fully enjoying our family Christmases. We savoured the build-up: the decorations, trying to find surprises for the children as well as satisfying their expressed wishes for gifts and the secret wrapping, often left until Christmas Eve or night. Every year they were determined to wait up for Father Christmas to arrive, unaware that we had set our alarm for three o'clock in the morning to carefully arrange the gifts downstairs, having requested that, if they were to get up early, they should leave us undisturbed until at least eight o'clock.

First-world problems. I know I am a terrible snob; I do wish that other parents had better taste. Birthdays, too, were occasions for family-centred generosity and the regular obligatory children's parties. We often baulked at the pointless, competitive events organised by some parents. Occasionally a family would propose that parents of guests make a charitable donation instead of giving gifts that were so often unsuitable and unwanted. We thought this to be a good idea, although it received little support.

I found the round of children's birthday parties to be an ordeal, especially those held in so-called 'soft-play facilities'. Badly behaved children and the combination of smells from junk food to smelly socks and trainers and the suspicion that some guests had urinated (or worse) in the ball pond...

AN UNEXPECTED SIGHTING

After leaving the printing press, I sat in the car wondering what to do next. I knew I had to do something about it. Bella was taking over my conscious thoughts.

I still carried a road atlas in the boot of the car. It had been there for several years and before that had been kept in my previous car. No one buys road atlases anymore; most people have Satnavs, although I choose not to. Something I may well now regret. The road atlas was, nevertheless, a sensible backup to have in the event of a breakdown, if my phone were dead.

I looked at the map and tried to recall my route from the printing press to Durncot. If I couldn't locate it from a map all those years ago, there was no reason to think it would be any easier today. I had to try to get her out of my thoughts, either by finding her or by proving to myself beyond doubt that it would not be possible. I made a reasoned decision as to where Durncot should be and set my mind to the task of finding it.

I drove through the countryside for some while, in no hurry and enjoying the views, until I felt the need for a break. As I passed through yet another attractive stone village, the sign hanging outside The Green Man pub caught my eye. Unlike many images of the Green Man, this one was smiling, kindly and possibly a little inebriated, in a jolly, convivial way, confirming the justification for his role on the sign. It was time to stop for a rest and some lunch.

The door was stiff. I managed to open it by turning the handle, placing my hand at the top of the door and pushing with my foot.

There were about twenty people in the bar. They showed little interest in the arrival of a stranger. I expect that they were used to visitors to the village and the surrounding area, especially at weekends.

'Good afternoon. What can I get you, sir?' said the landlord, I assumed, as he was the only person behind the bar. His polite greeting was lacking in warmth, but was not unwelcoming: more indifferent and weary. I glanced at the menu chalked up on a blackboard.

'I'd like your special of the day, please.'

'That's fine. And what would you like to drink, sir?'

'Just sparkling water, please, with no ice. I have a long way to drive.'

He took a bottle from the chiller cabinet and poured it slowly into a tall glass.

'Are you sure I can't tempt you to a pint of the local beer? Just the one? It's very popular. They do a bottled version as well.'

'No thank you. I never drink anything if I'm driving. I find it easier to have no alcohol than to be tempted to have more.'

As I picked up the glass, a chill tension ran down my back. At the time the landlord had recommended the beer, I had not looked at the label on the pump handle: 'Witches' Brew'. It was not the name of the beer that made me shiver - beers, in particular craft beers, are given strange names these days, presumably to attract attention and to mark them out from rival products. No, what took me by surprise was the symbol beneath the name. The symbol I had copied from the stone wall from the house in Durncot; the same as formed the design of Bella's mark, which I now recognised to be a Solomon's Knot.

I sat down at a vacant table in a window recess close to the door and opened my newspaper, not wishing to attract attention. The regulars were engaged in their own conversations, a low, grumbling discussion that travelled back and forth like a musical round.

I could not concentrate on reading; I was distracted. Should I ask about the provenance of the beer and why the label bore that symbol?

By the time my lunch arrived, my appetite had faded. I ate slowly and finished about three quarters, out of politeness. Why, I don't know. I was the customer after all.

I placed the knife and fork together on the plate, together with the screwed up paper napkin. No one had come in or left while I had been there. I looked out of the bay window, towards another on the far side of the pub. An elderly couple were seated in silence, their half-empty glasses in front of them.

As I stared in their direction, a young woman approached the door of the pub, between the two bay windows, from the street. She was having the same trouble as me in opening the door and quickly gave up. As she turned to walk off, she glanced in my direction.

I was convinced immediately that it was she: the woman at the window! And for a moment I believed that she recognised me. She smiled and walked away briskly. I stood up and clumsily moved the table, so as to dash after her.

I hesitated to take stock of myself. This was nonsense: to believe I could recognise someone from that far back in time. And if she and Bella were the same person, I had not been helped by her back being to the camera in the photos in the albums at the Walnut Tree Press.

'Can I get you anything else, sir?'

The landlord was blocking my way. I couldn't possibly

push past him. He would have thought I was trying to run off without paying and, if I had, he would probably have called the regular customers for assistance and all that that might entail. There was no time to explain my haste: the woman was turning a corner.

'I'm sorry. I thought I saw someone I know. No, just the bill please.'

I slumped back in the chair, disappointed to have lost such an opportunity. I should have been more decisive.

I thought about the woman. How could I have thought she was the same person I had seen thirty years ago, in a different village, albeit in the same general area? And then it occurred to me. As she had approached the window, while I had been looking at her face, I had, in my unconscious mind seen the mark on her wrist - a tattoo. And not just any tattoo: it was similar, if not identical, to the label on the pump handle, the same design I had copied from the gatepost - Bella's tattoo. This was a more plausible explanation for recognition.

The landlord returned with my change.

'Excuse me asking, there was a woman who was going to come in a few minutes ago, but she changed her mind. She had an unusual tattoo on her wrist, rather like the image on the Witches' Brew label over there. Do you know her?'

He looked at me in silence, expressionless. I felt embarrassed, regretting having asked the question.

'I'm afraid I didn't see her, sir.'

I left the pub and walked around the village in the hope of catching sight of her again. I veered off briefly into the surrounding countryside. I walked up and down lanes and then back into the village and into those shops where I could see a woman, or women, inside, with no success.

Before leaving to continue my journey, I decided to return to the pub to buy a couple of bottles of the Witches' Brew. If nothing else they would serve as a reminder of the symbol.

I coaxed the door open, as I had earlier. The interior looked different somehow. In a strange way, it was unlike the pub I had visited an hour or so ago. A younger man stood behind the bar. The customers were more varied in their ages than before. The Witches Brew sign had disappeared from the pump; it must have sold out. I asked the bartender if I could buy two bottles to take away.

'I've not heard of that one; it's new to me,' he replied.

'Witches' Brew', the same name as you had on this pump earlier when I was here.' I pointed to the now unlabelled pump.

'I'm afraid we don't sell that here.'

The ambient conversation ceased. I could feel the customers staring at me. Immediately I felt ridiculous. I was certain of my facts, or thought I was, but could see that there was no way of pursuing the enquiry.

'I'm sorry, I must have misread it. Excuse me.'

It seemed the most dignified way of withdrawing.

'Not to worry. We all make mistakes.'

I was about to walk out, my face warm from my blushes. I turned to ask, my question directed to anyone who might be listening. 'Can anyone direct me to Durncot, please?'

The customers were united in their collective response of frowns, shrugs and shakes of heads. It was time to leave.

As yet, I was no nearer to locating my destination. Still, the signs were ominous.

A MIDSUMMER NIGHT'S DREAM

I have always enjoyed the theatre. For me, it is the ideal medium to enjoy the classics: Shakespeare, Ibsen, Chekhov, Beckett, Pinter... Most of all I like the Elizabethan and Jacobean periods - The Duchess of Malfi is one of my favourites.

I was reading the Sunday papers and belatedly noticed a review for a travelling company production of A Midsummer Night's Dream. What attracted my attention was that the rude mechanicals' parts were to be played by actors operating string puppets. This was an interesting concept; I wondered how competent the actors would be and whether we would find the puppets to be believable, or a distraction. Would we be able to concentrate on the puppets rather than the faces of the actors manipulating them and speaking their words? Stephanie agreed that it sounded innovative and would be worth a trip. I telephoned to make a booking, excited by the idea of the intimacy of the performance in one of London's smaller old theatres. No tickets remained for our preferred dates, although there was a possibility of returns on the day.

We decided to take a chance.

The day arrived; Stephanie called the theatre early

morning. No tickets were available, but it was possible, even likely, that the situation could change during the day. We travelled to London and spent the late morning and early afternoon visiting galleries, taking a light lunch between.

We thought it best to go to the theatre in person, rather than telephone. The sympathetic woman at the box office told us that there were still no tickets available, in either of the circles (centre front row seats in the dress circle are our preference) or the stalls. Stephanie pleaded, unconvincingly I thought, that it was a special occasion and asked whether it would be possible to hire one of the eight small boxes. The woman explained that these were not currently in use, having been redecorated within the past few days. Stephanie begged to speak to the manager, who duly appeared and relented, possibly to rid himself of Stephanie's alternate haranguing and pleading. The transaction was concluded with good grace and an apology for the smell of paint we would encounter.

We had arrived in good time, an hour or so before curtain up. We decided to have a drink in the bar, something I was unaccustomed to doing for fear of dozing off during the performance and, worse still, snoring. The bell rang and we asked for directions to our box, at circle level. There is something about the carpets in these old theatres. They are frequently red, with a pattern you cannot ever imagine anyone positively choosing and give the impression that they have not been cleaned in all the years they have been there. They nevertheless have a density and springiness that suggests that it is the carpet, and not the ancient woodwormed floor and steps beneath, that support your weight. I have often had the same thought in solicitors' offices.

The door to our box opened onto the small seating area, with the stage beyond, designed so that the direction of the audience's gaze would prevent them from seeing the occupants enter or leave. One pair of red upholstered chairs sat diagonally in front of another, with a small step down to the forward pair. We took our seats. I leant on the brass rail to look around at the audience taking their places and filling the theatre to capacity. Presumably, those seats that would remain empty would do so due to illness, bereavement or travel difficulties.

I was pleased to see the orchestra pit occupied by ten musicians. I do love it when a production features live music, even when it is incidental to the play. Ten minutes before the scheduled time for the performance to begin, they started to play Mendelssohn's overture. While I recognise this as a musical cliché, I don't have a problem with Mendelssohn as a composer. To my mind he is in the category of 'quite pleasant, six out of ten', despite his lack of originality - he did not take music forward. If I have a criticism of this particular piece, it is that the overture is too fast a pace, at odds with the play it is intended to describe. It nevertheless served the purpose of encouraging the audience to take their seats.

The first act proceeded in the usual declamatory way, to set the scene before any real action takes place. This did not concern me; I was enjoying the atmosphere from an unfamiliar, privileged viewpoint, with the additional benefit of being able to observe the audience in an unobtrusive way, without their awareness. I enjoyed pointing out eccentric-looking characters to Stephanie and discussing observations with her without disturbing others.

My interest in the play began to focus with act two, which begins with Puck and a fairy entering from opposite sides of the stage. Puck is often dressed in a green tunic, covering his arms and shoulders, with britches or tights on his lower body - more like Robin Hood than Robin Goodfellow. He is sometimes portrayed with bud-like horns to suggest the devilish aspects of his character. This Puck was sparsely clad - no, wrapped - below the waist, with a collection of foliage covering the minimum amount of his body to achieve public theatrical decency. He bore no horns, just a thin garland, a slipped halo of oak leaves.

The fairy was costumed in a gossamer-thin, long, lacy dress with a token amount of foliage in the form of a flowery headband. I was pleased that wings formed no part of her dress. So often fairies are given huge unwieldy wings or small token appendages, incapable of initiating or supporting flight. The single aspect of her appearance that jarred was her heavy eye makeup, resembling two dark mirrored apostrophes.

I enjoyed the performance, so much so that I felt disappointed when the intermission arrived (rather early, I thought, at the end of act two, only a third of the way through one of Shakespeare's shortest plays). We decided against returning to the bar. Two drinks before taking our seats were enough and we had not placed an order for more. Far better to use the time to discuss our impressions than in trying to attract the servers' attention for more over-priced alcohol.

I could hear footsteps on the stairs, approaching our box, despite the carpeted floor and there being no other boxes in use. The door opened. We turned to see the fairy, in full costume.

'Good evening. How are you enjoying the play?' She crossed one leg in front of the other and curtseyed as she spoke.

We both stood up, silent in surprise that a member of the cast would take the trouble to come to speak with us, and especially before the end of the play. True, of course, that her part had been played (all of her lines appear in act two) and she was required to remain in costume for the final curtain call.

'Yes, it's wonderful, but what are you doing here? I mean, it's so unexpected.' I was lost for words. We had from time to time met cast members in theatre bars after performances, although nothing compared to this treat.

'Through flood, through fire, I do wander everywhere,' she quoted her lines in a flamboyant, jocular flourish. 'We were told that you had come a long way to see the play and that it was a special occasion for you. I'm so pleased they made the box available. It means a lot to us when people are so keen to see our work, rather than it being just something to do midweek.'

A susurrus spread through the audience, as they began to notice our visitor. I struggled to think of topics of conversation. I was keen to keep talking to her.

'Yes, we're delighted to catch the end of the run. It's had such good reviews. Where are you off to next?' I meant what was she or the company appearing in as their next production. She stood silent for a moment, then with a hint of mischief in her eyes, visible despite the black commas of her makeup, she whispered.

'Duty requires that I keep watch on that mischievous Puck, ere he misleads night-wanderers.'

She made another deep curtsey before reversing through the door, then turning and leaping out of view.

'What did she mean by that?' asked Stephanie.

'I don't know I'm not sure she meant anything significant; it's just a reference to the play - her lines that describe Puck misleading night-wanderers. Still, it was good of her to come to see us. There was something familiar about her, even with the stage makeup on. I'm sure it will come to me.'

The bell rang to announce the end of the intermission.

I was beginning to feel drowsy. Every few minutes my head would roll and I would jolt awake. I was aware of wandering into a semi-dream world, where the words of the play merged with my own thoughts to create an unreal world. This was not an unpleasant situation; I welcome it in the early mornings, or at night and, indeed, try to prolong the sensation, to remain more asleep than awake and to try to control my dreams. I knew that I should not do this here, however pleasant and interesting the feeling. Perhaps the early evening drinks had not been a good idea.

I resolved to concentrate on remaining awake.

As the play progressed, something odd happened. I was slow to notice it at first. The majority of Puck's lines occur in the third act. He is on stage for almost the entire scene two. It was during this scene that I noticed his costume becoming more abundant, leafier. The foliage grew, little by little, extending across and around his lower torso. The strange thing was how this happened so slowly, without any detectable movement or intervention and without him leaving the stage.

I have no idea how the effect had been achieved. The more I noticed it, the more awake I felt. I looked for evidence of some stage artifice, a Pepper's Ghost or similar, possibly a lighting projection. The odd thing was that I sensed no one else was noticing the change. The foliage grew and grew until, by the end of act three, it covered the whole of his body and head. He had become the Green Man.

I wanted to nudge Stephanie, to discuss it with her. I decided not to - she had seemed mildly irritated by my frequent lapses towards sleep.

'Now the hungry lion roars,
And the wolf behowls the moon'

An elbow struck my ribs. I must have fallen asleep. The play was now into act five and nearing its conclusion. I immediately focussed on the stage, without turning towards Stephanie.

Puck was no longer covered in greenery. His costume now appeared as it had when the play began. Why had there been a transition to and from the Green Man? I had missed the reversion and could not understand the point, either of this or the original gradual change. When had I fallen asleep? Perhaps the whole thing was a dream. Surely, if it had formed part of the play, I would have read about it, for its unusual aspect, in the newspaper reviews.

Oh well, not to worry.

'If we shadows have offended,
Think but this, and all is mended,
That you have but slumber'd here
While these visions did appear.
And this weak and idle theme,
No more yielding but a dream...',

The play ended. The curtains closed to loud applause, then opened to reveal the complete cast taking their customary over-exaggerated bow and retreat to the rear of the stage before rushing forward, hands linked, to take another.

After the third bow, the fairy stepped forward. She looked upwards towards the circle, to the left, then the right, then to the centre. It was an actor's trick to gain attention and silence.

I felt a frisson as her gaze now focussed on our box.

'Take care, night-wanderers, be warned, beware of shrewd and knavish Puck, that he should not mislead you as you return to your homes tonight, or on any other summer's eve. He frights the maidens, plays the goat and changes babes in cradles. Take care, beware.'

She bowed and made a sweeping gesture towards Puck. The curtains closed a final time to a comprehensive round of applause and cheers.

Never have I experienced a minor character giving an unscripted speech at the end of a play, albeit brief and containing references to the text. We discussed it on our journey home. Stephanie found it endearing: the idea that we should be made aware of Robin Goodfellow's potential unseen mischief in our day-to-day lives.

It had been an enjoyable evening out. I had not missed much during my nap.

THE GARDEN

I don't like giving up. If I decide that something needs to be done, I have to follow it through. It's a compulsion that, at the best, results in wasted time, repeated disappointments, or at least failing to achieve my artificial goals. In the worst cases, it can get me into trouble - I won't go into that now.

My inability to confirm the location of Durncot all those years ago was a typical example, if anything is typical. For almost a year I kept thinking that I should have persevered with my search.

It was the same today. To be told by two parties that there was no such place was just wrong, unless they had a reason to deny its whereabouts. Surely it could not be a conspiracy covering such a wide area, including the village where the printing press was located and the Green Man pub that I assumed lay between the press and the mysterious hidden village.

I was becoming more and more determined to return, to find it and solve the mystery. The mystery of thirty years ago, made all the more enticing by the new information I had learned today. I continued driving through the countryside. The contrast between open fields and wooded lanes with occasional hilltop views was a pleasure. To tell the truth, I did not have a realistic plan. I decided to trust my memory and instinct in the hope of recognising a long-forgotten landmark that would tell me I was nearing my destination.

After a long bend, the road arrived at a crossroad of equally narrow, but passable, lanes. I slowed to read the signpost. I recognised the name of the hamlet I had passed through a few minutes earlier, although two of the others were completely unknown to me. I felt a chill in my loins as I stared at the fourth finger, pointing to the right. The name had been obliterated by a piece of nailed-on wood. Apart, that is, from the initial letter 'D'.

I parked the car on the verge, amongst the wildflowers. I took a screwdriver from the car boot and tried to lift the covering strip, without success. I could not as much as lift it to reveal even the second letter.

Why should a destination originally selected as worthy of directions now be covered up, I asked myself? I tried to think of reasons. Could it have been abandoned? Could the road be blocked off, perhaps as a result of flood or landslip? Surely, in that case, there would be diversions in place. Suspicions of a conspiracy crossed my mind once more.

The randomness of my route was at an end. This was the way to go. Hardly a firm justification, given that the second letter could have been any vowel, or the letters, R or Y, or possibly W.

To my left, a long stone wall, a little over two metres high, stretched for a few hundred metres. I was surprised to find that it straddled a wooden door, enclosed by a cut stone arch and a wooden frame. Near the top of the door a square opening at eye level, protected by vertical and horizontal metal bars, divided the view into nine squares of equal size. I was curious to see inside.

Once more I parked the car, this time on a wider verge and walked through the thigh-level wildflowers surrounding the door. I was in no hurry and felt neither guilt nor apprehension. I had not seen another car, or a single person, in half an hour. Besides, there was nothing wrong with curiosity, as long as I remained on the outside.

I approached the door with growing interest and anticipation. The closer I walked, the more I could see through the grille. Hedges: my first impression was of the yew trees, neatly manicured to an appearance of sharp edges. I thought of the sculptures of Richard Long, in particular his stone circles, which create the illusion of perfect circular symmetry, whereas what you are seeing is a collection of surfaces, edges and shapes that fool the mind into seeing a perfect circle, being the image it most identifies with. As I drew closer, the tops of flowers added a variation of colour and shape, and the softening of the architectural framework of the hedges.

Once at the door, I stared down a straight, brickwork path, leading to a stone fountain in the middle distance, midway between the gate and a far wall beyond, above which rose the roof of a manor house, with its tall, angular chimneys. To the left, a wide herbaceous border ascended to meet another high stone wall. To the right of the path, a series of yew hedges, some four metres tall, defined three sections of equal size, with paths between, both ahead of me and to my right, suggesting a grid of nine enclosures of equal size. The hedge closest to me framed an opening, sculpted into its centre to form its own entrance. Side passages led off at regular measured intervals.

The warm early-afternoon sun, interspersed with light clouds, played on my shoulders as I gazed, in a hollow of time, down the avenue beyond the gate, teasingly out of reach, as though part of a secluded community, oblivious to the outside world. It was a view that encouraged daydreaming. I imagined the lives of the family who lived there. Were they as insulated from the external world as I imagined? Did they care about the day-to-day news of politics and social issues, or did they live their lives in complete isolation and indifference to their neighbours and the wider world?

I don't know how long I had been standing there, content in my musings, when a gardener, at least I assume that's what he was, with his weather-beaten navy-blue jacket, moleskin trousers and wide-brimmed hat, crossed immediately in front of me, pushing a wheelbarrow full of uprooted plants, whose season had passed and which had gone to seed.

'You startled me,' I said, as he looked up at me and put down his wheelbarrow. 'Are you in charge of the garden here? You certainly do a wonderful job. Are you open to visitors?'

'Good afternoon, Mr Merryweather. I'm afraid not. The garden is open for just one day a year, as part of nearby village festivities. It's for the benefit of local people. We don't advertise; admission is by invitation or recommendation.'

A frisson flowed over me. I tried my best to ignore the shock of unexpected recognition and continued to look him in the eye. He continued to look me up and down, discreetly, as he spoke.

'That's a shame. It looks so enticing. Even from here, on the outside, it makes you wonder what's around each turn. I imagine there must be quite a few of you employed to maintain it in this condition.'

He nodded. There was no reason why he should share this information with a stranger, whose agenda might include burglary or theft of garden ornaments.

'Have you worked here long?' I added. 'It must be a real pleasure for you.'

'Over fifty years. It's all I've ever known.'

'That's amazing! You must know every square inch of it.' I felt a bit sheepish, saying this. I had no idea how large it could be. The length of the stone wall suggested that the size of the whole property would run to several acres.

His expression mellowed.

'Have you come far? I've not seen you in these parts before.' He looked at the car, glancing at the number plate.

'Yes, quite a long way, actually. I've been to buy some books at a printing press about three-quarters of an hour away. The Walnut Tree Press - I don't suppose you will have heard of it. I've been there a couple of times over the years. They produce lovely books of poetry and prose, many illustrated with engravings of rural scenes and gardens.'

I didn't mention the altered signpost.

'I'm on my way to Durncot. I went there many, many years ago and decided I'd like to see it again. I can't locate it for some reason and no one in the area recognises the name. I've tried several times to find it, but with no joy. Not to worry though, it's all part of the day out, a bit of an adventure really.'

Another man emerged from one of the side passages. He was overdressed for the weather, in plus fours, a checked waistcoat and tweed jacket. The phrase 'keeping up appearances' came to mind. I imagined him dressed in this way every day, quite possibly in the same outfit. His grey hair and bushy moustache gave him an Edwardian appearance, and quite possibly reflected his values.

The gardener turned to face him, having noticed my gaze move from eye contact to across his shoulder. I waited as he walked over to his employer. After all, I had not been sent away, yet, and one, if not both of them, knew my name.

The gardener returned; his master stood his ground. He selected a large key from a bunch produced from his jacket pocket. He turned the lock and unfastened two bolts from the top and bottom of the gate. From the sound they made it was clear they were not in regular use. He opened the gate.

'Mr Wyrdstaff would like to meet you. I explained to him that you were keen to see the garden. He has invited you in.'

He closed and locked the gate behind me and followed me to the opening in the hedge, where his employer had remained, waiting.

'You can get on with your work now, Darnell,' said the country gentleman. 'Good morning. Welcome to Hefenwick Hall.'

'Good morning, Mr Wyrdstaff. I believe you already know my name.'

'You may call me Edmund. So, you'd like to take a look inside the garden. Well, your interest seems genuine enough and I imagine you will find it interesting, more so than you might imagine. Let me tell you a little about its history and design and then I'll leave you to walk around.'

I felt apprehensive at the welcome and kind offer. I was a stranger, whose true motives were being taken on trust. I was keen to show respect and to avoid undue curiosity that would hint at ulterior motives. For all he knew I could be planning a burglary... on the other hand, I had been recognised, perhaps even expected.

'Excuse me asking, do you have any connection with the bookshop and the Walnut Tree Press?'

'These days we're all connected. Six degrees of separation, I believe they call it. Let me put it this way. It's unusual for someone to discover certain places and things in this area. Finding it at all, by accident is peculiar enough. To recognise its special qualities and to want to return and rediscover it is exceptional. Believe me, we have ways of keeping ourselves to ourselves. You can regard yourself as privileged.'

What did they know about me? How did they find out? Most importantly, what was it that they had in mind for me? They must have some kind of plan. I consciously asked myself whether this was really happening. I had visited the general area only once before, thirty years ago. This was ridiculous.

I had to be on my guard. They knew my name and this provided them with the ability to create an air of mystery. Were they trying to draw me in, to some mysterious activity or for some nefarious purpose? Nonsense, I told myself. There must be a connection with the printing press. The owners there had welcomed me on both occasions and had given me a generous amount of their time. I did not need to worry.

'I am very grateful to you for agreeing to show me your garden.'

'No, I will not be escorting you. I will tell you a little about it and I will then leave you to walk around, alone, in your own time. Please take as long as you choose. The route you will follow is clearly laid out. There is one stipulation: that you at no time turn back. It is essential that you pay careful attention to what I have to say, in order to obtain the maximum benefit.'

There was no reason to disagree or to question the terms of my visit. Why should I not turn back? It was unimportant; I willingly agreed to the terms.

'What you are about to see is only a small, enclosed area of the grounds, centuries old. The route will lead you through a series of nine garden rooms of equal size that reflect your life, starting with your past, passing through the present and leading to your future, to terminate at the centre of the area. It represents what you think. It changes shape according to your destiny. It is a reflection of your soul. You must give yourself up to it. Remember, too, that a garden is a living organism, both its plants and design. Changes are possible, albeit often with a lot of hard work.'

It was an interesting concept, to design an outdoor space that every visitor could identify with. Was he referring to some form of mindfulness? Perhaps he had travelled to Hindu or Buddhist lands, as a geographer, naturalist or even a military man, where he had observed local practices and developed his own eclectic views and adapted them into a garden landscape.

'Follow the path, the natural route, in the same way that you would follow your destiny.' He gestured with his hand to the opening in the hedge, directing me to the specified route.

I assumed that the trail would be circular and would eventually lead me back to my starting point, where I could thank him before leaving. I wondered whether this was the reason I was not to turn back, to ensure that I would not become lost, although if what I was about to see was a 'small, enclosed area'…

I thanked him and shook his hand. He walked away in the direction of the house. To my left was a long brick path, adjacent to a wide bed of perennials ascending in height, sheltered by a high stone wall, similar to that bordering the road. My intuition told me not to take this, but to enter the first of three visible garden rooms, enclosed by yew hedges. I strolled from the gate towards the opening cut into the hedge.

I passed under the open arch, expecting to see either a low, formal arrangement or an area sub-divided into beds containing perennials, harmonious in their colours and complementary in height, with a continuous view through the arches of the next gardens.

The enclosure was much larger than I had foreseen from outside, perhaps ten times. It was heavily planted, both horizontally and vertically, the vertical space being defined by a canopy formed from horizontally pleached lime trees, each forced into a circular shape above a long, slender bole to give the appearance of a parasol. Some had had their trunks trained away from the vertical and overlapped in my gaze, making it impossible to see the exit, which, I deduced, must logically be on the opposite side from where I had entered. Head-high topiary formed a simple maze between the limes, interspersed with mirrors and other reflective surfaces: steel, glass, Perspex, plastic and acrylic, in shapes and colours designed to distort reflections and mislead the visitor in their quest for progress. It was not a true maze, more an avenue of hedges with alcoves, designed to lead the visitor in a fixed direction, with diversions.

It was as if I had awoken from a long, deep sleep. I felt relaxed and lethargic, slow in my thought. I put it down to dehydration from the long hot drive.

Sculptures and statues, also in predominantly reflective materials, intermingling with the brightest of flowers, added to the confusion. Red and yellow roses grew abundantly, as did a disproportionate number of delphiniums. What little I know of the plant world I learned from my mother, who had shared with me her knowledge of plant symbolism and had taught me to recognise a broad selection of flowers, trees, shrubs and herbs. As a young child, I had listened with interest. By the time I had reached my teens it had become tedious and I avoided such conversations when possible. For the first time in my life, I was now able to use the information which had been instilled in me by repetition.

I turned into an area housing a collection of mechanical devices, each separated from its neighbour by a low partition of perennials, whose flowers were about to bloom. There was a marble run, a miniature roller coaster, with a chain, on which shallow cups lifted the coloured balls and tipped them onto the metal tracks. They rolled along a series of slopes, loops and switchbacks, ending at the foot of the chain, to be lifted once more.

Another machine used winches to lift little pails of water that were tipped into channels. The water ran on to fill containers which, when filled, tipped into new channels, flowing in various directions. The streams emptied into a large wide bucket. When full, the bucket tipped over a model of a group of children, whose eyes closed with the weight of the water.

Other creations featured wooden puppet figures that operated simple mechanical machinery to humorous effect, sawing logs and watering plants.

I could hear a voice, speaking in a low moan, behind the next hedge. Perhaps there was someone else here, another visitor. I turned the corner to face a wall with a Romanesque alcove. At head height, a tortured mask of an open-mouthed grey face spoke repeated phrases. The mask was solid stone, apart from the lips, made of a pliant material to give the illusion of a living being speaking, in time with the recorded words. I struggled to make out what it was saying, until I realised that the words were in French: 'J'ai faim. Que j'ai du faim. Me donnez quelque chose à manger.' It took me a moment or two to realise that this was a mechanical talking rubbish bin.

In the next enclosure, the path forked either side of a fishpond. A bridge, made of three metallic strips crossed the water diagonally. 'Why walk around it, when you can take the direct route across the water?' I thought to myself. I stepped onto the first sheet of metal. It triggered jets of water, splashing me at head height.

The theme of this garden room was jovial, merry: playing tricks. I would need to be on my guard.

Interspersed among the humorous scenes and artefacts I found peculiar statues, one holding its head under its arm, whose glass eyes appeared to follow me and to blink.

The next compartment housed a low box hedge, raised in parts, designed in the form of a Solomon's knot.

I was startled by something that brushed the back of my neck. I was shocked. I imagined it to be someone's fingers touching me, stroking me. Startled, I spun around. Leaning over me, swaying from side to side, a topiary figure, trimmed to a near-human form, rustled in the light breeze. I had no idea of what shrub it was, that could be tailored to a recognisable image, yet be so flexible as to bow and sway while retaining its shape. It was certainly not box, yew, privet, or holly. Whatever it was, the designer had had a stroke of genius to find the ideal plant to create a moving, almost lifelike image to suggest the Green Man.

I had reached the end of the first section and was impatient to see what delights, or otherwise, the following ones would hold. I took a deep breath and walked slowly towards the gap in the hedge that would take me to the next.

The first thing I noticed on entering the second room was the swathe of purple carnations to my right, planted to look as if growing naturally in a miniature meadow of many grasses, attended by bees that hummed in drunken satisfaction. I had never seen so many planted together, of any colour.

To my left, in a triptych of tableaux, low box hedges separated groups of statues and ornaments, interspersed with flowers and shrubs.

In the first tableau, a group of three marble statues was set together in the foreground. One, a male figure, was covered in ivy, except for his eyes, nose, mouth and hands. His right hand was raised, as if in blessing, or to signify peace. The foliage gripping his face had grown, or had been trimmed to look like a beard, giving him a smiling, saintly look. Another Green Man...

In his left hand, he held the wrist of a statue of a woman, who appeared untroubled, or unaware of her nakedness. Her gaze travelled across the Green Man to a seated figure, equally unconcerned by both his and her absence of clothing, who looked up at her in admiration. The three were located in front of a shallow pond. On an island at its centre, surrounded by water, stood a sculpture of a building, whose height was disproportionate to its girth and appeared to incorporate designs of fantastic beasts, unknown to me.

Behind the lake roamed topiary animals: a giraffe, a lion with its captured prey and a work in progress of an elephant, the trunk not yet fully trained to a wire support.

A flock of tiny birds flew in and out of the flowers and bushes. Two rabbits ran in front of me, followed by a cat carrying a mouse.

I looked towards the statues once more. They had

changed their positions. The Green Man was holding the woman's hand forward, as if presenting her to me. The seated man now faced in my direction; the woman avoided my gaze.

I blinked. When I opened my eyes, all three had reverted to their original poses. My imagination was playing tricks; I had become the object of a merry jest.

The larger, central tableau was composed of many collections of smaller figures, gambolling naked in a pleasurable, unselfconscious way, many embracing with an air of innocent affection. Contrasting with these figures, giant topiary fruit and birds lay among cherry and plum trees. An electric model of groups of people riding an assortment of animals rotated anti-clockwise, up and down as if on a roofless carousel, on the banks of a pond where bathers frolicked. At the rear of the tableau metallic sculptures, some flask-like, some built of phallic components, floated in a larger pond.

In the foreground, oversized open shells attracted the curiosity of yet more naked figures, who were looking or crawling inside.

There were many plants in strange and sensual shapes that I could not recognise, and giant fish, some with wings. The entire scene was one of feasting and sensuality, yet sporting an overall air of innocence and genuine shared pleasure, amidst bright and vibrant flowers.

The third installation was a similar size to the first. It was a sinister affair, a dark garden, hellish in nature, hell represented by a metal brazier from which a stylised fire of illuminated orange and red material blew upwards in a jet of air. The joys of the previous section were supplanted by images of war, torture, pain and death.

I recognised an interpretation of the seven deadly sins, with animals inflicting death and torture upon human figures, their punishment designed to fit their sin.

Two tree stumps, like massive, gnarled legs, bore a stone figure, whose gaze of resignation stared from beneath a pointed hat. Its buttocks were open, revealing a painting of drunken revellers.

Demons and unfamiliar creatures abounded, devouring people. A figure of a giant rabbit carried an impaled and bleeding corpse. A creature with a bird's head feasted on a human body.

Some statues doubled as fountains, the water flowing from their mouths and buttocks, to represent vomiting and defecation. Giant musical instruments lay scattered about, including a harp bearing a crucified figure.

The few plants and shrubs that grew in this area were dark, unflowering, wilting. How peculiar that the sculptures, models and statues should take precedence over plants and nature in this area.

I remembered Edmund's words, that the garden reflected my past, present and future. This room, the triptych, was a microcosm of that idea. It represented my beginning, my current life and foretold the end. There was a message here. I must choose whether to heed it, or to ignore it at my peril.

Onwards. I had to move onwards. I wanted to learn more of my future!

The third room housed an open-air theatre, the stage and auditorium laid out on the diagonal. Being the third room of the grid of nine, the square lent itself to the layout of an entrance and an exit on adjacent sides, opposite to the stage in the far, north-western corner. I entered the passage and descended half a dozen steps between the rows of grass terraces. Tiers of stone slab seating arced to my right. From the front of the auditorium, an adjoining aisle led at a right angle, up another flight of steps to the exit and the entrance to the next room. Above the midway point between the entrance and exit, a high opening housed the control booth where the sound and lighting would be balanced.

The front rows sat in a hollowed-out area, such that

the sloping stage was at head height for those spectators. The stage was similarly grassed; the curved front of the apron edged with precisely cut granite blocks. The wings and rear of the stage were formed from bamboo screens. Mounted on the proscenium, which was covered with a heavy white canvas, was a network of scaffolding bearing lights, rows of curtains and scenery. A mask of a Green Man looked down from the centre of the arch with a smiling, kindly expression. Bright yellow coreopsis flowers bordered the stage.

The bright sunlight, appearing between occasional fast-moving white clouds, showed the theatre at its best. This was a fair-weather theatre, in immaculate condition, looking at the height of its preparation for an imminent performance. I walked across and upwards to sit above the control booth, to take in as much of the view as possible. With the late morning warmth at my back, I enjoyed a feeling of gratitude. I was blessed with good fortune to have found this place.

The white backdrop of the stage lit up, yet I had seen no one, either in the garden or in the control booth. A kaleidoscopic projection of melting colours lit up the screen. A caption appeared in the centre, growing from a tiny image of letters to fill the illuminated area with the word 'Title', before adding 'A Harmonious Life'.

Was this perhaps a rehearsal, not for a theatrical production, but a film screening to be held this evening? Unlikely, given that on my way here and at the gate through which I had been admitted there was no sign of publicity, although I acknowledge that most visitors would arrive using the main entrance and drive, wherever that may be. It was odd, nevertheless, that there was no evidence of anyone watching, other than me. I reasoned that there may well be hidden cameras allowing the organisers to monitor what was happening remotely.

I decided to relax and take advantage of the free screening. After all, I would not be here when the scheduled event took place.

My feeling of relaxation was not to last long. The play began. I was immediately engrossed. The subject of the film was my family or, more precisely, scenes from my life with Stephanie and the children. A large-screen home movie, with flickering black and white grainy scenes, in the style of a nineteen-fifties hand-held amateur camera, whose source I could not imagine. Once or twice I imagined I saw subliminal images of the Green Man, smiling, benevolent, like the mask over the stage.

Over the next fifteen minutes, I watched a series of chapters from my family life, all happy. The final shot was a slow zoom to a close-up of Adam's smiling face. The film then faded to darkness.

These scenes were from my past. There must be more to come before my future would be revealed.

I felt a tear roll down my cheek.

I walked on, to the right, through the hedge to the next section. It did not open directly onto a view, but onto a screening hedge directly behind the opening, passable at either side. I remembered the aling-aling I had seen widespread in Balinese domestic architecture, designed to screen off the interior courtyard of a home from the outside world and to prevent evil spirits from entering the house compound.

A window had been cut into the centre of the hedge, to provide a teasing, framed view of what was to come. I paused at the opening, entranced by the delights of what I was about to experience.

As with the previous rooms, the interior dimensions were greater than could have been guessed from outside. A miniature landscape of mountains, waterfalls, a valley, streams and forests, spread before me, creating an illusion, not of a Balinese garden, as I had expected, but of a Japanese rural panorama. It had been constructed with such care and attention to the detail of perspective that my brain automatically interpreted it on a grand scale, as if looking at a photograph. Despite the miniaturisation, the effect was of a natural landscape. I imagined I could sense the kami, the spirits, who inhabited this glade. I could not wait to explore.

The design was laid out on a north-south axis (I knew the house was to the north). I passed to the left of the hedge, where a Torii gate marked the entrance to a sacred space, representing the transition between the finite world and the infinite world of the gods.

From there, a gravel track led in what promised to be a clockwise route, to arrive at a building in the south - I could just make out the ridge of its roof. The landscape had been created principally by digging down into the enclosure, with a raised area, almost opposite me, representing a mountainside, with the top of a cascade at its centre, falling behind the low trees ahead and beneath me. To my left, pines reached up, almost to the top of the main, framing hedges. Below them, oaks, cherry, apricot and maple, and cypress, cedar and camellia trees tumbled down harmoniously and in proportion to their size to meet a stream that entered from the east and flowed towards me at the western end. That so many varieties of tree were enclosed harmoniously in such a space drew me into a tranquil and relaxed state of mindfulness. I walked slowly down the winding descent into the valley.

New vistas opened up. A bank of azaleas tumbled down the hillside. At the foot of the hill, in a flatter area, I saw bushes trimmed into rounded shapes, the group combining to resemble a pattern of waves, lapping up to a bamboo gateway, where the tips of both sides touched high above me.

I could imagine how the view, this brainchild of some brilliant garden designer, inspired by travels to Japan, would change colour and form with the seasons: cherry blossom and azaleas in Spring, irises in June and rich foliage colours in autumn.

I passed through the bamboo gateway to the side of a stream, where a pair of cranes walked with grace and dignity, untroubled by my presence.

The stream opened onto a lake, whose irregular shape was bordered by a pavement of large flat rocks. A plain wooden bridge arched gently across to an island, covered with white sand, raked into patterns of waves: delicate crests rising above curved ripples. Three grey stones of differing heights, rested in apparently random positions, their yellow veins flowing upwards. The tallest resembled a temple; the shortest nestled, snug, in the sand. To one side, low woody bushes with angular stems and branches crouched like a troupe of ageing ballerinas.

Ahead of me, a level stone bridge connected to a second island. I stopped midway on the bridge to gaze at the goldfish and carp, which surfaced in expectation of food. Into the bamboo tube of a shishi-odoshi, water flowed from a bamboo half-pipe. When full, it tipped with the weight of the water to clack against a stone bowl and emptied, presumably to inhibit birds from stealing the fish. A third bridge, made of logs and covered with earth and moss, led me on to the far shore.

I could hear the distant (though it could not be far away) sound of a waterfall. No, a cascade; it was the gentle sound of water tumbling between rocks that I could hear, not that of water dropping from a great height.

I felt calm - serene and contemplative - in this secret landscape, whose illusions continued to engage me as to how they were formed. I stopped and stared. It was partly the compartmentalisation, the concealment of what was to come, and also the scale of objects in visual planes. Each vista was constructed in the perspective of a Japanese landscape painting. Large objects, such as upright stones and taller trees, were set in the foreground, with progressively smaller features in the intermediate and distant planes. Yet every element seemed natural, perfectly positioned to envelop and cocoon the visitor from the outside world, moving him or her to a feeling of serenity.

I reached the cascade, with its lapping pool beneath, in which stepping-stones of hard volcanic rock, the veins of which were aligned in a single direction, invited an adventurous, yet safe, crossing. Pines of various sizes, their trunks twisted into graceful flowing shapes, clung to the gaps between the rocks, their finger roots digging deep to drink from stray drops and rivulets. I peered into a gap between the rocks, where a continuous trickle dropped into a dark, descending cave. I could not see how deep it was. The edges were too slippery to tread close.

The path led to the right of the waterfall, to approach the shady southern edge, sloping gently upwards between rows of azaleas. A series of stone lanterns was set between the path and a gently flowing stream. I was curious to reach the source of the flowing water.

On turning to the left, I discovered a pond, again full of fish and lotus flowers, flanked by a rocky wall. I continued upwards, towards an inviting fork to the right, which I could not resist. Hidden from the view of the rest of the garden, a simple wooden building, with a thatched roof, stood diagonally on the opposite side of a damp, mossy lawn, strewn with leaves. It had no windows, just a single wooden vertical shutter, propped open with a stick.

It was a teahouse. I could imagine a hermit living there, away from the gaze of any passers-by, living in contemplation, undistracted by the view. The building's placement, in the corner opposite to me, framed by the rocks and trees, drew me into it, as if I were following a flock of wild geese in flight.

A sturdy wooden bench to the left sat adjacent to a compact structure, which I found to be a privy. Between this and the teahouse, I noticed a stone water basin. I was hot; I washed my hands and splashed my face before approaching the open shutters. Inside, two tatami mats lay waiting.

I climbed upwards, behind the teahouse, into the

trees, where celandines bloomed, out of season. I passed the statue of a Buddha in a meditative pose, its light-coloured stone almost covered with thick green moss, so beloved of the Japanese people. Though I could no longer see the teahouse beneath me, a new, retrospective view opened up, creating a sense of belonging and an instant nostalgia for what I had seen and experienced. I felt a longing, a sadness that I had just passed beyond one of the most satisfying experiences of my life, without having realised it at the time. I wanted to remain, but I knew that it was already in the past, that my ongoing journey could not surpass what I had not until now acknowledged to have been the best of times.

The temperature dropped, as a tangible mist rolled in. I heard a distant rumble of thunder. It was time to move into the next themed section.

I looked behind me. I knew I must not turn back.

The chill mist descended within a few minutes. I felt the moisture on my arms and forehead. I had reached the fifth room, at the corner of the northern side of the matrix.

Whereas open gaps and arches cut into the topiary had defined the entrances to the previous rooms, a full-height metal turnstile gate now interrupted my progress. It looked new and fitted snugly into the hedge. I did not understand the need; it was not as though the garden was often open to visitors, and why stop them from retracing their steps?

The turnstile was difficult to operate. I pushed hard with both hands, bracing myself against the frame. Eventually it gave, emitting a pained screech, like a bird caught by a cat. There could be no return now.

Inside, a convex marble wall, two metres tall, sheltered a delicate, slender rose bush. I stopped to admire its single, deep chocolate flower. When I moved closer, it became clear that it was black, with no hint of other tones. Drops from the mist were beginning to cling to the buds.

An unseen robin began to chirp; the shrill melody pierced the mist. I love their high-pitched song - they are one of the few birds to sing throughout the year. I prefer the spring and summer song, so positive and confident, to the autumn song, with its quieter, melancholic air, hinting of winter.

Birdsong raises my spirits. Chirp, chirrup… Cheer up!

This was a ghostly garden, a haunting garden. My footsteps crunched the gravel underfoot, with a sound like distant muffled gunfire. I meandered between groups of shrubs, selected to complement each other and at different peaks in their annual cycle to provide continuity of interest. Each section of the room contained a unique artefact. Some looked out of place in such a setting. I wondered whether they were placed as a puzzle for the visitor to solve, a rebus.

Enjoying my exploration, I was becoming accustomed to the idea of a hidden set of clues to be solved. I had identified several relating to my past. Those symbols that were unfamiliar I could contemplate later. From this point onwards I had to concentrate on interpreting the themes of rooms I had yet to visit.

A bronze-green Victorian post box leaned, lop-sided, half-hidden. I followed the short, muddy track that led off to it. I had only ever seen one in a museum. I admired the hexagonal shape and the rich colour, offset by a gold cypher and coat of arms, and the leaves and acanthus bud decorating its cap. A bouquet of slate envelopes stuck out from the aperture, as if the box were full. Another single missive, also slate, lay on the floor, its address etched in distressed characters, as if the ink had run in the rain.

Cobwebs stretched between the low trees and bushes, rendered visible by the now vanishing mist. Dense accumulations of the wispy, silvery threads formed shrouds over the upright conifers, made eerier where they extended to neighbouring growth, creating half-seen images of ghostly forms through gaps in the foliage. Trees creaked in the intermittent light breeze, branches moaned as they rubbed against each other. Squirrels chattered in a sinister rebuke, as though plotting something. I heard a distant sound of someone sawing with a squeaky blade.

I passed a fingerpost, leaning to one side. Three of its digits were completed obliterated and unreadable. I smiled as I looked at the fourth, pointing upwards to '….cot', the leading letters reduced to four black smudges.

A statue, in the Greek style, poured an urn of gold coins and water into a pool, which in turn fed into a drain. Its neighbour, a Buddha figure, looked on, hands together in prayer.

I walked on, to discover a grassy rectangle, where an oversize bronze bull crouched, as if about to charge me, its head low, displaying long, handlebar horns and a twisting torso, showing off its exaggerated muscular strength.

Behind the bull, a fountain played. Beyond the fountain lay a square gravelled area, dominated at the centre by a tree, like no other that I had seen. It must have been three metres in height. Its thin branches curled upwards, then over to droop in the manner of a weeping birch or willow. Indeed, the branches were as thin as those at the extremities of a willow. It bore tiny leaves, barely covering the twigs that bore them. The breeze sifted through the tree to make a moaning sound. But it was the fruits, or seeds, that were most unusual.

They hung in strands, with ten or more borne by the same string-like branch, each spinning in alternate directions, shaped like lace bobbins. From time to time one or more would drop to the ground, making a noise, a splash in the gravel. The dropping seeds exploded as they hit the ground, scattering a mixture of seed and black dust.

I walked carefully past it and around the final bend, from where I could see the opening to the next garden room. A brick-based glasshouse faced the sun, its roof windows propped wide open. I stepped inside. It was filled with jasmine. The scent calmed my senses; I am sure my heart rate dropped. I breathed deeply. Jasmine, Yasmin; truly a gift of God.

Black clouds began to gather, bringing the threat of a thunderstorm. The rain was holding off for now. A flash of lightning and another roll of thunder urged me to move on. There may be troubling times ahead.

In the next area of the garden, a bed of purple and pink tulips spread before me. I would have expected these to be planted in a bed. Here they grew wild, between fallen trees, laid out as if awaiting the return of the woodman after a storm. I was about to discover the garden of lost and broken objects.

Ivy had claimed cracked and shattered terracotta pots, its aerial roots invading their crevices, drawing them towards the earth from which they had been fashioned. Broken crockery, some decorated in the styles of Ironbridge manufacturers - Coalport, Jackfield and others, willow pattern - lay in recognisable fragments among the flowers.

I admired sculptures made from broken glass, carefully constructed to represent human or animal subjects, their bright mosaic skin reflecting snapshots of the sky, the flowers and trees, the soil. An image of Pegasus made of broken mirror shards and stained glass glinted in the sunlight from the diminishing breaks in the cloud. Pegasus reared, one front hoof raised higher than the other, a quiver of thunderbolts strapped between his wings.

Two dilapidated wooden sheds, their paint distressed, housed vintage tractors, surrounded by agricultural and garden machinery and tools. None of the machinery appeared to be in working order.

I walked along an avenue of cordoned fruit trees, attached to parallel rows of posts and wires, leading to an octagonal greenhouse. Its benches were filled with potted bonsai trees, their stunted branches, like the cordons, disciplined, forced, into unnatural shapes.

Beyond the greenhouse, a shorter row of similar fruit trees came to an abrupt end. Suspended from the naked wires hung dried out carcasses of dead moles, magpies and other deemed pests. A swarm of ants teemed beneath. A green woodpecker startled me with a mocking, two-tone call. I must have disturbed it from its feast.

The birdcall unsettled me. My mood changed. I felt a sense of sadness and disillusionment that the earlier pleasures and the joy that I had taken from the well-tended garden, were deteriorating into chaos and despair. It was as if my trust, previously unquestioning, had been betrayed. Something had changed and would never again be as before. Everything was starting to go downhill.

The threatening storm broke. I ran to the greenhouse for shelter.

The storm quickly passed. The sun shone again.

I looked up to the sky as I entered the seventh room. There was no rainbow. As with the garden, I needed to modify my expectations and to think about consequences and outcomes.

Aloe, asphodel, marigolds and cypress were the trees and plants I identified first. As before, there were many plants in flower that should not have been, with an increasing number of bushes and trees twisted into cruel, tortured shapes.

A fast-flowing stream lay ahead, amid jagged rocks set close together, forcing the swift waters to twist and turn, producing a miniature rapid, where the waters broke into foam and spray. Clear and shallow, the stream's swift current conveyed a sense of implied danger.

A simple bridge allowed me to cross in safety. I stepped gingerly across the wide, ridged, alternate black and grey planks, taking care on the wet surface.

On the far side, next to the path, a single, tall tombstone, flanked by lesser, upright stones, leaned at an angle. I struggled to read the faint inscription, barely visible beneath the lichen. I took my keys from my pocket and stroked gently, taking care not to scrape or deface the aged stone. I managed to reveal a few of the letters:

'In mem**iam, **a*'

The second line was indecipherable, aside from a few numbers, no doubt dates. I worked patiently at the third line, until I uncovered the following fragment:

'A tr*sting **mpanio*'

It was a pet cemetery: a dog's grave. The occupant must have been missed more than its present neighbours, whose burials were recorded with simple, unmarked stones. The memorials were arranged as a group, beneath an ancient gnarled oak, whose dead branches exposed rotten extremities. A large lightning gash in the trunk revealed a hollow interior.

I noticed that one of the stones, at the far side of the group, bore a miniature carved scroll. I stepped towards it, in what I considered to be a respectful manner, to examine it, taking care not to tread upon the graves. I knelt down to read the deep cut words: 'The child that might have been'. Surely not! I shuddered at the idea of what lay beneath. I could not bear to think about the torment the parents must have suffered. I looked away, then walked on.

I heard a faint sound coming from the cemetery behind me. Its timbre suggested a cuckoo, but it was not birdsong. The same three repeated notes, rising, descending, rising, and then rising again. It sounded familiar. And then I recognised it. It was organ music, the motif from Fauré's requiem: the In Paradisum movement. I knew it well and had often followed the score when listening to it at home: the organ stops marked 'voix céleste, gamba'.

I knew that my visit was approaching its end. I felt sad, both at this realisation and the pathos of music. I was fearful too.

I am not good at being strong in adversity. I must try harder, for the sake of others.

As I passed through the exit, the oak tree creaked and groaned. A branch snapped, then fell across the gap.

I had reached the penultimate stage in my journey. Beyond the gap in the hedge, the path swept to the left, then again to the right, twice. I wondered whether I might be about to enter a maze; I discovered instead a long avenue of roses, which met overhead to form a tunnel. They stretched ahead in a straight parallel border, lined on both sides with an inner row of hornbeams, growing to head height. To my left was a stone tablet bearing the following inscription:

> "... go not astray in her paths.
> For she hath cast down many wounded: yea, many strong [men] have been slain by her.
> Her house [is] the way to hell, going down to the chambers of death."

Proverbs 7:25-7.

I could not understand the geometry of the overall garden design. Each room varied in size and shape. Each was ushering me to my destination: the final room at the centre. The eighth room, in which I now stood, was long and narrow. The roses, trained into dense arches, grew so profusely as to block out the overhead light, and to focus the visitor's attention on what lay ahead. As the path proceeded, the colours of the flowers changed, becoming darker, from white to cream, peach, yellow, then to red, indigo, violet and black, and back to white again.

At the far end, I could see brightness, a shaft of dazzling light radiating downwards, its rays spread as you might see in an art deco window, appearing as a ramp leading up to a light source located in the final, ninth room. I walked slowly, with feelings of apprehension, acknowledgement and resignation.

My progress had at first been casual, relaxed, with a sense of freedom, to be able to choose to go where I pleased, as long as I complied with the instruction not to turn back. The latter rooms hinted at a lack of alternative, with no option to retrace my steps, no second chance. It was as if I had not realised that there had been choices, alternatives that I could have made earlier. It was worrying that these were in the sections represented by my past; the future offered no such consolation. I had missed my opportunity. I must now live out my life as it was mapped. I was resigned to what lay ahead.

There was nothing I could do. It was too late. I was compelled to submit to whatever the future would bring. I had no options; there was just the one way to go, with no escape, no other means of exit. My return was barred. The path was dark, with scant light passing through the intertwined rose arches overhead. Ahead, the light shone brightly from the direction of the next and final room.

I stared at this brilliance before me. I began to walk forwards again, unsettled, as if in a trance. Though my feet were moving, I sensed that some invisible resistant force was hindering my approach. I remember a floating sensation and feeling as if I were walking in the wrong direction along a travellator. I was aware of the ground beneath my feet, yet I was making no progress.

I looked again in the direction of the final room, knowing that soon I would enter. A bronze bell rested on two stone pillars in front of a fountain. Behind the fountain, a Corinthian column supported a golden urn from which rose gold and orange flames.

And then, the silhouette of a woman moved into the aperture, obscuring the beams of light at its centre. I was sure it was Bella.

The light grew brighter; she beckoned to me to approach and enter. I took a step forward.

'He's coming round. Are you all right, Oliver? Here, take some water.'

I opened my eyes. I was lying on the grass, looking upwards at a clear bright sky. Peaceful: that's what I remember, peaceful. From either side of me, Darnell and Mr Wyrdstaff leaned over me.

'You passed out. We were worried about you,' said Mr Wyrdstaff.

I sat up onto my elbows. I was on the grass near to the gate where I had originally come in. They must have carried me here. I took a sip from the glass.

'Yes, thank you. It must have been the heady smell of the flowers.'

'You take it easy and rest there for a while,' said Darnell.

'Thank you. I have to be going. I have to be somewhere.'

'Are you sure you are well enough to drive?' said Mr Wyrdstaff.

'Yes, yes, I'm fine. I'll be all right. Thank you for allowing me to visit - and for looking after me just now.'

'Well, you didn't quite make it to the end,' said Darnell.

I wanted to ask if I could return to look at the ninth garden, half-hoping to catch another sight of Bella but decided against. I stood up and brushed myself down. I thanked them once again for their hospitality and apologised for any inconvenience and for the disruption to their day.

'I must be on my way to Durncot. It's been rather a rushed walk round. I'd love to come back another time, if I may. Perhaps if I come back this way, if I have the time.'

I noticed them exchange conspiratorial glances. I said nothing.

'Well, I doubt we'll see you again. No one ever returns to the garden; it's not possible,' said Mr Wyrdstaff. His eyes narrowed. 'I do wish you luck with your search. I hope you're prepared.'

Startled by his response, I was about to ask what he meant, then hesitated. He clearly knew or had heard of Durncot. I sensed both men were withholding information they could readily have proffered either now or when I had first arrived. Their words were friendly, but I felt an undertow of concealed purpose. How had they known my name? Mr Wyrdstaff – Edmund - had been evasive when I had asked about a connection to the Walnut Tree Press.

Edmund and Darnell continued to exchange enigmatic smiles. I was convinced they knew something; there must be a link between the Press, the garden and Durncot. For the first time, I felt threatened, not by them but the growing evidence of a conspiracy, of which I was at the centre. I decided against asking further questions. I thanked them a final time and turned to leave.

They showed me out of the gate and bade me goodbye with a formal courtesy and handshakes. I heard the locks turn behind me.

I started the car to continue my journey, relieved to have escaped from an unidentified sense of imminent and growing danger. Now I had time to think rationally through the events of the past hour.

There was something odd about Mr Wyrdsatff's parting comments. I couldn't quite put my finger on it. Why had he made a point of stating how it was so difficult to find certain places around here, let alone return to an area where people were intent on keeping themselves to themselves? Yes, of course, it was unlikely he would see me again. It had, after all, been a chance visit, after having taken an unplanned diversion. But why did he say no one ever returns and that he hoped I was prepared for Durncot? Was Durncot a source of danger and was that the reason I would not be returning?

This was nonsense! I reasoned that my mind was starting to play tricks on me and resolved to dismiss the idea.

But I couldn't. I recalled his words before I began the tour. He had said quite clearly that the route would lead me through a series of nine rooms of equal size that reflected my life, beginning with my past, passing through the present and leading to my future, which he said would 'terminate' at the centre. I had not reached the centre - it was the one room I had not entered before I passed out. I have never fainted in my life. Was it possible that...? No, they couldn't have done that.

I took a few deep breaths and felt calmer, almost serene. I was determined to think positively. The tour had been an interesting and worthwhile diversion. The experience had been more than a garden, it had been a thought-provoking theme park. I had understood a little of the imagery, yet by no means could I claim to have fully interpreted the meaning of everything I had seen and encountered. The latter sections, in particular, were a mystery to me. I felt a mixture of apprehension, excitement, as well as the sense of danger about what the future might hold.

I had seen glimpses, hints at my future that were both cryptic and worrying. It was at present a mystery that I could not decode. I had spent too much time in the garden; I now had to press on and find Durncot. I wanted to be sure of reaching my destination before nightfall. On my original trip, all those years ago, the journey from the Walnut Tree Press had taken not much more than thirty minutes. Why was it taking so much longer? I was no wiser as to where I was heading. It did not look to be a happy place.

BLESSINGS

We met at a party, Stephanie and I. Well, more of a social gathering really, of colleagues at the large IT company where we were working in different departments. I had seen her before, several times. We had passed each other in corridors or had found ourselves in the same lift. Until then we had not had occasion to speak, other than when exchanging polite greetings when holding doors open.

I am not a party person. I find it difficult to introduce myself to strangers and to make small talk. I don't think I have much of interest to say to other people. It's easier to wait for them to speak to me and to respond to what they have to say, to encourage them to talk.

When I arrived, around eight o'clock, I told my hosts that I would probably only stay for a couple of hours, that I had an appointment in the morning and wanted to feel fresh and alert for it. I don't know why I felt obliged to give an explanation; it was unnecessary. The party-givers were living in the moment and were unlikely to be interested in the reasons for a guest's early departure when announced on arrival. It was true that I had an appointment: a routine check-up at the optician's. Not a very credible reason. It's all part of my problem. I have to justify things and I refuse to tell a lie, however small.

As the evening went by, I began to feel less self-conscious. I had floated between most groups and had been able to contribute something small to each discussion. It had been hard work. I decided to sit down in one corner of a long sofa and take a quiet minute to consider whether to leave now or stay longer.

I looked around the room at everyone enjoying themselves. I felt both envious and out of place. I don't understand why I have these inhibitions. I am not a negative person; I just recognise that I am different. I was released from this reverie when Stephanie sat down at the opposite end of the sofa. We exchanged smiles; she shuffled along to sit next to me.

'Hello, I'm Stephanie. I've seen you about in the office. You're looking as though you are not entirely comfortable in these situations,' she said. 'I've noticed a couple of times.'

'Oh, I'm fine. It's good to meet colleagues I've not spoken to in a social environment.'

She laughed and linked her arm through mine. Not in a flirty way: it felt like a gesture of friendship.

'I don't believe you,' she said, patting my hand. 'Don't worry; I like to keep a little distance from people I work with, too.'

I felt tense, for no reason at all. I am not a good conversationalist. It was difficult enough to join in with the groups, let alone hold a one-to-one discussion with a relative stranger. Stephanie was completely at ease and totally uninhibited. Socialising came naturally to her. I don't remember the detail of what we talked about - nothing too serious. I do remember that she led with questions, for which I was grateful. I constantly reminded myself to feed questions back in and not just to talk about myself.

Eventually, the conversation came to a natural end. I used the opportunity to make my excuses to leave. I had enjoyed meeting someone new, who was charming, interesting and completely open and relaxed.

'Lovely to talk to you,' said Stephanie. 'I'll look out for you around the office.'

I collected my coat and was shown out by my hosts. As the door closed behind me, I realised that I hadn't told Stephanie my name. I walked home briskly, excited, almost daring to hope...

A few days later I met her in a corridor at work. As soon as she saw me she broke into an enormous smile.

'Hello, Oliver. I wondered when I would bump into you again. I enjoyed our little chat at the party.'

I tried to appear at ease and not overly enthusiastic. This was difficult, knowing that she must have found out my name from someone else.

'I was thinking, after you left the party... Why don't we go out for a meal somewhere? I'd like to get to know you better.'

I was sure she noticed me swallow, involuntarily.

'Don't worry. Just a friendly, private get-together. No expectations or obligations on either side. I'd really like that.'

'Yes, so would I. I'd like that very much, too.'

We made an arrangement, there and then. Stephanie offered to book somewhere and to pay, as she had made the suggestion. That would be out of the question. I was not going to agree to be treated on a first outing. It was not the right time to discuss it. I could pick up the bill at the end of the meal.

At the restaurant, we talked about all the usual things: our backgrounds, interests in music, cinema, books and the theatre. When she moved the subject on to politics, I was wary of how best to respond. However much I was growing to like her by the minute, I am not one to betray my principles. An unnecessary worry, as we broadly agreed on the big topics and were able to hold a reasoned, intelligent debate about alternative solutions to social problems, occasionally disagreeing, without arguing, on points of detail.

At the end of the evening, I contrived to pick up the bill, despite her protestations. I offered to take her home. She declined, reminding me that her flat was a long way from mine and that it would take too long for me to get back, especially with work in the morning.

'Perhaps another time, I'd love to do this again, or something similar,' I said, emboldened by the pleasurable evening we had spent together. By then I was having to suppress hopes and expectations of where this could lead.

'You'd certainly better!' she said. 'Otherwise, I will have to come and seek you out and embarrass you.'

I walked briskly to the tube station, full of energy from the evening. It had been a perfect first date. I had felt at ease and under no pressure to be anything other than myself. I was pleased, too, that she had not accepted my invitation to escort her home. I would not have wanted to have gone through the ritual of being invited in and to have felt obliged to explore physical possibilities. It's not that I am old-fashioned, prudish or inhibited; I prefer relationships (not that I had had many) to develop organically, to let desire take a natural course, rather than go through the motions because 'it's what people do'.

This was not to be a problem. As we enjoyed more and more dates, our relationship developed, to discuss personal aspirations, including families. We discussed what each of us might consider as potential barriers to a long-term relationship. I shared with Stephanie my problem with anxiety and self-consciousness. One of my few friends had advised me against admitting any personal weaknesses, saying that this would turn her off me. I did anyway. I like to be open with people. She said that she thought this might be the case. It was not a problem, as I was 'a very nice man'. I think she noticed my expression change as she spoke these words and then added, 'I think I could fall in love with you.'

From that day on our relationship moved forward quickly. Soon we were discussing moving in together. Stephanie announced that she had found another job, with better career opportunities and the possibility of working from home when we started a family. This was the first time she had mentioned the subject in such positive and definite terms. It was another step up. Within a week I had proposed and she accepted. We would move in together immediately and start to explore buying somewhere of our own. We were both earning well and were fortunate to have gone into IT when it was a relatively uncommon career. Stephanie's idea made sense. As well as the positive aspects she had identified, we would be less at risk in the future, in the unlikely event that the company were to fail and we would both be out of work at the same time.

Believe me, I do understand that other people's accounts of how wonderful their relationships are can be boring, so I shall say little more. Many other pleasures followed, including the birth of our first-born, Freya. I was overwhelmed by a whole range of emotions, from joy to fear: the realisation that I was responsible for the life of a real human being. I cherished the thought. Finally, after so many years, I had come to recognise that I must take control of myself and to become a role model to my, our, child.

I tried so hard to do the right thing yet, despite my efforts, I was never satisfied I was doing enough. There always seemed to be something missing, a feeling that I should have done more. I wanted everything in life to fit perfectly, like a giant jigsaw. Some pieces were in colour. I had to find a way of dealing with those that obstinately remained in black and white.

'Do you think we will stay together, for the rest of our lives?' I don't know why I chose that moment to ask. For some months I had been feeling uncertain in the warmth of our loving relationship, despite acknowledging it as a ridiculous thought. I was so blessed and happy to be able to enjoy a family life: to make my, our, children happy in a home of our own, with relative career security and us all in good health. It seemed just too good at times, incapable of lasting.

Stephanie shrugged her shoulders. 'I expect so.'

She sounded disinterested, though not uncaring or antagonistic. Nor did she seem evasive. Her response was timely, if unconsidered, and open. I should not have asked the question at a time when my level of interest in the matter was not in step with hers. I had sprung it upon her, without first preparing her for a discussion of a subject that is at the heart of a relationship. I should have given her time to open up and examine her feelings; to offer her own thoughts, both positive and any negative ones, which I am sure she would have done.

It was not my intention to put her on the spot, or to appear demanding or clingy. I know that at times I can disappear down a rabbit hole, without checking whether others are following. This was the reason for my question. It was not intended to be selfish or self-centred. I was looking for reassurance that we were communicating, to restate what I hoped and believed was the status quo. Stephanie was becoming used to my sudden crises of doubt. I don't think she minded. Right from the beginning, she had been supportive, in subtle ways, without drawing attention to herself. I was so fortunate and did my best not to appear weak or demanding. I always tried to remember to explain how important the family was to me and how I wanted to deal with any potential problems or misunderstandings as they arose.

Oh, what wonderful times they were. It was a blessing to be alive. There were so many sources of joy and pleasure, some arising from unlikely incidents, including those that threatened danger.

None more so than the time we visited a cave in the South of France.

We were staying in a house in the Var and were looking for a day out away from the sea and the water parks, where regular visits were essential to avoid the children becoming bored. In past holidays, in other regions of France, we had occasionally visited caves and had in general found the trips successful. From our guidebooks, we decided on the Grotte de Baume Obscure, near Grasse, which featured a sound and light tour. We would go the next day, as heavy rain was forecast: ideal in the sense that we would be under cover for the main part of the visit.

We had not expected the rain to be so unrelenting - we were thoroughly soaked running from the door of the villa to the car! The first part of any journey from the house was a half-hour drive through mountain roads. These were not dangerous as such, but our progress was slowed by the poor visibility from the strength of the downpour and the interior of the car steaming from our drying clothes.

I couldn't wait to reach the A8 autoroute, where the road would be wider and faster. It was not to be. Almost immediately we joined, the rain came down even harder. I would not have believed it possible. The windscreen wipers at full speed could not cope with the volume of water. Visibility was down to ten metres, owing to the volume and heaviness of the downpour and the force with which it bounced off the windscreen and bonnet. Despite this, cars and lorries continued to overtake at speed in the two outside lanes. Yet still the rain became heavier and heavier, punctuated by thunder ricocheting from the mountains, and lightning, which could barely be seen through the mist and downpour. It did not take long for me to decide that it was too dangerous to continue. I was afraid that someone would crash into the rear of the car, as I was only travelling at thirty miles an hour. I pulled onto the hard shoulder, as close to the edge of the road as was safe, and turned on the hazard lights. Some other motorists followed suit - I was pleased to see one some thirty metres behind us, providing a shield. Traffic was still passing, though thankfully now at a much-reduced pace.

After about fifteen minutes the rain eased enough to continue. I set off cautiously, still in the slow lane, ignoring the flashing and hooting of impatient followers.

Grasse is a hilly town. By the time we arrived, torrents of water were racing down the streets, bearing a variety of vegetation, plastic, saturated cardboard and more. Water had built up behind walls, causing some to burst and leave stones and mud across the roads. I was beginning to wish we had chosen another activity. We had come too far now to turn back; we were less than twenty kilometres from our destination and the children were excited by the effects of the water and the prospect of the caves.

The route took us out of town on progressively smaller roads, and then, as we entered a forest, onto a narrowing track, some three kilometres from the caves. I was becoming concerned about our return journey, as streams were developing on the tracks that crossed the one we were following. I was worried that, as the water continued to run off the mountains, they could be impassable by the time we returned.

We arrived at the car park just as a coach was departing, leaving only one other car, an old Renault. I could not tell whether it was a functioning vehicle or a dumped wreck.

I parked as close as possible to the signpost to the entrance. I put on the child carrier and placed Adam in it before we stepped out into the rain. We must have paid using a credit card machine - I don't remember - as I am sure we hadn't seen a single person that morning. The entrance to the caves was inconspicuous: a single, heavy metal door embedded into the rock face. It was closed and could not be opened using the handle. Stephanie pointed to the sign above, which stated that it would open automatically once the preceding tour was complete.

We waited, shivering in the rain. Although it was May and the South of France, it was unseasonably cold, exacerbated by the deluge. After fifteen minutes, we heard a mechanical noise from behind the door. It opened automatically, as indicated, to reveal another, which opened once the first had closed behind us. We stepped through. There was no one to be seen.

Today, the tours are either guide-led or unaccompanied, in which case groups of up to five are admitted with a lantern. Perhaps it was the same then and the guide had not turned up. We passed inside, into a narrow passageway at the top of stone steps, slippery from a combination of water and a hard sandy surface. Hidden lights began to play on the walls, ceiling and floors, beckoning us in. A weird, electronic soundtrack began to play a hypnotic, tuneless theme, constantly varying in volume and tone. The son et lumière show promised by our guidebook had begun.

A sign warned us of the slipperiness of the path we were to follow, particularly after rain. Another advised of the automated nature of the tour and the need to keep up with the lights as they moved ahead of us, illuminating the trail.

The path began its descent immediately. It was more slippery than we had imagined, even while holding onto the metal railings. Within a few metres, our feet were wet. Not to worry; we were here now and were determined to enjoy the experience. No sooner had we started, the lights beckoned us forward towards a steep staircase. Already I could see that the lights behind us were extinguished. We moved as quickly as was safe in the treacherous underfoot conditions. I had the additional responsibility of carrying a young child and ensuring we did not collide with the rock walls.

We descended through tunnels, some so narrow that you had to turn sideways, towards a small underground river. We had visited cave systems before, in several regions of France. The general pattern is a descent into a large cavern, which is suddenly revealed in full lighting, followed by diversions into side passages to see the notable and unique features, such as minerals, fossils and cascades, before ascending once more to the surface. We had read the description in our guidebook, now confirmed, that in this case, there were several corridors to pass through before reaching the main chamber. These started in a small side chamber at the point where the underground river met a tributary before emptying into a pool in a grotto, behind which was a drop into darkness. We had learned from the guidebook that, if a person were to fall into this pool, their body would be sucked into an underground river system, from which they would emerge, some three months later, many kilometres away in the mountains. Freya and Alex found this prospect exciting and were keen to find it as quickly as possible.

Once more, after a short pause, the lights insisted we moved forward into new passages to either side of where we stood. Once more we struggled to keep up. Once more the children joked about getting lost underground, never to be found alive.

Each section displayed its own attractions: the expected stalactites and stalagmites (I reminded the children how to remember which was which, by the 'g' for ground and 'c' for ceiling) and a slow dripping waterfall, beautifully lit and audibly enhanced with abstract music. I remember well the challenge of keeping up with the lights continued, as they continually led us onwards. I was at the rear (it was the responsible place to be, to ensure no one was left behind). On more than one occasion I had to scramble forward urgently, in near darkness, to catch up.

We reached the chamber with the grotto and the pool that led to the underground river. Freya and Alex dared each other to stand close to the edge. At last, there was an opportunity to rest, to catch our breath and to actually enjoy the scene, rather than just keeping up with the tour.

It was not to be. Already the guiding lights were moving onwards. The lights began to dim. And then…

…And then the lights went out.

For a few seconds, I could make out the fading glow from the route we were meant to take, but the floor of the cave was now in complete darkness. It was slippery underfoot. I could feel Adam's body tense in his carrier, as though he knew there was danger. He must be sensing my anxiety. I reached out to take hold of Freya and Alex in the darkness. We stood in silence. I instantly thought, how long would it be before another party came into the cave? It was possible that no more visitors would arrive, given the weather conditions and the difficulties of driving here. Despite feeling on the verge of panic, I was careful to hide this from the family. The priority must be to keep together, to ensure no one was lost or in danger of falling into the chasm, which was so close to where we were standing, now hidden in darkness.

I wished we had never come here. It was like everything else I planned: an unintended failure. This was no time for self-analysis and pity. I had to do something to keep us all safe and alive. I had no idea what to do. We could stay where we were, in the dark and wet. At least there was water to drink, but for how long can you keep children safe and amused like this? There were three alternatives, to remain where we were, to go back to the entrance or to go forward in the hope of reaching the exit.

What happened next was a miracle. A light shone in my face, and then on Alex's. Unbeknown to the rest of us, he had brought a small torch and was shining it with pride and glee all around the chamber. Stephanie, Freya and I shouted with joy. It should have crossed my mind that Alex almost always carried with him a selection of objects that might come in useful. The prospect of exploring a cave system would have ensured he would think of every possible option for adventure. His essential kit would be composed of a miniature spanner and screwdriver, some string, and of course a torch, which no explorer should be without. We were still in danger, but at least we could now see where we were.

Our joy was heightened within seconds, as the lights came back on, followed by the sound of a man's voice, asking in English, spoken with a French accent, whether we were all right. We had had no idea that the caves were monitored from a control room. The light from the torch must have alerted him.

Had the man really known all the time that we were there? Was he watching his CCTV? Could he hear sounds from the cave? Would we have been found if we had not had the torch?

We continued our tour, now able to enjoy it in the knowledge that we would be safe. The lights remained constant, presumably overridden by the controller. We passed through the Fairy Gallery and the bat cave, and on past the green pools and the Palace of the One Thousand and One Nights.

How we laughed at this, relived it, shared it with others, both in the following days and in the years to come.

For much of our life together we lived close to National Trust woodland. The children loved to play outside in all weathers. They invented their own games, laying trails of twigs and stones, which no doubt mystified other children discovering them on the days that followed and no doubt led them into their own games.

Building a tepee, using fallen branches stacked against a tree or, as the children grew and gained experience, self-standing, was another favourite, as was wading along streams in wellington boots, pretending to be explorers in the jungle. I remember the excitement when we first followed one stream to its source, a rusty-coloured trickle bubbling out of the ground, prompting all sorts of questions as to where the water came from.

Another activity we enjoyed regularly was playing with

a rope attached to a tall oak, whose branches began conveniently close to the ground, allowing them, or more usually me, to climb the tree to adjust the length of the rope by increasing or reducing the number of times it was coiled around the supporting limb. The tree grew from near the top of a slope, making it possible to tow the end of the rope uphill before launching into the air. The trick was to try to take off in an arc, so that you could swing round in circles or an oval trajectory, delaying the moment when you dropped to the ground, while throwing the end of the rope to the next in turn.

We discontinued this pastime when, a few days after thoroughly enjoying ourselves, I read in the local newspaper that someone had hung themselves from an oak tree in the same woods. An early morning dog walker had discovered the suspended body. Police said that it was the third such occurrence in ten years, in each case using the same tree. The article described it as the 'hanging tree'. No clue was given as to the exact location, other than the name of the particular wood, one of a complex of National Trust woodlands in the area.

I pictured our tree and tried to imagine how anyone would go about ending their life in this way. I could not shake off the thought or image. Though there was nothing to suggest that it was our tree that had witnessed both riotous fun and tragedy within the space of a few hours, I was so grateful that we had not gone the next morning. It could have been us who found the body.

I chided myself for the selfish thought. How miserable does a human being's life have to be, how apparently hopeless, before they resort to this? I used to get angry during my commutes when, on a delayed train, the driver announced a fatality on the line and other passengers would complain about how selfish the person was. Once, a woman called someone on her mobile and complained to her friend, in full hearing of the carriage, that such people should be more considerate. My anger was directed more at myself, for not having the courage to point out how desperate the victim's circumstances must have been and that they probably would have left behind distraught loved ones whose lives would be forever changed.

I knew I could not possibly take the children to play at the tree again.

School and university years passed quickly for Freya and Alex, following the pattern I would imagine is common to most families, of difficulties and achievements, occasional problems that would make us wonder how they would turn out - completely unnecessary worries, with hindsight. We were proud parents.

Some of the problems we had to deal with made me feel disappointed and ashamed. These are in the past now. They are never mentioned and I would not repeat them nor would I ever remind the children. It would serve no purpose and no good would come of it. They have all turned out well. Besides, we had other, far greater problems to preoccupy us. I can't go on with this. The reasons will become clear.

We dealt with the teenage years, the boyfriends and girlfriends. I was both proud and sad to see them go off to university. The house seemed so empty while they were away. In some ways, the saddest thing about children growing up is that you don't at first notice the transition from childhood to adulthood. When they returned after graduation, it took time to adjust to the effect of these missing years and to recognise that they would never be children again.

But that too is selfish. You have no choice than to acknowledge their decisions and accept that the best you can do is offer advice in as subtle and non-intrusive ways as possible. I knew that Freya had made a bad choice in Simon. It was as well that Stephanie was at hand to prevent me from interfering.

Freya and Simon married. I'll say no more of that now.

Weddings are of no interest to those who are not part of the family.

I found the transition into adulthood regrettable in some ways, whereas I know it should be celebrated. I, more than most, should continually remind myself of this. I felt in a way that I had lost Freya. I had lost Alex too, as he moved abroad to start a career and returned less and less frequently.

And I had lost Adam.

A SERIES OF WEIRD EVENTS

At last, I was on my way again, in my search for Durncot. As I drove through the undulating countryside, I reflected that, throughout this period, from the time my memories of Durncot were reawakened by the night-time vision, I began to have dreams, disturbing dreams. Most of them I forgot within a few minutes of waking, although they often left me with a feeling of dread and depression. I experienced both strange dreams and dreamlike encounters, including some quite weird and unusual events in my waking life. Whether all of these were a consequence of this new focus in my life, or a hyperactive, over-suggestible imagination, I do not know.

It's easy now to recognise that they were not real. I should have made an effort at the time to remind myself of this, and that I would feel better later in the day, or sooner if I took some exercise. I knew too that I should remind myself to be mindful at all times, particularly if in an unstable state of mind, or when hovering between the varying degrees of depression I felt most mornings. I could have decided to ignore them for what they really were, yet I was convinced that they were in some way connected, not only to each other, but to a grand scheme in which the woman, Bella, and the Green Man were entwined in a common conspiracy.

I was beginning to be worried by the way that external events, real or imagined, were having an effect on me. I had never paid attention to concepts like 'The Old Religion' and had only been vaguely aware of the Green Man. To my mind, these were ideas or entities taken seriously only by people whose lives were lacking something. People who could not bring themselves to accept the beliefs of conventional, established religions, or did not see themselves as fitting in with the communities and rituals that these entailed. Perhaps they preferred being adherents to a New Age group, with a credo based upon myths of dubious origin, so as to feel they were outsiders and that they were in a way superior to non-believers.

A few dreams did remain in my memory. Each was surreal and haunting, slow and yet fluid in the way it evolved and with a common theme. There were too many to recount them all, and so I will describe the few that I recall most vividly, telling them in the way I remember them, as I would a real experience.

Strange Music on the Radio

I started the car and drove off. It would be a long journey, which would pass quicker if there were something interesting on the radio. I didn't want to listen to the political news programme and switched channel to the local radio station. The music was not to my taste: I prefer to choose what I listen to, unless there is the promise of discovering something new, whatever the genre. I was about to turn it off when the presenter announced that he would be interviewing a local author, whose work was familiar and whom I admired, in thirty minutes time.

I left the radio on. The music was tolerable and I did not want to miss the studio guest. Whether I would get to hear her was uncertain, as I had just crossed into the next county and the signal was beginning to fade.

As I drove further, short bursts of interference intruded into my chosen programme, an indistinguishable mash of words and music that washed over the broadcast then receded, like the waves of a falling tide, breaking over and under the surface, rising then descending, like a pod of dolphins gliding through the water. The effect was distracting: not unpleasant, almost hypnotic, with a babble of voices irrupting from time to time. One of the voices was distinct from the others. A woman's soft tones: calm, soothing. She spoke short sentences, each in a similar rhythm, whose pitch and volume descended and faded towards the end of each phrase. I could only make out a few individual words.

There was something familiar about what I was hearing. It was almost in reach. What did it remind me of? Someone giving directions? Soothing a small child? Stroking a cat? The radio broadcast began to fade more frequently as I drove through woodland and further from its source. The more it faded, the clearer the woman's voice became. I could recognise a few more words. Not enough to make sense of what she was saying, or even to construct a complete sentence. Some clues began to emerge:

'You have to go…'
'You will find it…'
'It's important that…'
'There isn't much time…'

It was an entreaty. She was urging someone to go somewhere, quickly, and giving directions, although I could not make out where she was trying to send the person. There was an incongruity between the calm, insistent firmness of her voice and the presumed importance of the subject matter, yet I was aware I was making this judgment without full knowledge of the facts, the context, or a proper understanding of the message she was attempting to convey.

The programme was dissolving into a gurgling soup of buzzes, rushes of song phrases and Aeolian hisses, like reeds in a breeze, giving way to the relentless perseverance of the woman's voice. It was as if she knew she could press home her message through persistence and repetition. And it was working. I was trying harder and harder, with increasing success, to make out more and more words until, with a jolt, I thought I heard her say my name. I realised it was not the hearing of my name that shocked me (it's common enough), it was that I knew, yes, knew, that the words were being addressed to me personally. How, I do not know. I tried to reason this away, telling myself it was a radio broadcast, a second station supplanting the one I had originally tuned in to, as I passed into a new reception area.

My foot instinctively touched the brake. Fortunately, I did not press it. I say fortunately as I noticed in my mirror a car close behind, flashing its headlights, the driver irritated by what I now realised was my slow speed. I raised my hand in acknowledgement and sped up. I saw a sign indicating a layby half a mile ahead.

I turned into the layby, once more making a polite wave to the motorist behind, who hooted his horn as he passed, whether in recognition or as an admonishment I didn't know and didn't care. I was by now intent on concentrating on the female voice in the safety of the layby.

'Oliver, I need to talk to you.'

Anyone else would have taken no notice and not have thought anything of it.

'We have to meet.'

'How can we do that? Where can I find you?'

Her voice evaporated once more beneath a rhythmic buzzing and crackling, in waves and bursts.

The interruptions subsided.

'Durncot. You have to go back to Durncot.'

I sat up in my bed, shocked. Immediately I wished that I had not. I had lost the chance to remain inside the dream and possibly to have found some answers - or some more questions.

The Eddy

In another dream, I found myself in a building, one unknown to me. I was drifting from room to room, as though floating. The walls and floors appeared to be made of a strange metal, with variations of colour from white, through to silver and pearl, with a matt sheen that reflected the light, shining out from somewhere distant, hidden from view. The interconnecting rooms were empty. The floors and ceilings sloped to create variations in room height. Every room had at least two doors. Some had three or four, so that either I was led through a single exit, or had to choose, where there was more than one option. I felt a compulsion to move forward. At any given time, only the room I occupied was illuminated; the next would remain in semi-darkness until I decided to enter. Once I had taken a few steps forward, light flowed into the next room. Not uniformly, it was like a wave, as if to confirm the direction I had chosen, or should take.

I had no sense of time passing. After I don't know how many rooms, I entered a circular chamber, whose vaulted roof was formed as a tunnel. Through the opposite exit I could see a passageway stretching into the distance, towards a small, brilliant light source. The internal light was different here: low-level lighting that illuminated the lower half of the room more brightly than the ceiling, with a yellow - no, golden - luminescence that created a calming, ethereal effect.

I stood, calmly, feeling my mind and body relax. The light brightened, then began to dim, uniformly, as in a restaurant, late evening. The temperature dropped, in apparent harmony with the light. At first I did not notice, and then I felt an involuntary shiver. My gaze, which until that moment had been focussed on the distant point of light through the tunnel, drifted down to the centre of the room.

Something strange was happening. An almost imperceptible series of ripples began to flow from a central point of the solid floor, as if a stone had been dropped into a pool. The colour of the floor was changing from pearl to a greenish hue, gradually darkening. As it did, the outward flowing ripples slowed to a standstill, then changed direction, to reverse their flow towards the centre, and to turn slowly anti-clockwise, with a dip at the core, like a whirlpool. I was standing close to the outside edge, wary of being sucked in.

The colour darkened. The eddy filled, then began to flow upwards, creating an amorphous, as yet unrecognisable, shape. It was as if it were being fashioned by an invisible potter on a wheel. It seeped across the floor, its deep oily, green, thick, viscous form shining, inviting touch.

The hypnotic spell melted. I felt a tremor in my bones as I realised the shape was morphing into a human form. As the base of the liquid spread across the sloping floor, defying gravity, so the upward growth took shape, developing arms, a head and definition of a bodily shape, a caped figure. On reaching its final height, a half metre taller than me, the outer skin burst into a chorus of writhing foliage, a liquid medusa. It filled me with horror.

'Don't let that happen!'

As I screamed, I heard my voice change form, from that in a dream to an echo in my room. The nightmare had ended. Its physical impact remained.

The Lake

In a similar dream, sometime later. I was standing on the bank of a lake, watching the dark clouds passing over the mountains behind the far shore, the low sun illuminating their peaks and ridges. As the sun began to set beneath the hilltops, a mist rolled in from the left of my view, thin and translucent at first, then thickening to a dense miasma. I watched, as the sky darkened, the clouds turning to the black of night.

The mist settled in the centre of the lake. A white pillow of cloud balanced upon the surface, condensed, compacted to a neat shape. It looked as though it could be touched, stroked, caressed.

I stepped into a small rowing boat, tied to a stake beside me and rowed out towards it. The surface of the lake at my back was still. I turned frequently to check the cloud was still there. I stopped rowing when I reached a point one hundred metres from the cloud. I trailed a single oar in the water to turn the boat to face it and then dropped the other to steady the boat.

As I did, the mist began to darken to match the deep green of the lake. As with the oily fluid in my earlier dream, it began to grow and spread, as it changed into a towering Green Man. My sleeping brain had produced a variant of the liquid monster. This time I had no fear. I had exhausted my dread and surprise on the first such encounter.

I awoke calm.

The third such dream was different still. I stood in a narrow forest clearing, alone and opposite a fully formed Green Man, the sun at his back, his foliage rustling in the breeze. I sensed that I had been watching him for a complete afternoon, although my perception of time had compacted the elapsed interval to an instant.

Once again, the sun set towards a starry twilight; once again I sensed an unseen danger. From beneath his evergreen skirt, the foliage began to grow and change form, mutating into serpentine tentacles, which crept and slithered in all directions. As the longest reached the adjacent trees, they whipped around the trunks to ensnare them, then extended upwards, their tips prodding at the bark as they wove higher and higher.

I stared, uncertain where this probing growth would end. The figure himself remained still and silent - not once did I hear him speak, or utter a sound.

And then I jumped, pierced with shock as a tentacle touched my foot, and then lashed around and up my leg, gripping me, immobilising me.

I awoke with a start, breathing heavily between the sweat-drenched sheets.

The Stained Glass Window

I enjoy visiting churches. I am not a religious person, nor am I anti-religion. I have on occasions attended church services, other than at Christmas, weddings and funerals, and I enjoy singing the hymns. The problem I have with Christianity centres on two main areas where I cannot accept the established dogma: the doctrine of the Virgin Birth and the resurrection. Once you reject those, not much remains.

The main appeal of churches is the architecture: the variations on a common theme, both in design and materials. Graveyards are another source of interest. I like to read the inscriptions on older tombstones and monuments and imagine the lives of the deceased and what their descendants might be doing now.

Stained glass holds a particular attraction for me, especially that dating from the medieval period. I love the deep reds and blues, which I discovered were created by adding copper, and sometimes iron and manganese to the ingredients. It was only when I did a little research into the history of the manufacturing process that I discovered how expensive it must have been. Most of the glass was imported, in sheet form, from Flanders, to be decorated locally and fashioned into panes. My interest is not exclusively in the medieval period. I have made a point of visiting several of the churches that are home to panels designed by the Pre-Raphaelites.

Unusually for a static medium, stained glass can convey images of movement. I remember visiting a country church that I later realised was not far from the Walnut Tree Press. Despite its modest size, the church housed several detailed and colourful windows. Judging by the quality of both the glass and the narrative design, I am sure that they must have been commissioned by the lord of the manor, or another wealthy benefactor.

I was struck by one in particular, in which an image of Jesus, floating in the air and surrounded by his disciples, was standing in front of a tunnel of yellow light, framed by trees in a number of shades of green. I stood admiring it for I don't know how long. The sun shone through the window at an angle, projecting beams of light into the darkness and dust inside, downwards towards the floor of the nave. It flickered through the trees in the churchyard, close to the window, its slow movement from left to right marked by the changing angle of the beams. As I considered how the moving light source also created a sense of movement in the glass image, I drifted into a dreamlike state, oblivious to all but the movement of light and the warmth of the shaft of sunlight in which I stood.

I contemplated the group of disciples, clustered around the Christ figure. One of the disciples (I could not have named any of them) stood behind Jesus with his left arm extended at waist level to the left of Jesus' body, his elbow directly behind that of his master. The effect of the dancing light through the trees was to alternately illuminate the arm firstly of one subject and then the other. To me as an onlooker, it appeared that Jesus was lifting then lowering his forearm, beckoning the viewer closer.

As the sun moved further round, Jesus' face changed from pale yellow to a faint green, then darker. I wondered how this could be happening. Was I imagining it? I was not. The green must be coming from a denser clump of leaves from the tree. I began to feel a familiar anxiety. Jesus had become the Green Man. He was beckoning me.

The feeling quickly passed. The image was soothing, not threatening. I was being called. I had never experienced a calling before. The sun passed beyond the window. With a feeling of sadness, I re-entered the living world.

The Masks

I was walking through narrow, winding streets, late at night, admiring the stars, with no other person around, in what might have been either a French or an English village, populated with stone buildings, centuries old.

The world was in its bed; all was quiet. No lights shone from the houses. What light there was, came from an unseen moon, casting sharp shadows on the grey stone. At first, I did not notice the breaking of the silence, interrupted by the intermittent faint pulse, a sound like a crowd exhaling in brief, exaggerated bursts. It seemed imagined, then distant, stopping and starting again, mounting slowly with each iteration, until I realised that the source of the sound would soon be within sight.

I became, fearful, sensing danger. I wanted to retreat, to retrace my steps, yet I was drawn by curiosity to discover what was driving the approaching crowd, whose feet I could now hear, marching, with a purpose I did not understand.

They were nearing the street corner, a hundred metres away, still out of sight, their appearance imminent. They must be carrying torches - I could see reflected light illuminating the house opposite the street from which they were about to emerge.

I stood rigid, dreading what I was about to see.

They began to turn the corner. Many were carrying flaming torches and wearing elongated white masks that displayed a uniform, evil grin. The masks covered their faces completely and stretched down over their dark green cloaks. I felt my body tense, as if I were being crushed from either side. The tightly-grouped crowd marched slowly, stamping their feet in exaggerated steps. As they did, their knees rose and fell in unison beneath their garments.

I had expected to see a small band of people. They just kept coming until hundreds had turned the corner. I could not move. Closer and closer they marched, the top halves of their bodies swaying from side to side as though one.

As they came to within inches of me, I thought I would pass out. The front row divided as they reached me. I could feel the heat from their torches. I could see, a few rows back, a taller, dark figure, whose shape I could not make out, carried on a platform raised above them. I felt threatened. Something bad was about to happen, which I might not survive. Within seconds it was upon me. Two of the crowd threw torches to the figure, which caught them with outstretched hands, to illuminate the seated torso of a Green Man, his white eyes and teeth ablaze with the reflected flames. No other parts of his face or body were distinguishable beneath the dense foliage that clothed him. The platform stopped directly in front of me, the Green Man, still seated and towering above me, leaned forward, his head ever nearing mine, his eyes and lips widening to a menacing leer.

I felt faint; I passed out, or so it seemed. I lay trembling in my bed, afraid to close my eyes in case he reappeared. I snatched at the light switch. I was safe.

The Photograph

I am told that I have a natural eye for a good picture. I do believe that I am fortunate to have an ability to see the potential for a shot in an instant. I had assumed this was down to luck, or coincidence, until I read an article that described how some people are able to see a three-dimensional image in two dimensions, and so are able to envisage the content of the photograph they are about to take.

When I say luck, I have found that there have been occasions when the photograph I took turned out differently from how I intended, purely by chance. This happened to me recently. I was driving through the countryside, on a familiar route not far from home. It was a fine day and I was in no rush to get to my destination. As so often before, I passed a turning to the left with the name of Nine Bridges Lane, which is signposted as a narrow road, unsuitable for heavy vehicles. I had often wondered whether it really did cross nine bridges and decided that on my return journey I would take a diversion and see for myself.

I had no idea where it would lead. It would be interesting to take the turning and explore a new area and to be surprised. I imagined it would lead to another major road about ten miles away. I would not check its route on the map. There was no possibility of becoming completely lost; it would be a little adventure. I was looking forward to counting the bridges. I knew they must be small, crossing streams and possibly a narrow river. After all, I live in a flat county.

And so, a few hours later, I took the untravelled lane.

I quickly counted three, four, five low stone bridges. I remember hoping the journey would not end too quickly. The afternoon sun was low in the sky, casting a clear light, with sharp shadows. Years ago I used to carry a small camera in the car, to record unexpected or unusual landscapes and moments. Nowadays there is no need, with the quality of the cameras built into mobile phones. The scenery looked attractive in the sunlight, although there was nothing sufficiently striking or unusual as to make me want to stop to take a picture.

I crossed the sixth bridge. Up until now, the road had wound through commonplace hedgerows and fields. Ahead, the landscape was changing. A long, gentle incline led to the top of a hill, where the sun sat between two woods, through which the lane would pass.

I approached the top of the incline. I could see a farmer, or agricultural worker, busy with a chainsaw, taking the branches off a felled tree at the edge of a copse. The sunlight reflecting from the blade contrasted with the woodland behind him, where the trunks, beneath the leaf line, appeared as a gateway to the darkness between them. I could see the photograph in my head. I needed to find a place to stop.

I was fortunate to find a passing place, where I pulled in. I was sure it would be fine to park there. I had not seen another vehicle since leaving the main road and besides, there would be plenty of room to pass.

I leaned against the side of the car and set the magnification on the phone's camera to the longest setting. The man with the chainsaw was still far away from me. His height occupied only a quarter of the horizontal screen. This was not a problem; I could crop and magnify whatever shots I chose to keep later. It took several minutes to capture the image I sought, to include the reflecting blade and the angular way he held the chainsaw. I checked the images to ensure I would be satisfied with the result and continued on my way. After a couple of miles, I rejoined a familiar main road and drove home. I must have missed one of the bridges, as I had only counted eight.

That evening I loaded the photos onto my laptop. It took no time at all to reduce the number of shots I might want to keep down to a maximum of three. I began to edit each of these in turn. The first task was to crop them, such that the figure occupied one-third of the vertical height and thus divided the photo into three. I then adjusted each horizontally, to place the felled tree at the centre, offset by the small group of prominent trees to the right. I then checked the histograms to correct the exposure, adjust the highlights, blacks and whites, and then fine-tune the clarity, vibrance and saturation. I find this process very relaxing; I become totally absorbed in the task and forget the outside world, sometimes losing track of time altogether.

As I worked through the images, the choice of my preferred photograph became clear. The final task was to examine the shot in close-up, at one hundred per cent, to check for camera shake or blemishes that may have resulted from dust on the lens.

And that was when I saw it...to the right of centre, at the top of my screen: the Grim Reaper! Among the vegetation of the trees which stood forward of the copse, a group of dead branches, bearing brown, lifeless leaves, stood out from their background to form the shape of a ghostly figure, with dark eyes, a prominent nose, mouth and chin, and sloping shoulders. It even appeared to be holding a scythe in its left hand, as it looked down on the man with the chainsaw. It was eerie to think that this was created in my mind from the random arrangement of leaves.

I checked the other two photos. They were not the same, only parts of the figure were visible and I would not have made the connection from these alone. I returned to look at the first of the three. I felt a mixture of exhilaration and apprehension. I was excited by the happy accident of capturing a unique, striking image. I had an irrational feeling that I was receiving a message, whose meaning I did not comprehend.

The Flickering Film

One summer's evening, Stephanie and I thought it would be a good idea to go to an open-air cinema screening. We were staying in a seaside town, on a fortnight's holiday. We had spent most days sitting on the beach, watching the children. Freya and Alex were now nine and ten; Adam was four. It was the summer before... No, I'll come to that later.

During the days at the beach, Stephanie and I took turns to read, while the other looked out for the little ones (they will always be our little ones). Freya and Alex were always willing to look after Adam. They played joyfully together, with the occasional tease. We interspersed trips to the beach with occasional outings to local attractions, most of which were overpriced and uninteresting, prompting calls from the children to return to the sea.

After several days of following the same pattern of activities, Stephanie and I were in need of more stimulating, adult entertainment. The outdoor cinema looked to be a promising solution. The screening area was located in a compact green space on the esplanade, enclosed by canvas walls, giving the impression of a roofless tent. The audience was invited to take a picnic and to bring blankets to sit on. We agreed that this was preferable to formal seating. If Adam became too tired, it would be easier for him to sleep on a blanket or cuddled up in our arms.

There was a choice of two films, scheduled on alternate days. Stephanie and I would have preferred to have seen Cinema Paradiso which, although we had seen it before, would be ideal for a balmy summer's evening outdoors. We decided that Freya and Alex were a little young to appreciate it and there was nothing about it that would appeal to Adam. Instead, we chose an evening screening of a children's film, whose title I no longer remember. Stephanie and I agreed to forgo a cultural outing; the children would love staying up late to watch a film they would enjoy, out of doors in the darkening evening. We could augment the adventure by encouraging them to choose the ingredients for our picnic.

We arrived early enough to select a good spot and set out the blanket. Most families had chosen to sit close to the screen. We chose to sit further back, in the centre. The screen was mounted high enough for the whole audience to be able to see well, without having to peer over or between other people.

We finished our picnic just as the lighting dimmed, prior to the screening. An unseen presenter introduced the film over the PA system. He added that, as a bonus, after the main feature, they would be showing a short film made by students at the local sixth-form college. No details were given, other than that it was suitable for families. We wondered why it was not scheduled before the main feature, when a larger crowd would be present.

The performance began. The film was not memorable, although I acknowledge I was not the target audience. I was thankful to have the students' production to look forward to, provided our children were not too tired at the end of the evening. This turned out not to be an issue.

Towards the end of the film, a few drops of rain began to fall, soon turning to a steady drizzle. We had brought umbrellas, as had some other parents. We were hesitant to raise them and obstruct the view of people behind, a consideration that did not occur to the family directly in front of us. By the end of the film, Freya and Alex were complaining that they had been unable to see much of the closing scenes. All three complained of being wet.

I suggested we remain to watch the short film. Most people would be leaving at the end of the main feature and there would be a better view of the screen. The family were not interested. I was grateful to Stephanie for offering to escort the children back to where we were staying, to allow me to watch it in peace.

It took a while for the students to set up their equipment. They had shot their production on reel-to-reel film, which, even in those days, was a dying medium. By the time they were ready, the audience had dwindled to about fifty, mainly hardy couples and individuals, who were by then standing among puddles in the persistent rain. I thought about leaving, but it would have been discourteous. I wanted to show support for the young people's efforts, both in producing something creative and having the courage and belief to show it to an audience.

It began simply, with a still shot of a painted background of a lit domestic interior with a starlit sky visible through a window. A clay figure of a girl entered from the right, walking, stopping to look up, down and around, her movements filmed in freeze-frame motion. Another figure, of a boy, emerged from the left. I say a boy, it had a boy-like face but, unlike the girl, its body was made of flat geometric shapes.

The sound consisted of blips and other electronic noises to emphasise footsteps and the characters' interaction with objects. Their sparse, clipped dialogue was shown in sub-titles. They walked back and forth across the room, performing domestic tasks in bursts of a few seconds, with a brief pause between each. The rapport between the three-dimensional girl and the two-dimensional boy began to develop. The boy started to bounce up and down, without bending his legs. He then stopped, walked around and repeated the actions. After a few iterations, the pattern changed. He would stop still, bounce on the spot twice and on the third bounce leap high in the air and change shape. While in mid-air his limbs, head and torso folded in on one another and then unfolded, revealing him having changed into a new shape, a new figure.

He became a dog, a cat, a rat, a bird. The girl looked

on as though patiently waiting for him to stop. After several more changes, he jumped once more and turned into a man holding a baby, at the same time as the girl turned into a woman.

He was now three-dimensional, as were all three. He cradled the baby in his arms, rocking it back and forth in a jerky rhythm, smiling at the baby with a loving expression. He offered the baby to his wife, kissing her as the swaddled child passed from one pair of arms to the other. The woman rocked the baby and then placed it in a crib on the floor.

The scene flickered, alternating between light and black. A bolt of lightning flashed outside in a cartoon-like fashion. A row of exclamation marks extended one by one across the sub-title box. The baby woke and waved its arms in distress, its head rolling from side to side.

The woman began to grow in height, writhing a giddy dance as she did, while the man and the baby, to either side of her, remained their original size. I was beginning to be drawn into the film and wondered where the plot would lead.

And then the film snapped with an audible crack. I, we, the audience, stared at the screen, now showing a strip of film in two-tone shades of green and yellow, its perforations shivering as they flowed at a slight diagonal down the screen, partially obliterating the story. One spectator booed, another couple turned to leave.

In an instant, I realised that the film had not broken. Had it done so, we would have been looking at a white screen. It was all written into the script.

I assumed that this effect would not last more than a few seconds. I was wrong; it marked a change in direction. The strip of film continued to flow down the screen, in its several shades of green and yellow. It continued to hold my interest as I watched the frames peel downwards, with the newest appearing from the top, so that you could see the underlying film in a short window in time, several instants concurrently, whereas in daily life we see just one frame at a time, albeit merged into the next. If only we could do this in real life, I thought to myself.

The flashes of lightning continued to shine at the window, alternately illuminating and darkening the interior scene. The green woman continued to grow. She juddered over to the baby in its crib, lifted it and shuffled over to her husband, as all the time she grew, the edges of her silhouette becoming serrated, tree-like and fuzzy. Still holding the baby, she embraced the man, or so it appeared - it was more like the absorption of his body. The three began to spin, as one, slowly at first, then working into a whirl, bouncing on the spot, as the man had done earlier.

She grew and grew, filling the screen - no, not the screen, the individual frames. The camera panned in to the topmost frame of the strip, effecting a transition to fill the whole screen with the single image.

Cut: to the woman's face, and a subliminal shot lasting a fraction of a second, showing two eyes peering from foliage superimposed upon her cold, hypnotic stare.

The word *FIN*, white on grainy black, announced the end of the film.

RANDOM ACTS OF KINDNESS

I try to be good. It doesn't always seem to work.

When I look back, I see so many things I wish I had handled better. I could have done so much more for so many people. The problem was the stress: the pressures of daily life, worrying about job security and being able to do my best for the family. And, so often, I was frustrated when my best efforts failed to achieve the intended outcome.

Let me tell you about some of my disappointments.

I was walking through the centre of town on my way to the station, when a woman nearly collided with me. She seemed to be looking straight through me, oblivious to the fact that I was in her path. I was in a hurry to meet Stephanie in London and was irritated by losing a few more seconds and the possibility of missing the train. A selfish thought; I should have set off earlier. I stopped and apologised profusely, despite not believing myself to be at fault, if indeed there was a fault, rather than being a simple accident. She looked at me, unsmiling, and nodded in recognition of the gesture, still staring beyond me and not truly meeting my gaze.

'Cheer up!' I said, smiling, hoping for a more

responsive reaction, though I don't know why. I wasn't trying to make a point and I was definitely not making a pass - I don't do that sort of thing. I regretted saying anything, other than my apology and should have known better than to be too familiar with a stranger.

'I'm sorry. I'm not really with it at the moment. It was very rude of me,' she replied.

'Are you OK? Do you need any help? I don't mean to intrude on your private business. It's just that you look quite distressed.'

'I… I've got a few problems, that's all. Nothing I can't sort out.'

I considered leaving it at that. I could see, looking over her shoulder at the Town Hall clock, that I was going to miss the train. I verified the time on my watch. Never mind, it couldn't be helped. The next one was not for an hour - I would have to phone to excuse myself.

'Look, forgive me for being so direct. I find it sometimes helps to talk to someone - even a complete stranger. If I may say so, you don't look at all well. May I buy you a coffee? Just a coffee. I've no agenda; I'd just like to try to help, if it helps you, that is.'

She thought for a moment. I assumed she was weighing up the potential dangers and benefits of talking to a stranger, taking into account that it was before ten o'clock in a moderately busy high street. She was taller than me, I think. It would have been impolite at that moment to look to see whether she was wearing high heels.

She nodded, staring downwards, and then smoothed her neat, tinted blonde hair with the back of her hand. She was in her early thirties. From her appearance, I would have described her to be a quiet sort of person, with a kind face, perhaps a little shy (this was only a first impression, of course; how could I possibly know?).

'There's a coffee shop just up here, to the left.' I gestured the direction, putting my right hand behind her, without touching, ushering her. I made innocuous comments about the weather to keep her attention from the possibility of changing her mind.

The coffee shop was about a third full, in that hiatus between people buying a drink to take to the train or the office and their mid-morning break.

'What can I get you?'

'A macchiato, please. A double, if that's all right.'

'Just what I was going to order. Why don't you find us a quiet seat?'

The one person in front of me was reaching for his wallet to pay. One of the two baristas, a short, smiling woman with a Mediterranean appearance asked me for my order. I often wonder how these places make a profit. It takes so long for the coffee to be ground, prepared and poured. This was an occasion when I wanted to be served quickly, to not want my temporary new companion to be kept waiting and then to decide to leave.

I paid and took the drinks from the counter on a tray. I looked around. There was no sign of her. She must have changed her mind after all and left. I felt a moment of panic and disappointment.

'Your friend. She went upstairs.' The male barista gestured towards the staircase, which I had not noticed.

I was surprised to reach the top of the staircase without spilling any coffee. She was sitting in a corner table, close to a window looking out to the rear of the café. I had braced myself to appear calm and relaxed and to ensure I walked upright, in a calm and confident manner. I placed the tray on the table and sat down opposite her, drawing my chair in.

'I'm Oliver.' I reached across the table to shake hands.

'Holly,' she replied. Her hand was cold, her handshake limp.

I passed her coffee from the tray. 'I'm sorry, I should have asked if you'd like something to eat.'

'You're very kind. No thank you,' she responded, as I expected.

'Do you live locally?' I asked, after the brief silence. I wanted to allow her the chance to open the conversation in her own time.

'Yes, we live just outside town,' She took some froth from the coffee with her spoon.

'Do you have a family?'

She blushed. Her eyes began to water. The tears defied gravity. She shook her head slowly, still looking down.

'I'm sorry. Is that a part of the problem?'

She nodded sharply and sniffed, then reached in her bag for a tissue. She blew her nose quietly, deliberately, as if trying not to attract attention. I stirred my coffee slowly. It was not sugared; I suppose I wanted to create some sort of focus of attention, to avoid rushing into more questions.

'Take your time. I'm in no hurry.'

'I'm expecting a baby.' She blew her nose again.

'Well, that's wonderful. You must both be so happy.'

I wanted to reach over to touch the back of her hand, to shake it gently, in affirmation of my sincerity and good intentions. I thought better of it. She turned her head to one side and ejected a sneer - not at me: she was playing through a scenario in her mind.

'Would you like to talk about it? If it helps?'

She took a deep breath and gathered some composure.

'It's my husband. He doesn't want children. He wants me to have a termination.'

Her choice of word disclosed her feelings. It is softer than 'abortion' which, even in today's politically correct world has an abruptness and clinical connotation. I thought later that this might just be my imagination, interpreting the comparison of the softness and hardness of the vowels in the two words. One implies bringing something to an end before its course has run; the other, as in a rocket mission, suggests an emergency or a system failure, perhaps the difference between two types of event: one where a normally functioning process is brought to a close, in contrast to ending something which is not viable. Whether she consciously chose the word for this reason, I do not know.

'I'd love to have children, but I want him to want a child too. I had hoped he would come round, to change his mind. I was prepared to wait; I didn't mean to get pregnant. He says I did it deliberately, to defy him. He says he'll leave me if I keep the child.'

Another significant choice of word. Most women would have said 'baby'. She was looking at a future well beyond a foetus, a baby… to the time when her, their, son or daughter would become a young person, growing in independence, while reciprocating parental love.

'How do you feel about that?'

'I love him. I don't want him to leave me. I've always believed we would spend our whole lives together.'

'Do you believe he would go through with it - to leave you?'

'Yes, it's something he feels strongly about. He's a good man, but obstinate. He has fixed views. Once he's decided on something, it's impossible to persuade him to change his mind.'

'And what about the baby? Have you made a decision?'

She sighed, undecided how to respond.

'It's not right. It's not at all right to…' she hesitated, 'to end the life of a healthy being. It's not fair to me or to the child. I shouldn't have to make such a choice.'

'Have you said this to him?'

'Many, many times. It doesn't make any difference. He won't listen.'

'Did you discuss having children before you married?'

'Oh yes, of course. He knew I would like a family,

right from the start, and he made it perfectly clear that he didn't. The trouble is, you think that someone you love will change their mind, that as the relationship develops they will feel the same way - to want to share the love through creating and caring for a family. I suppose I was foolish.'

'Do you have friends or family you can talk to? Have you told anyone else what you have been telling me?'

'No, not really. It doesn't seem fair to ask people to take sides in a private matter. If they were to take my side, he would dig his heels in even further. We have a small group of close friends going back to our university years. We don't see as much of them as we used to as not many live close by. Most of them have young families of their own.'

'Has he set a deadline for you to make your choice? I mean…'

'I know what you mean. No, he hasn't. He doesn't need to. I suppose you could say the deadline is twenty-four weeks. Can you imagine? Doing that at twenty-four weeks? But that's not the point. Every day that goes by, the child is a little older, steadily becoming a complete person, continually growing towards viability. Every day the idea becomes more unthinkable. You may find this strange: I feel a bond with my unborn child. It's as though he or she knows what I'm thinking, what I'm going through.'

She dabbed at her nose and looked up towards me.

'Does he try to control you in other ways?'

'Not really. Not intentionally, anyway.'

'Do you think you've considered all of your options, and thought them all through?'

'I believe so. There just isn't a good solution, one that would make us all happy.'

I was moved by the inclusion of the word 'all'. I suppressed the involuntary welling of tears.

'How about the future? Are you able to imagine how

you will feel about each of the options in years to come?'

'I've thought about most of them in that way. I can't bear the idea of looking back and regretting having a termination. And if he were to change his mind at some point in the future, to decide he would like to start a family, how awful it would be to live with what I'd done. Can you imagine living with the knowledge that you had deprived your children of an elder brother or sister, for no reason and that, even worse, you now regret it?'

'I can see that where you are now is not a good place to be. How do you think your relationship will be affected by whichever way you decide? Do you think it will survive?'

She toyed with her spoon, stirring the dregs of foamy milk in her cup.

'I don't know. I don't think it could ever be quite the same again. One of us will have been coerced into something they didn't want.'

'Do you think there could be any other options open to you? Choices you haven't considered?'

'I could just do nothing. The child will continue to grow until there is no other alternative than to run the full course. He can't force me to do what he wants, but by then he will have left me. I want him to be there, as the father of my child. I want to have a normal happy family, whatever that means. If I were to leave him, I'm too old to go through the cycle of finding someone else who's suitable to start a family with. I'd be better off as a single parent.'

'Would you be capable of supporting yourself financially?'

'Yes. I'm self-employed. I work mainly from home. I'd need to find someone to help with childcare on an ad hoc basis on the occasions I have to visit clients. I'm sure that some of my few local contacts with children would welcome being paid.'

'It's beginning to sound as though you have the basis

for a Plan B. You're in quite a strong position, on the whole.'

I didn't want her to respond to this, at least not immediately. I changed the subject, to describe some of my own challenges, and how I had overcome them by focussing on the key issues and being mindful. To be frank, I wasn't being completely honest; I over-egged it a bit. It's odd how so often I knew what I should be doing to put my own life back on course. I found it easier to advise others than to put the advice into place for myself.

She looked calmer now, less tearful. She pushed the screwed up tissues into her handbag.

'I'm so grateful for this,' she said. 'You have been very kind.'

'Not at all, I'd like to be able to help. You said that you felt unable to talk about the subject to friends and family. I'd be more than happy to give you my mobile number in case it would help to chat again, either on the phone or to meet somewhere like this. Really... as I say, I've no agenda, I'd just like to help.'

The receipt for the coffees lay on the tray. I wrote down my mobile number and passed it to her. She put it in her purse.

'Thank you so much. I really ought to be going now.'

I stood up and offered her my hand.

'I think I'll stay and have another coffee. It's been a pleasure meeting you. I do hope you'll get in touch.'

'Thank you.' She formed the words with her lips, silently.

I hoped that she might call. For the next few weeks, my heart would beat faster whenever my mobile rang and announced an unidentified caller. I would hurriedly think about what I would say if I were to recognise her voice before she gave her name. If she had found our conversation helpful, then surely... I thought about her at night and even dreamed about her, though the detail of the dreams was lost within seconds of waking. For a while, she became almost as mysterious as the girl at the window.

I did not hear from her again.

I could understand that she might not want to contact me, living in the same area. She may have thought better of keeping my number. If her husband were to discover it, whether or not we met, the explanation, however innocent, would be potentially damaging. I thought I might meet her by chance in town again - if it could happen once... I found myself seeking her face in crowds. Once, I was sure I caught a glimpse of her, diagonally from behind, and called out to the woman, a stranger who turned and glared.

Perhaps she had moved away. I would never know.

I drove to the sports field close to Freya's primary school, to collect her from the after-school reading club. I was early and sat with the roof and windows open, enjoying the warm sun. A trickle of parents ushered their children and their belongings into their vehicles. Some of the younger ones complained that they had not been allowed enough time on the swings, or to play with their friends on the field.

The father of a young girl, about seven or eight years old, comforted his sobbing daughter. She was upset that her friends would not talk to her after she had allegedly got them into some form of trouble with their teacher, the detail of which I did not catch. He had to lift her into the high passenger seat of his pickup truck.

'People do that sometimes, my darling. They know they've done wrong and look to find someone else to blame for it. Don't you worry about it. It'll all be better tomorrow, once they've slept on it and had time to think things through.'

His voice was calm, reassuring. He closed the passenger door and walked round to the driver's side, continuing to talk to his daughter.

'Let's take you home and see what we can make you

for tea. Then you can tell me about the rest of your day.'

He closed the driver's door and started the engine. As he did, I noticed that some papers had fallen out of the car. I dashed out from my car to draw his attention to them. It was too late, he had pulled away and was turning left onto the road and so could not see me in his mirrors.

I picked up the papers. There were some leaflets and a large, stamped, addressed envelope containing, by the feel of it, several sheets of paper. I wasn't sure what to do. It was a Thursday afternoon. Tomorrow was a scheduled non-pupil day: I would not be able to catch him until after the weekend. I had noticed his company name on the side of the truck - something Brickwork - but hadn't remembered it. Should I post the letter, or wait until after the weekend? The letter was addressed to a construction company. Perhaps he was responding to an invitation to tender, or returning a signed contract. Next week would be a new month. Perhaps the closing date for responses was the end of the current month.

I was undecided. Supposing he had not intended to post it. There was a post box by the school; he could have dropped it in when collecting his daughter and may have chosen not to, although why, in that case, attach a stamp? There might be other reasons for not having done so. He may have been unsure of the correct postage for the weight. Or he may have changed his mind about posting it, for whatever reason. Of course, it might not have been an important document.

I made up my mind. I walked back towards the school with Freya and put the letter into the box, just as the post van pulled up to make the daily collection.

What next? Should I wait for him in the car park on Monday, to confirm, to explain...? No, I did not know whether I had done the right thing. On that day I had been presented with a one-time opportunity to take immediate action, whether for the best or not. I had made a decision. I expect he would have noticed the letter was missing, later the same day. I will not know whether he was unconcerned or anxious. Nothing would have been gained from him knowing that it was I who took the decision on his behalf. It could not now be undone.

Early on Sunday mornings, I walk to the village centre to buy a newspaper. It is just over a mile; to complete the return journey takes an hour. I prefer walking to taking the car. Aside from environmental considerations, the walk wakes me up and takes me out of my post-sleep stupor of fading dreams and depression. I have noticed that the weather for the day is often at its best in the early mornings, before the promise of clear sunlight is betrayed by treacherous clouds. The senses are keener at this time of day. If I focus on being mindful of the light and sounds around me, my other senses will fall in step.

This was the case early one winter's morning. I left the house just before the late midwinter sunrise, taking care as I walked along the unlit road with no pavement. Even at the best of times cars travel far too quickly and are oblivious to the possibility of pedestrians.

I had almost reached the village when I noticed a young woman, about a hundred metres away, walking slowly in my direction, gazing at something she was holding in her hand. The dawn had not yet broken and I wondered what she was reading in the half-light. As I was about to pass her, I saw that she was looking at a letter.

'Excuse me,' she said. 'Could you please tell me how to find Parsonage Lane? I don't know the area and I don't want to be late for an appointment.'

I was puzzled. Why would anyone have an appointment early on a Sunday morning, a day when no buses run, in a village several miles from the nearest town? It was none of my business. Perhaps she had driven and left her car in the centre, believing herself to be quite close. It was unusual too, that a young person was not carrying a mobile phone. It may have run out of battery.

Oh dear… Stephanie often chided me for over-analysing situations, when all I should do was to accept things as they are.

'Now, I know the name - I'm sure I've seen it somewhere. I can't think where.'

'I've been walking around for fifteen minutes. You're the first person I've seen to ask and it's too early to be knocking on strangers' doors.'

'I do know it; I'm struggling to think where it is. Ah, yes, I think I have an idea. If you go back towards the duck pond and turn to your left just as you reach it… Go down that road for about half a mile and I think it's off to the left. By the time you get there, there should be more people around, so I would ask again.'

'Thank you so much. I was told to arrive early. It's for a job interview, before the lady goes off on a business trip. I'd hate to miss her and lose the job.'

That explained it. And I was pleased to be able to help, or at least point her in the rough direction. 'I'm walking as far as the corner. Follow me and I'll point you down the road that I mean.'

Why on earth I didn't walk with her, instead of dashing ahead, I don't know. It wasn't as though I was in any real hurry. With hindsight, I think that subconsciously I was wary, as an older man, of walking along with a young woman and that she might feel uncomfortable with me. At the time it seemed better not to.

I reached the duck pond and turned to point down the road I suggested she take. She waved back to me in acknowledgement. I walked on to the newsagent, paid for the paper and set off on the walk home. I was still thinking about Parsonage Lane. I could almost envisage the road sign, although I could not place it. I was halfway home when it came to me. Where I now remembered it to be was not at all close to where I had directed the young woman.

I increased my pace and walked briskly home to

check online. I quickly located it. In fact, she had been heading in the right direction when I met her. I had now sent her the wrong way; I had to try to find her. By now half an hour had passed. I dashed to the car and drove back to the village and took the turning I had sent her along. I followed the road to the furthest point that I judged she would have walked to before giving up. There was no sign of her. I felt ashamed that I had let her down.

I turned back towards the village, constantly chiding myself. Approaching a junction, I slowed the car to look to either side for emerging traffic - unlikely at that time of morning. I remember being surprised that I was sufficiently focussed to check. I looked to the left and then the right. I could see someone walking towards me, some way off. I turned down the side road and, yes, it was she.

I wound down the window and apologised profusely.

'Jump in. I'll take you there!'

She looked hesitant (not surprising when a stranger has given you wrong directions and then seeks you out), before crossing in front of the car to open the passenger door.

'Thank you so much for coming back for me. I'm very grateful.'

'It's the least I could do. We'll be there in less than five minutes.'

I made some small talk about where she had travelled from and how she had managed to get to the village at that time of the morning on a Sunday. She had taken a taxi from the station, some seven or eight miles away - the unhelpful driver had dropped her off at the centre, not being familiar with the village and inexplicably having no mobile phone with him to check.

'Here we are. Would you like me to wait for you, to take you back to the station afterwards?'

I was trying not to appear pushy, or worse still, creepy. I was pleased that she took the offer as it was intended.

'That's very kind of you, but the lady has agreed to take me back to the station when the interview is over. Thank you so much for taking the trouble.'

'Not at all; I'm pleased to have been able to help eventually. I'll wait until you are inside. Good luck!'

She rang the bell. The door was opened. She turned and waved as she stepped inside. I drove home, feeling a mixture of relief and exhilaration. For once, I had not let someone down. Not quite.

Much later, after Freya left university, she met her partner, Simon. I didn't take to him. He was vague about his business affairs - something to do with property investment and development. He liked to boast how successful he was, without citing many specific facts. To me, it sounded dubious, to the extent that I wondered how close his dealings were to the borders of morality, let alone legality. I was worried that Freya could be drawn into a bad situation out of love for someone whose motives were self-centred.

I had to keep this to myself. Freya was in theory old enough to make her own judgements of character and I did not want to risk a rift with her. The most I could do was to ask open questions in the hope that she would deduce any problems and find the solutions for herself.

I was not surprised when, only a few months after their marriage, Simon asked me to lend him some money. He was 'a few thousand short' of acquiring sufficient funds to buy a property, a disused warehouse built at the height of the Industrial Revolution, that was now a derelict shell, albeit, so he claimed, with a solid structure.

'It has the potential to make millions. It's only a mile or so from the city centre and could be converted into a multiple-purpose building: a shopping mall over three or four floors with offices above. There's quite a bit of space outside for parking, although we would probably need either to dig down and create an underground car park or, alternatively, use the lower floors and have less office space.'

My eyes were already starting to glaze over, both from boredom and my reluctance to have any involvement. I've always been risk-averse and had no intention of changing, not even for my daughter's husband.

'So, you need some money to buy the building, which is one thing. How will you fund the redevelopment?'

'That's sorted, more or less. I've found a business partner who will provide most of the funding for that stage of the project. The exact amount will depend on how we agree the split in the equity and the proportions that they and I put into the second stage. So, what I wanted to discuss with you amounts to two opportunities. Firstly, to provide me with a loan to buy the building outright and secondly to give you the option to invest in the redevelopment.'

'I can understand the loan for the building. What exactly are you proposing for the other part?'

Simon sat back to take a breath, then leaned forward, forearms on thighs and hands apart.

'We could become partners. If, say, you were to mortgage your house and I were to take out a loan on my, sorry, Freya's and my house, you and I would have a much larger stake in the ongoing project than if I were to go it alone.'

'And Freya, of course.'

'I'm sorry, I don't understand.'

'If you were to be borrowing against Freya's equity in her home, then she would be entitled to a share.'

'I haven't actually discussed it with her yet. I thought I would talk it through with you first. Once you agree, it will be easier to convince her.'

'Tell me, how much of your own money are you putting up, towards buying the building?'

'Well, almost all of it. I've arranged to borrow against

Owen W Knight

other properties I own, or have an interest in. I just need to make it up to the final sum with a few extra thousand.'

'What experience do you have of managing a project this large?'

'It's true that all of my previous developments have been on a smaller scale, but the principles are the same. The potential return is enormous; I can get my accountant to go over it with you if you like.'

'When you say "a few extra thousand", exactly how many is a few?'

Simon fidgeted, then clasped his hands together.

'A quarter of a million.'

I have always kept my financial affairs to myself, apart from sharing information with Stephanie, when she was alive and we were together (which she was, at that time).

'Simon, I'm sorry. I just don't have that kind of money readily available. Yes, I have the house and our mortgage is close to being paid off, but I'm not prepared to borrow against it. You will understand, I'm sure, that I am a lot older than you and need to be looking at securing my financial future, and Stephanie's.'

I suppose this was almost a white lie. I had investments in funds and premium bonds, which totalled not far short of the amount Simon was asking for. I decided to use my own definition of 'readily available', to mean cash in the bank. It's true that I could have realised these investments within a week or two, far less than the amount of time it would take for Simon and his associates to draw up contracts.

'That's exactly what I'm offering you - an opportunity to secure your future with the return on the investment.'

'I would love to help, especially with Freya as a beneficiary. But I have to say that, apart from not having anywhere near that sum of money to hand, I believe that there is too much risk involved. So much could go wrong. Okay, you could buy the building but, from what you've told me, it looks as though you would be a junior partner in the redevelopment and would therefore have little or no control. All sorts of things could go wrong, starting with the planning process. If there are delays, there will be additional costs and interest. With those delays, building and materials costs will increase. You could find the project then competes with similar new ventures. You haven't explained anything to me about the cash flow and what will keep the project going in the meantime. You could be left with an empty, derelict building, whose value ends up far less than you paid for it.'

'I can't believe you won't do this for your daughter!'

I did not react directly to what I considered to be Simon's provocative remark. It was a clever ploy. He guessed, correctly, that I would feel some degree of guilt towards Freya, the implication being that he would tell her that I had rejected his request, no doubt putting his own spin on the account.

'I've already explained my financial position. What I am prepared to do is to lend you twenty-five thousand, subject to a legal contract between us, with the money to be paid on signature of your contract, once I have confirmed Freya's interest is recorded, and without any liability on her part, should the scheme fail.'

I had no idea what I was talking about and whether it was legally possible. It would have been easy enough to take advice, if it were to happen. Honour had been done. I had made an offer, only one-tenth of the amount requested, and with conditions attached. Simon was not impressed and said so, using colourful language I had not heard from him before. Freya had alluded to Simon's temper. Not in any detail. She would not have wanted to worry me.

My discussion with Simon deteriorated. I will not bother to relate it, even in general terms. He became irritated, then angry, repeating his assertion that I wasn't doing the best for my daughter and was letting her down. Finally, he recognised I was not going to change my mind, to increase my offer (which he declined as being totally inadequate and insulting), either now or later.

He stood up to leave. 'One final thing,' he said.

'What's that?'

'I'd appreciate it if you didn't share this discussion with Freya. I don't want to worry her.'

I had no intention of telling Freya. I would have to find a way, nevertheless, of keeping an eye on Simon's future activities and somehow alerting her to the dangers he and his schemes posed, in a way that would not cause her to turn against me.

Within weeks, Simon's plan fell through. He was unable to buy the building. I felt relieved, yet I took no pleasure from the outcome. I felt guilty for having deprived Freya of a possible opportunity for security. I was grateful, nevertheless, that their relationship was not damaged and that we were all able to remain friends…

…for the time being. A few years later the relationship broke up. Freya discovered that Simon had had a series of affairs. Despite his promises to reform, Freya eventually decided she had had enough. I was pleased that she had taken decisive action, yet I felt disappointed that the union had failed. I want so much for the people around me to be happy and fulfilled. I wish I could have done more to help them to stay together and to make it work.

This was not the only occasion I found myself exposed to the world of property dealing. For a while, Stephanie and I lived in a suburban area of a medium-sized town. This was before Adam was born.

Our modest, nineteen-thirties house backed onto a former sports field, privately owned by a local company that had moved to a new location in another part of the country. Now long abandoned, its pavilion demolished, the site had reverted to nature: a wilderness of shrubs, grass and small trees. It was surrounded by houses, similar to ours, with a single point of access, an entrance drive running between our house and that of our neighbour.

A pair of chained metal gates blocked the drive. These had been in place ever since we had moved there.

All of the houses enclosing the field had tall, chain-link rear fences, allowing a view of the field while giving some protection to their windows when two football pitches, or cricket pitches in summer, had been in use at weekends.

The field now served a different purpose, as a safe, sheltered playground for the children of residents, accessible only through the gardens of the adjacent properties. Owners had cut openings through the fence, allowing their children and their friends to come and go as they pleased. The arrangement suited most people, other than the criticism levelled at some dog owners who allowed their pets to foul the area.

Things changed when, one day, we all received notice of a planning application to develop the site and to build one hundred and fifty houses on what I learned was a three-acre site. To be honest, I could understand the logic of the proposal, which had the support of the majority of local councillors, given that it did not eat into green belt land and was arguably wasteland.

On the other hand, the nearest public park was a mile away and, perhaps selfishly, the majority of the surrounding residents enjoyed the relative privacy of backing on to an open space and the amenity it provided for their children.

The developers had agreed a price with the owners of the land and were keen to press ahead. There was talk of mounting and funding a residents' campaign to block the application. After months of deliberation, it was conceded that this would be too expensive and that, as they were the major beneficiaries of the status quo, it was unlikely that wider support for an objection could be raised. The application was approved and contract negotiations to complete the purchase got under way.

To our great surprise, Stephanie and I received a letter from the developers' solicitors. We had been unaware, or had disregarded, a clause in the contract for the purchase of our own property specifying that the locked driveway to the field passed over land that we owned, and that a right of access, agreed with the original owners, would lapse with any change of ownership.

The developers offered a sum of money for the parcel of land we owned - several thousand pounds, which we declined. This was not to be the end of the story. Over the next months, they made, and we turned down, ever-increasing offers, that eventually reached an amount that would almost double the value of our property.

There was no question that we were tempted. The money would buy us additional security against financial problems, redundancy, or whatever unexpected shocks we might encounter. We remained adamant that we would not sell. Whatever value was now placed on the land would not go away. The driveway was the only point of access; the only alternative open to the developers would be to buy another complete property, demolish it and create a new entrance. Even if they were to consider that option, it would be simpler for them, both in terms of cost and planning, to return to us with a yet higher offer.

We thought we had achieved the best of many worlds. Without taking any action, we had saved the field, increased the value of our home, which would ultimately benefit our children, and gained the thanks and respect of our neighbours.

More was to follow.

We did not hear from the developers for a while. Life returned to normal, better than before, as we made new friends with neighbours to whom we had not previously spoken. People would stop us in the street and thank us, and invite us to dinner and to their parties, not that I am comfortable with parties - I prefer the company of my family.

Everything was going well, until the winter's evening when there was a brisk knock at the door at about eight o'clock, shortly after the children had gone to bed. I answered the door to find two tall, heavily built men dressed in quilted jackets, their raised hoods partly obscuring their faces.

Without any greeting or other polite formalities, the larger of the men stated they had come about the driveway. The developers were about to make another, final offer and it would be 'in our interest' to accept it.

The manner in which he spoke left me in no doubt that this was a threat. I felt afraid in a way I had never felt before. I had never experienced anything like this and had never expected to. My instinctive reaction was to be firm and assertive and send them away, telling them not to return. But when you are responsible for the lives of others... Not only did I have a wife and two children, I was delighted that Stephanie had recently been confirmed to be pregnant with Adam. Within seconds, a vision of the future played out in my mind, of fear and anxiety that something would happen, something violent. It is difficult to describe to others how, when you have not been exposed to violence, whether real or threatened, you are suddenly aware that is not just something that happens to other people in the news. It could be about to happen to you or your family and that life will not be the same until the source of danger is removed.

'It's not for sale, I'm afraid. If you give me your contact details I can pass them on to my solicitor.'

It was a ridiculous statement. One look at these men, one sentence from them, told you that they were not creatures of reason. They wanted just one thing and were not going to be swayed from their purpose by refusal or logical argument.

The man who had spoken cocked his head to one side, his eyes narrowed. His silent companion took a knife from inside his jacket and began to pick his fingernails with it, the blade glinting in the porch light.

'Who is it, darling?' Stephanie called from upstairs.

'Nothing. I'll be up in a minute.'

The man with the knife smiled and looked at his companion, who spoke again.

'I don't think you understood me. You… are going to sell that land, if you know what's good for you. We've been watching your family and know all about you.'

'Don't you threaten me; I'll report you to the police!'

The pair grinned, each baring his teeth in a forced, aggressive way.

'And what will you say? And what do you think they will do? I'll tell you: nothing. Because there'll be no proof. And meanwhile, you'll be shitting yourself every day, wondering when we're going to turn up again, whether it's the next day, the next week or in a few months' time.'

'That's it. I'm calling the police now!'

I stepped fully inside the door and went to close it. The man who had spoken put his foot inside to prevent me. I was by now terrified that they would force their way in and up the stairs. The man gripped my shirt with both hands, tearing it. His expression hardened, his stinking breath flowed over my face.

He drew me towards him. I thought he was going to head-butt me. He pushed me away, into the hall. Somehow I retained my balance and managed not to make a noise.

'Just do it! Or you don't know what might happen.'

They both turned and left. I shut the door, bolted it and put the chain on.

My first thought was not to tell Stephanie. I could persuade her that we should sell the land and the problem would go away. I knew this was not the answer. We couldn't possibly continue to live in a house where such a threat had been made. How could I keep it to myself, with her not knowing that she and the children were in danger?

Stephanie agreed that we had to report the incident to the police. I took the next day off work so that we could explain the situation to the plain-clothes officers, whom we had asked to arrive separately, reasoning that if they came together it would be obvious to anyone watching the house that they were police.

The officers were sympathetic, they explained that there was little they could do with there being no evidence to connect the unidentified men with the developers. They gave us advice on personal and family safety and told us to contact them immediately if any further threat, or suspicion of a threat, were to occur.

The following days were the worst of my life (apart from what was to happen in a few years' time - I'll not discuss that now). We remained on guard, twenty-four hours a day, looking carefully at anyone suspicious or unknown who passed near our house. Proper sleep was out of the question. It did not take long for us to decide to move. Stephanie agreed that it would not be enough just to sell the land. The house was tarnished; it could never be a true home again.

We instructed an estate agent to value the property and to put it on the market for a quick sale, telling a few white lies in the process. I despise untruthfulness and deceit in any form, but reasoned that this was an exceptional circumstance and therefore pardonable.

I told the agent about the offer that had been put in on the driveway land, but that we believed it could take a while to finalise. I told him that we needed to move quickly for reasons of a career move and to complete the sale and a new purchase before our child was born. We invited the agent to confirm the offer with the developer and to put the house and land on the market at a price that would allow a purchaser to make a quick profit on the sale of the strip to the side. He must have thought we were insane or foolish not to see the partial sale through and to retain the full profit ourselves.

I was worried that the threats directed at us might be repeated towards the new owners. Stephanie reassured me that, if someone were purchasing with a view to making a quick profit, then they would ensure the sale of the driveway materialised, otherwise they would be buying an overpriced house. She also said that it would save us from the embarrassment of being seen by the neighbours as having given in for the sake of personal gain. We could explain the 'career move' argument. Appeasing the neighbours was the least of my worries; Stephanie's words were, nevertheless, wise and reasoned.

The sale and move went through quickly. The threat had been averted. Stephanie's pregnancy progressed to a normal and happy conclusion and the family would benefit from the inflated proceeds of the sale. All was well again.

If only I had been able to save the field.

I sometimes think that feeling guilt is my signature emotion. I make regular, modest donations to charities, mostly for the benefit of poor people in developing countries, to people who genuinely cannot help themselves through no fault of their own who, by an accident of birth are living their lives at an enormous disadvantage to people like me, who have nothing of substance to complain about.

I also, through a charitable organisation, make small loans to people with an entrepreneurial spirit, also in developing countries, to assist them to work their way out of poverty. This is a cause close to my heart, and something of a no-brainer, as the money is always repaid. It costs me nothing and it does seem to make a real difference to people's lives. Yet there are so many occasions when I feel guilty that I am not doing enough.

People will sometimes ask me to donate to an animal charity. I class myself as an animal lover, although I prefer to give to human causes. I prevaricate when asked to give for animals, and then, out of guilt, will give an additional sum to a people charity instead. Recently, I had made a larger loan than I usually do to a particular entrepreneur who had endured enormous challenges to support her extended family. A few days later a major humanitarian disaster occurred. Donations were sought to provide relief urgently. Having just given some money I ignored the appeal, believing it was such a large event that there would be no shortage of donors and that the target sum would be raised quickly. The appeal remained in the media for several weeks, with the emphasis moving from relief to rebuilding. I still had not given. Eventually, I gave a small amount, only to find I felt even guiltier that I had not given more.

Stephanie told me that I should not worry about it and to forget it. She said that I had given something, which was more than most people had done and that many more individuals had benefitted from what I had done elsewhere.

I kept dithering as to whether to increase the donation I had given to the disaster appeal, until we were hit by a cluster of unexpected domestic bills, which demanded immediate attention and financial management. I felt no less guilty; at least the decision had been taken out of my hands.

We used to go on long walks as a family. Well, not exceptionally long - typically between five and eight miles. Long enough to make it worthwhile taking a picnic, which was often the highlight for the children, whose complaints of tiredness or feigned boredom acted as a barometer of when and where to find a good place to stop.

I looked forward to these outings and enjoyed researching and planning new places to visit, preferably taking a circular route so as not to have to counter complaints of 'we've seen this bit already', usually answered by 'no, it's different: you're seeing it from the other way round'.

Even these family walks I found carried an element of stress. The responsibility of ensuring everyone was enjoying themselves, that they were not too hot or too cold, and especially the responsibility of ensuring no one was injured or endangered.

This sense of duty would lead to protests from the children, and sometimes Stephanie, that I was spoiling their day. There were, nevertheless, occasions when my foresight proved justified and I was able to salvage a little credit.

I remember one such occasion well. We had driven some distance from home to take a new route. Where we lived was flat and we wanted a few hills to climb - nothing too steep - to give the children a different experience and to take them out of their comfort zone.

By the time we arrived at the start of the loop, a steady drizzle had set in, bringing with it a light mist. There were no complaints as we put on our waterproofs and changed into suitable footwear. Our picnic was distributed among the rucksacks we carried, as well as spare jumpers, gloves, hats, carrier bags for rubbish and the various items the children had concealed to assist in exploration and alleviating boredom. We had brought a child carrier for Adam. He walked well, although he would no doubt become tired after a few miles.

Stephanie and I took pride in being competent map-readers. We took it in turns for one of us to be in charge of the Ordnance Survey map, while the other read from the guidebook, on the occasions when we brought one. We had learned from experience that guidebooks can be inaccurate, or out of date, with routes blocked or diversions or rerouting introduced. Bad weather can be a factor too, making it difficult to spot or identify landmarks. This was to be one such occasion.

We were past the halfway point when we realised we had taken the wrong route. We should have crossed a ford, a quarter of a mile after the previous landmark and had now walked a half a mile on. We looked at the map and identified where we had gone wrong and our approximate current position. We decided to take a short cut through a field back to a footpath shown on the map, rather than retrace our steps.

The field sloped uphill; we couldn't see the top, where our exit would be found. We opened the wooden gate and passed through. As I lifted it off the latch, one of the hinges broke away from the rotten wood in the opposite post. When I tried to close the gate, the end dropped too far and rested on the ground, leaving it slightly ajar; there was no way I could fix it. The field looked empty, so it would not be a problem.

We trudged up the hill in what had become steady rain. I pretended to be exhausted, to encourage Freya and Alex to compete and beat me to the top. As the upper section of the hill flattened out, we could see cattle. We could only make out the upper parts of their backs; their heads were lowered and grazing.

We kept walking; the hill started to level out. The cattle were cows, except for a lone bull, which turned to face us. It stood, fifty metres away, close to the gate at the far end of the field. I gestured to the others to stay silent and remain still while I assessed the situation. The bull sniffed at the air, nodding its head up and down. Steam from its nostrils evaporated into the cool moist mist. It began to walk towards us slowly. I tensed, aware that it might become aggressive to protect its cows.

I spotted another gate to our right, partly obscured by an overgrown hedge. If the hedge had not been trimmed, would the gate be open or locked? There was no time to walk back to the foot of the hill. I reasoned that, if we turned, the bull might take it as an invitation to chase. I decided we would take a chance and walk slowly towards the right-hand gate. If it were locked and if the bull did charge, I could help the others climb over and take my chances. I told the family to walk calmly towards it. It was not chained and was sturdier than the one through which we had entered. We opened it and passed through, taking care to close it. We had crossed within twenty metres of the bull. It had chosen to disregard us.

'That was exciting, children, wasn't it?'

'I was really scared,' said Freya.

'I wasn't,' said Alex.

No one believed him. It didn't matter; we were safe. I remembered the open gate at the foot of the hill. I would have to return, taking a route through the field we now stood in, to try to secure it against the possibility that the cattle would escape. It took a great deal of effort to lift it back onto the latch. I was fortunate to find a piece of rope on the ground and used this to tie it to the post. I walked back to the family, retracing my steps. As I did, I heard the rumble of hooves on the other side of the hedge as the bull, followed by the rest of the herd, dashed downhill towards the gate.

'I'm glad we took this route,' I said to Stephanie.

'That was a lucky escape,' she replied.

We followed the footpath to rejoin our original route and continued our walk without further incident.

For many years I had a successful career, in a company where, for most of the time, I enjoyed working. There were inevitably times when things did not run smoothly.

I had risen to the position of director. This was a software company, with several divisions, organised by vertical market sector. This was a good thing in many ways, as the clients all had broadly similar requirements, with some bespoke tailoring to provide them with what they believed to be a competitive or operational advantage. It also meant that it was possible for my team to acquire expertise within that sector and to give confidence to existing and prospective clients that we understood their business and IT requirements. In this way, we were able to develop and expand our company's business. The downside was that all of the clients were affected by shared problems affecting their marketplace.

This was the case during one of the deeper recessions a few years ago. Some of the client businesses survived, others failed. Those that continued to trade were forced to cut back on expenditure, including systems development and operations.

Our company had a strategy for reducing the effects of a downturn, by linking product prices to inflation and employing freelance staff whose contracts would not be renewed if there was not enough new work to justify employing them. This time the recession cut much deeper and the decision was taken that several permanent staff would have to be 'let go' across the board, to reduce costs and to ensure that profits continued to be acceptable to shareholders.

I won't go into the rights and wrongs of a capitalist society, save to say that I recognise that a business has a number of stakeholders, all of whose needs should be respected. The most important of these are the investors who provide the capital and the employees who provide the products and services that enable the company to trade. Others include the customers of the business, who depend on those goods and services and the suppliers of the necessary materials to create those products and services or to allow the company to function. Even the office cleaners should be regarded as stakeholders.

I digress.

A meeting was arranged to announce and explain the problem to the whole staff and to warn them that redundancies were expected. One of the reasons for this was the hope that some staff, who might already be going through an interview process with another company, might decide to leave sooner rather than later, reducing the number we would have to release. Regular management meetings, involving the participation of every division of the company, discussed and tried to agree where 'savings' (redundancies) could be made.

Eventually, the board decided that I had to reduce the number of my staff by twenty-five, a quarter of the total team. Reluctantly, I drafted a list. No one in my team, apart from my senior managers, knew who was on the list, creating even more uncertainty and discontent. Some staff came to ask me if they were on it, something I could neither confirm nor deny before it was finalised. Once it was, it was only fair to get the process over as quickly as possible.

It was one of the worst times of my working life. I had known many of my team for ten years or more and in some cases their partners. Being a locally-based company, they would sometimes be collected from the office by their spouses, who would come into the office, occasionally bringing their small children.

I knew that it was not simply a matter of a business reducing the number of its employees. It would affect the lives of real human beings. I tried to suppress the selfish thought that I was pleased that Stephanie no longer worked at the same company.

Briefly, I thought through what would happen if I were to refuse. The answer was simple: I would be obliged to resign, causing hardship to my own family, while my replacement, whoever that might be, could well take the decisions in a different way, not taking into account both the individuals and the consequences for their families.

In some cases, it was straightforward to evaluate the role of the person and the financial contribution their work made to the company's profits. It was not necessarily within the power of the employee to make a difference in the revenue they produced. I was determined to examine imaginative ways in which to keep as many of the twenty-five on the payroll, while turning the business around.

Part of the irony of the situation was that, at the same time, we were interviewing for an intake of graduate trainees. It was ridiculous to be encouraging young people through the front door while we were ushering loyal and dedicated staff through the back door. Unfortunately, several of the older staff were supporting legacy systems, which were being phased out, the clients being migrated onto newer platforms. Once this had been achieved, those employees would no longer be required and their skills would have no use or value. These were the ones who would find it the most difficult to secure new employment. The responsible thing would be to retrain them.

Eventually, I managed to devise a plan to retain or transfer twelve of the twenty-five, leaving thirteen for whom there would be no option other than to give them the bad news.

Redundancy payments were calculated which, although well in excess of the minimum that the company was obliged to pay, would be little compensation to those who had worked loyally and diligently, in some cases for many years. The announcements were scheduled to be coordinated for a single day. It was only fair to get it over quickly.

The day arrived.

The atmosphere in the office was awful. Instead of the usual good-natured banter, there was a depressed silence. It became worse as, from time to time, someone from another division would come to our floor to report that a colleague had just been told they had been selected, and that in some cases this had been unexpected.

Throughout the day people watched for who was being called into my office and exchanged silent glances, assuming that person was about to go. This was not necessarily the case, as some of them were being asked to consider transfers to other departments.

The final interview of my day ended at six-thirty. Not a single person had worked past their normal day. This was most unusual in our business, where it is the accepted norm to work eight, nine, or more hours in a day, willingly, out of job satisfaction.

I was alone at my desk. I burst into tears. It was one of the worst days of my life. The task itself had been upsetting for all concerned. Life in the office would never be the same again. A few weeks before, we had worked together as a friendly team. There were the occasional differences of opinion and discontent over salary reviews yet, on the whole, we worked as a close-knit unit offering support to one another.

I sometimes feel I am on a slippery slide, that whatever I do in life will result in failure, or at best disappointment, whether for me or for others.

I can't keep on letting people down.

THE DISAPPEARANCE

I was convinced, from the amount of time and the direction in which I had been driving, that I must be approaching the general area where I would eventually find Durncot... or not. I decided I would take a short break from driving before what I hoped would be the final stretch towards my intended goal. I was pleased to find, as I entered the next village, that it was large enough to support a main street with several shops, including a teashop. This was just what I needed. I parked the car and went inside. It was about half full. I ordered a pot of tea and a slice of cake and took a window seat, away from the counter.

As I poured myself a second cup of tea, a man came in and sat down at the next table. He noticed that he had placed the same order as me. We exchanged a half-smile. He asked me if he might join me.

'By all means,' I replied. 'Please do.' I gestured to him to take the seat opposite me.

He asked how I came to be in the village - quite politely, I should say - he had not seen me there before and was merely curious as to why an outsider should be visiting.

I explained, as concisely as I could, avoiding too much detail, while doing my best to avoid seeming weird, deranged or otherwise in need of medication or confinement. To my surprise, he appeared to accept my intentions and continued to talk to me in an interested, unpatronising way.

We talked for perhaps five or ten minutes, until he looked over both shoulders, lowered his voice and moved his chair closer to the table. He leaned across, as if about to share a secret.

'Listen! Let me give you some advice.'

His head was lowered almost halfway across the table in his concern not to be overheard. I remember thinking that his body language was more likely to attract attention. I remained seated upright, to defend my personal space, resisting the temptation to lean back.

'You need to be aware: to be sensitive.'

He looked over both shoulders again. No one was facing in our direction.

'Aware of what?' Why would anyone take any interest in an adult stranger searching for a woman from their distant past, other than to offer assistance and advice?

'Let me tell you a story, a true story of something that happened close to here a few years ago. It left a deep impression and the village still bears the scars, as I'm sure you will understand when I tell you. I think you will find it relevant to your search. If you have the time, that is?'

He phrased the words as a question that I would have to answer.

I was now beginning to think that he might be the weird one: that I had walked into a conversation with someone who was not going to let me go. What was his motive? I didn't think he was looking for money, yet I couldn't be sure. I had other business to attend to; I didn't want to be stuck with a bore or somebody who would make demands on me that I was unable or unwilling to fulfil.

I could not risk the possibility of dismissing possible useful information.

'Very well. I need to be on my way within the hour. Where can we go to talk in private?'

'Come with me and I'll tell you my tale, on condition that you do not speak until I have finished.'

Without hesitation, I agreed. We left the café and our unfinished tea and walked the short distance to a park, where we sat on a bench out of earshot of the few other people enjoying the fresh air. I was eager to hear his 'tale'.

...It was May Day. We celebrated in the usual way, with a maypole, Morris dancers and the crowning of the May Queen. Even today people here leave gifts of baskets of flowers on neighbours' doorsteps, anonymously.

The festivities would be over by lunchtime, other than for the one little girl in the village whose birthday fell on that day.

The family lived on the outskirts of the village, beneath the hill you can see over there, in the far distance. The house had seen better days. It was quite large and spacious: eighteenth-century, I'm told, in need of more love and care than the parents could realistically afford. It had a couple of paddocks, each containing a horse chestnut tree. No horses, mind - they couldn't run to that. They were as happy a family as you ever could meet. There was nothing the parents wouldn't do for their three children.

Rachel was the youngest; it was her tenth birthday. For as long as she could remember, her mother and father had organised a birthday party, an occasion she and her friends looked forward to. When the sun shone, as it did that year, they would spend the afternoon playing games and chasing in the paddocks and beyond, towards the woods that climbed from the bottom of the hill. Often the celebrations would go on until dusk. The parents and their friends would flow in and out of the house, enjoying wine, food and conversation, while keeping an eye on their own children and attending to minor disputes, cuts and grazes and demands for food and drinks.

That year, Rachel was especially grateful to her parents for allowing her to have a party. Her friends would remember it not only for the fun and the excitement of playing in the twilight but as a double celebration: her cousin Claire was to be married in the morning of that same day to Nigel, her childhood sweetheart. Although the wedding was the main event, Rachel would be able to invite her friends as a reward for the dedication she would willingly devote to her duties as a bridesmaid.

The ceremony went as planned. Bride, groom, families and guests returned to Rachel's parents' house to celebrate.

It was as though summer had arrived early. The evening was unseasonably warm as the light lengthened before the approaching summer solstice. The children looked forward to playing outside as late as possible, enjoying the creeping thrill of descending darkness.

Rachel looked around, still wearing her bridesmaid's dress and floral hair garland, occasionally sighing with pride as a doubly important host, as she watched and participated in her friends' chases and tumbles and hugs and kisses. A string trio had been engaged to play under a sheltered canopy. Their competent, unobtrusive, musicianship was praised and applauded by guests.

The best was yet to come. Her parents had promised a treat: a surprise visitor, something traditional for May Day. She had found it difficult to remain calm when telling her friends at school, pretending to keep a secret, when she was not herself aware of what it would be.

'When's our surprise going to arrive?' her friends asked repeatedly.

'Soon. When it begins to get dark.'

The children were engrossed in their games, interspersed with copious party food and drinks served from the small marquee; games that became darker and scarier as the evening progressed. At first, they did not notice the tea-light lanterns being set out around the edges of the two fields. Soon they discovered ways to incorporate them into their play.

They were interrupted by the sound of hands clapping to attract the younger guests' attention.

'Come now all of you. Listen to me. Claire and Nigel are about to leave and they want to thank everyone, including all of you children, for making their day so wonderful and memorable.'

A few groans were drowned by cheers and squeals from the excited children.

'Will we be allowed back out to play?'

'Of course you will, and you have the surprise to look forward to.'

They broke off from their games. Several, red-faced, looked grateful for a rest. They gathered, some in groups, some with their parents, to listen to the bridal couple make a final speech before their chauffeur-driven car drove them slowly away to the applause and tears of the guests.

Everyone returned to their chosen activities. Glasses of wine, punch and fruit juice were poured. The conversation and laughter resumed and gathered in volume and jollity. It was one of those evenings you didn't want to end, and so you shut out the sad prospect that eventually it would.

The collective sound of animated children quickly rose to its previous peak and beyond, as they were startled by a new arrival, who announced his presence in the fields. A small girl ran into the house, calling, 'Mummy, mummy, come and look. Outside!'

Her mother walked slowly, unconcerned, glass in hand, towards the door onto the terrace, followed by her husband. Others joined them, curious. And then, as they began to discuss what they saw, most of the whole room followed.

They could hear before they could see. Standing beside the horse chestnut tree in the further field, a drummer, dressed in the red and cream costume of a soldier from a couple of centuries ago (possibly Napoleonic times, I couldn't say) beat out a vigorous rhythm on a military field drum, as if entreating a division to prepare for an attack.

The children bounced up and down with excitement, some clasping their hands in front of them. It didn't seem to me to be much of a surprise, although I was pleased that they were enjoying it. Or rather, I was, to begin with.

The drummer beat a roll, loudly then diminishing to near silence, continuing for near to a minute, then raising it to a crescendo, while slowing the rhythm until the individual beats became distinct and emphatic. He paused, raised his sticks as if about to begin again, then crashed them together to hit the drumskin and frame simultaneously.

Some children jumped, others screamed and then stifled the sound with hand over mouth.

It was not the drummer who startled them.

From behind the tree, a figure, the top of a figure, until now unseen, leaned out: a monstrous being, three metres tall, of foliage and flowers. It was broadly human in shape, with a distorted, abstract face peering from close to the top of its form, yet much lower than that of a human.

'It's Jack in the Green,' a parent exclaimed. 'I've read about him, a May Day character from folklore. I didn't know they still existed. I thought they'd stopped well before the twentieth century.'

'What a lovely idea, to have traditional entertainment,' said another.

The parents kept their distance, close to the terrace, allowing the children to enjoy the spectacle without interference.

Jack leapt out from behind the tree. His shape was conical, a tall bush, arms covered with leaves, as was every part of the body - you couldn't see the feet. He waved his arms stiffly, up and down to one side then the other, in time with his legs, in a way that suggested a star shape. He jumped in a continual bounce, turning and weaving an erratic path as he did so.

The children quickly joined in, copying his movements and following his serpentine trail around the field, taking care to keep their distance, wary of his sudden turns and lunges in their direction. He cut a jolly figure, though with an eerie air.

He began to bounce from side to side, arms and legs wide, in the shape of a letter X, all the while turning and twisting into his crooked path. I'm sure he didn't touch the same blade of grass twice. It was as if he were fixing his bearings, covering every inch of the field, learning the landscape of the enclosed field and its boundaries.

The parents trickled back indoors; just a few remained on the terrace.

Darker and darker, the twilight descended. The Green Man's rolling jig grew frantic, bouncing and cartwheeling. The remaining parents glid from the now cooling terrace towards the lights indoors. Time passed, unmeasured. Perhaps a quarter of an hour went by.

Until… Until a child, one of the youngest present, ran indoors, tearful, in her anxiety to find her mother.

'Mummy, mummy!'

'What is it darling?'

'A strange lady was in the garden. She's taken them all under the hill. I was following them, but then I stopped to watch the stars twinkle. When I looked down they were all gone.'

By the time the parents had reached the garden it was empty. The tea lights continued to glow around the edge of the silent fields.

'Tell me, what do you mean, they've gone under the hill?' Her mother grasped her by her upper arms and shook her to ensure her attention and her understanding of the urgency of the question.

'That's what she said; I heard her while I was looking at the twinkling.'

'Did she say anything else?'

'Yes. She said, "Come with me. I know a place where moonbeams grow".'

'What did she look like? Try and remember, it's important.'

The little girl burst into profuse tears.

'I don't know. I can't remember,' then added, 'She had a funny mark on her wrist.'

A search party was formed, spontaneously, in panic, with scant attention to organisation. Almost all of the remaining guests ran quickly through the fields, towards the woods. The little girl stayed behind, seeking comfort from her mother.

While they were searching, they saw a light through the trees. They rushed towards it to discover a group of masked men and women, naked, dancing around a fire. That sort of thing is common around here - the Old Religion, not to be confused with Wicca - it's considered harmless, as are its adherents. The searchers asked the revellers whether they had seen a child, or children, or a woman with an unusual mark or tattoo on her wrist. They had not. They offered to break off from their ritual and assist.

An hour later the children were discovered wandering, dazed and distressed; except for one, who never returned... that was Rachel.

'And that is the end of the story.'

'Let's go back to the tearoom,' I suggested. 'I'll buy you another cup of tea.' He agreed.

The tearoom had now emptied of customers. We took the same window seat as before. My companion sat back in his chair, resting his overlapping hands on his thighs.

'How long ago was this?'

'Oh, about ten years ago now.'

'I don't remember this. It must have made the national news - a small child abducted - there must have been a national appeal for information or witnesses.'

'You would think so, wouldn't you? That's the whole point. The villagers didn't want outsiders coming and poking their noses about. However distraught they were, and I can tell you there was no end of grief, there was no way they wanted the news to get out.'

'That's just not possible. Even ten years ago, someone outside the village would have missed them. There would have been birth records, health records, education… Someone, or some organisation, would eventually have noticed a child had disappeared, let alone a whole group.'

'In most places that would be the case, yes. It's different here. People keep to themselves. They don't often travel outside the local villages. When there's a problem they keep it within the community. The vicar of their church, in a neighbouring village, a young man, newly-ordained, advised them against reporting it to the authorities. He warned them that there would be months of media attention and speculation of guilt that would divide the community and aggravate their grief and pain. It would destroy their lives completely, beyond the stress they would continue to endure.'

'And so what happened next?'

'The villagers decided to close up against the outside world. They agreed that it would never be mentioned again. They conspired, successfully, to hide the girl Rachel's disappearance and to fabricate her death, or rather an explanation of her presumed death.'

'What was the name of the village where this occurred?' I asked.

'Dymwold, close to Durncot.'

I was curious. How had he heard of this hidden village that was not on any maps, that no one else I had spoken to admitted to recognising?

'May I ask how you came to know of this, if it's not a rude or insensitive question?' I asked.

He clasped his hands together, his forearms resting on the table. His facial expression showed distress.

'I'm sorry, don't worry. It's not important,' I added.

He looked up at me, taking a deep breath before he spoke. 'I was at the birthday party. I am one of the parents, one of the fortunate ones whose child returned. I was so grateful, yet felt so selfish at my feelings of relief that it was not my child who didn't come back, who was lost forever.'

'I'm so sorry.'

'I felt so guilty that I was determined to find out what happened, who did it and whether there could be any possibility that Rachel was still alive. And so I've made it my mission to keep on searching until I've found answers.'

'Do you share your findings with Rachel's parents?'

'No. It would only intensify their grief: drag it all out longer by raising false hopes. But I do sound people out - in particular strangers such as yourself.'

'In case they were involved in some way?'

'I suppose that's true. Outsiders rarely come here, to this part of the country, cut off as it is. They've no reason to.'

'Well, I can assure you that I have no connection. Let me rephrase that. I have no direct connection to the events you've described, but we do share a common interest in certain elements of the mystery.'

I decided to confide the reasons for my presence with this complete stranger. I needed both to put his mind at rest and to find out whether he had more information that could be of use to me.

We agreed that it was possible that Bella and the abductor were the same person although, unless she could be traced, there was no way of proving the case.

I was no closer to meeting Bella, although I was getting closer to Durncot. My companion at the table had confirmed it as being close to Dymwold, which lay beneath the distant hill, in sight of where I stood at that moment. And the woman that the little girl described, could she be…? There was not enough to substantiate her being Bella. I was tempted to offer to combine our resources in the search. I decided against the idea. As much as I empathised with his aims, I was too focussed on my own agenda and did not want to put myself in the position where, with the best of intentions, I started something and then let him down.

I stood up and prepared to leave.

'Thank you, it's been most interesting, and you've helped me a lot. I wish you luck with your own search.'

THE CREATURE BEHIND THE CURTAINS

Many years ago, when I was a young child (very young - it was before I had started school), I would creep down the stairs in the time between dawn and my parents and my sisters waking. I would go into each of the downstairs rooms and examine things. I found this exciting: having the freedom to do what I wanted, in secret and without interruption or censure. My father was strict. He would often tell me to leave things alone, that I would break them or injure myself. As spring grew into summer, with the sun rising earlier and earlier, there was more time to explore without fear of discovery. The light shining through the thin curtains made it easier to avoid both colliding with furniture and other objects and incurring the anger of my father for waking him.

It was not a large house. Upstairs there was a bathroom and separate toilet. My parents had their room; my sisters shared another. These days an estate agent would describe my bedroom as a box room or study. A dining room, living room and kitchen, all leading off the hallway, comprised the downstairs space. The dining room served both as a place to eat meals and as a family room in the evenings. The living room was reserved for entertaining infrequent visitors and was to be kept tidy at all times. The door was kept closed and it was understood that is was out of bounds except for special occasions. I did not explore the living room, for this reason, and another, which I shall come to.

The expectation of making a new discovery was not often realised. From time to time I might find a letter or an invitation to a family event or, occasionally, a list of items to be purchased for a domestic project. There were two mysteries to which I hoped I would eventually find a solution: the contents of a locked metal box, to which I couldn't find a key, in an alcove cupboard in the dining room and the contents of a heavy wooden chest stored under the stairs.

The sense of danger, descending the stairs while the house was asleep, was augmented by a fear of what I might encounter if I were to explore the living room. Perhaps it was because it was a forbidden area: that I was anxious that a trap had been set or that a terrible event would occur if I were to enter.

This fear was to manifest itself in a real and tangible way. Some mornings, just a very few, as I turned the corner from the stairs and passed the door, I would hear a strange noise, as if someone were saying 'gobble, gobble, gobble,' to imitate a turkey in a non-too realistic way. Sometimes I thought I could hear someone shuffling around.

There was, of course, no way I could tell my parents or sisters the circumstances in which I heard these things. What was peculiar, on reflection, was that I reasoned that whatever was making the noises was contained within the room and could not escape, provided the door was left closed: almost the reverse rule to that followed by the family. Provided I did not enter, I would be safe from confrontation and harm.

This was not a daily routine. The first thing I would do on waking would be to guess the weather, from the way the light played on my curtains. On wet or overcast mornings I could not be bothered to get out of bed but, when the sun shone, I was awake and up with anticipation. I would crawl across the bed to the window and peer out from the lowest part of where the curtains met. Usually, there would be nothing interesting to see: a cat or two, some birds. Sometimes I would catch the milkman rushing from house to house. These were the days when milk was delivered by a horse-drawn cart. The horse knew the round so well that he would walk forward to the next house with no need for a command from his employer. He seemed contented, particularly when his nosebag was attached. The thing that would give me most pleasure was the infrequent occasions when the horse relieved himself outside the house of the two elderly ladies opposite, who so often found an excuse to complain about me to my parents, or to report things they claimed they had seen me do that would get me into trouble. Such events included catching me gleefully waving at them as they crossly took a shovel to the still-steaming heap of manure in the road.

The morning pattern continued for a couple of months, until the day something changed.

I had been sent to bed early, by my mother, unfairly, for something my father had done. After tea, which was the evening meal in our family, my bath was run. In those days most ordinary people took a bath just once or twice a week. I played with boats in the bath until my father came up and told me it was time to get out and dry myself. Although I was too young to go to school, I was considered sensible enough to be left for short periods to bathe myself and wash properly. Despite this, my father was insistent that I cleaned my teeth thoroughly.

I dreaded teeth cleaning. My parents bought Gibbs toothpaste in tins. There were two flavours, I remember from trips with my mother to the grocers: 'standard' and mint. My father dictated to my mother that she bought standard. I detested the strong flavour and its intensity, which, if I applied too much, would make my lips and gums sore. What I hated most was that the family shared the toothpaste. A tin would last for months. The tin contained what started as a hard block of cleaning material, to which you would rub your wet toothbrush in a circular motion until it moistened, then foamed enough to adhere to the brush. You would then apply it to your teeth and repeat, then close the tin to keep it 'fresh' and moist, ready for the next family member. After use by several people, a small hole would appear in the centre of the paste to reveal the bottom of the tin. With further use, the hole would become larger and larger until only a small amount of paste was left clinging around the edge of the base. Even then, the paste would still be used until chunks broke free and had to be chased around the bottom of the tin - often attracting unwanted little hard bits you had to spit out.

Each time I cleaned my teeth I forced myself to suppress the thought that my father, and less so my mother and sisters, had loaded their toothbrushes from the same surface.

That evening, I braced myself, as usual, making my mind go blank, and started to brush vigorously. I had almost finished counting the required number of seconds of brushing when my father asked me to show him my teeth, to check that they were clean. I wanted to finish and ignored him.

'Show me!' he shouted and pulled my shoulder to turn me around.

With teeth clenched I opened my lips in a grimace.

'Look up at me so I can see.' He lifted my chin.

That did it. As I looked up I swallowed a mouthful of foaming toothpaste and at the same time lost my focus on keeping an empty mind. I could no longer keep out the thought that I had swallowed my father's saliva, nor could I keep down the toothpaste.

With a single belch, I vomited a mouthful of foaming pink mush down my pyjamas and onto the floor.

My father slapped my face. I don't recall it as a hard slap, but I felt the heat in my cheek and the tears well as I let out a cry. I felt ashamed and embarrassed, and a sense of disappointment that I had let my father down again.

My mother and my elder sister rushed upstairs. My sister ushered me to my room. She sat me on the bed, then fetched a hand towel to wipe my face. She brought some fresh pyjamas and then gave me a hug and offered to read to me. I was vaguely aware of hearing my father and mother in an agitated discussion and my father denying striking me. Perhaps I had imagined it. I would have to try to do better to please him.

It was in this remorseful frame of mind that I descended the stairs the next morning, tiptoeing, as usual, and placing my toes on the parts of the stair treads that I knew would not creak.

'Gobble, gobble, gobble.'

It was there, without a doubt, and louder than on previous occasions. It had a determined tone to it, as if it were embarking on a course of action. It had a plan.

Emboldened by my shame at disappointing my father, I was presented with the opportunity to atone for my faults by confronting the intruder.

It fell silent. Did it sense my presence?

I opened the living room door cautiously, my boldness already waning. I pushed the door to a half-open position and peered into the room. The curtains were closed; weak sunlight shone in through the fold and a small gap between them at the centre. The room was in silence with nothing unusual to see.

Until… Until I noticed a shape behind the curtains, a still, grey shadow. I stared at it, unsure from my memory of the infrequently visited room, of what ornament sat on the windowsill. I tried to think whether, when looking towards the window from the front garden, I was aware that there was anything there - surely I would have noticed. No, I could not remember any ornaments, vases, or anything else to be seen from the outside.

My body tensed, then froze. The shadow shape moved, almost imperceptibly slowly, as though turning sideways. Its profile now clearly resembled an elfish figure, like a garden gnome. Slowly, silently, it edged, glid, towards the gap at the centre of the curtains.

'Gobble, gobble, gobble!' it said, then 'Puck, puck, puck', or so they sounded. The words were not as fear-provoking as the implication, the projected thought: 'I'm coming to get you!'

It was now almost at the gap in the curtains.

'Gobble, gobble, gobble!'

From behind the right-hand curtain, a green sleeve emerged. From the sleeve, a grey claw was visible, like a chicken's foot. I screamed and felt a stream of urine flow down my legs, soaking my clean pyjama trousers.

My mother, father and sisters rushed downstairs and into the room.

'What on earth are you doing down here?' my father shouted.

'It's there - behind the curtains!' I cried.

My father drew back the curtains; there was nothing there. The windowsill was bare.

'Leave him. Go back to bed. I'll look after him,' said my mother. After some discussion, my father and elder sister went back upstairs after redrawing the curtains. My mother and younger sister tried to comfort and reassure me and led me into the hall.

'You go back to bed too, mum,' said my sister. 'I'll look after him.'

'He doesn't have any more clean pyjamas,' said my mother.

'Don't worry. I'll sort him out.'

Alone with my sister - my favourite sister - I tried to explain what I had seen and heard.

'You were probably just dreaming, in some form of sleepwalk.'

'No, I saw it and heard it. It was there.'

'Of course, there is another possibility.'

'What's that?' I said, my fear beginning to rise again.

'We think mum has an assistant, a sort of elf that tidies the house at night.'

Whether she was trying to reassure me or frighten me more, to this day I am still unsure. It was the latter possibility that engulfed me.

'You don't need to worry; it's here to help. Unless…'

'Unless what?' My eyes and sinuses tensed.

'Unless you say the wrong thing. Then all hell will let loose.'

I ran back into the room and pointed towards the curtains, where the shadow now reappeared. My sister ran in behind me and picked me up without listening or looking towards the window.

'Come on, little man. Let's take you back to bed.'

I was determined to look behind the curtains again, to reveal the creature, under the protection of my sister. As she carried me out of the half-open door I made a desperate attempt to stop her closing the door. I knew that I could make doors open further by pushing the door edge at the hinge end. What I did not understand at that age was the principle of how levers work and that her pulling on the handle generated far more force than I could counter with at the other side. I screamed again, as the door edge closed against my fingers.

My mother and father rushed downstairs once again. My mother took me off to bathe my fingers, the bruises already starting to appear beneath the nails, under the cold tap.

Now, not only had I got my sister into trouble for not noticing the unwise manner of my attempt to keep the door open, I had disappointed my father again, by disturbing his sleep, twice in one night.

DISTURBING NEWS

The chance meeting with my café companion had confirmed that I was nearing the end of my search for Durncot. I was travelling deeper and deeper into an area of mystery. Of course, I had known that this would be the case before I had embarked on my journey. I could not have predicted that so many strange events and happenings would occur as the day progressed.

The man's account of the child Rachel's disappearance was harrowing. I found it astonishing that, in a time of such distress and pain, the villagers had been able to suppress what had happened and had maintained the deceit for ten years. I also found it hard to believe. Not because I thought he had lied to me; it just seemed beyond comprehension that no one had ever let the secret escape, either deliberately or by accident.

I was certain there must have been some newspaper coverage. Why could I not recall it? Could I have been on holiday? Even had that have been the case, the investigation would have continued for months, years. There must be many cases from that period and earlier that have not been closed; disappearances that resurface and are given publicity every now and then. New evidence is found, someone comes forward who, for whatever reason, was unwilling or afraid to do so in the past, to identify a new suspect. These days it is common for new DNA evidence to emerge, though that assumes the recognition of a crime, possibly involving a person reported missing, whose family home will have been thoroughly searched and clothing and personal possessions tested for the DNA.

I remembered that, as I had driven into the village, I had noticed a library. Even in these remote parts, I thought that it might well maintain a local newspaper archive. It was worth a try. I would search their collection for the abduction.

The library was open. The librarian tried to be helpful; unfortunately, their newspaper collection only went back five years. I would have to go to the county library for older editions. I explained that I did not have time for that. He asked what I was looking for and whether he could help. It was better to give a simple answer: I explained that I wanted to look through crime reports.

He suggested enquiring online and gestured towards three computer terminals behind a screen in the corner of the room. I could have used my phone, although a large screen would be easier.

I discovered the existence of a national newspaper archive. I was disappointed to learn that this was a paid-for service. An annual subscription would be expensive, as was the 'pay as you go' option that would limit my search to a ridiculously small number of articles. A single month's subscription offered the most sensible route. I could concentrate my efforts over a few days if need be, and still be able to return for more after following up any discoveries. Once I had built up a few leads (it was like a criminal investigation - indeed that's what it was!), I could enquire further, using a more specific and generalised online search. I would still need to visit the area, where I might be able to follow up my findings with local people and to explore any evidence of rumours and hearsay.

I registered for the service and paid the subscription. I was quite excited at making a real start and the prospect of making real progress. It was not as easy as I thought it would be. I should have planned in advance what I was searching for.

I made a list of promising search terms. Missing children, disappearance, unsolved, unexplained, group, woman, Green Man, Jack in the Green, May Day, 'under the hill', the name of the village in the man's story, the name of the hill that he had pointed out to me.

I searched without success. I began to wonder whether the man had been lying to me, that he had made it all up. This had not occurred to me at the time, despite the tale being fantastic, in particular, the account of the villagers covering up the disappearance. Had I been gullible, wanting to believe a fantastic tale, because it seemed to fit well with the other strange things that had happened to me? The association of the Green Man and a mysterious woman, coupled with an unusual event in the broad area where I had encountered strange things had perhaps led me into a susceptibility to believing what I wanted to believe; a loss of objectivity.

The more I thought about it, the more I was convinced that it was just too much of a coincidence. Why should a stranger tell me this tale with these associations? And why would he choose to tell me? I suppose he could be telling the same tale to everyone from outside, to give the place an air of mystery. If this were the case, why would he risk his listener reporting the matter to the police, when the villagers had agreed to adhere to a code of silence? It's not as though he was after anything in return. I have said that he did not ask for money, or food or favours or any kind. All he asked was an audience: to be listened to, uninterrupted.

I decided to widen my search terms. If there really

was a connection between the woman who led the children under the hill and my mysterious woman, I should search on her attributes.

I made a new list: woman, tattoo, witches' mark, including Durncot and Dymwold, the Walnut Tree Press. I started the search process again. As I expected, the name Durncot yielded nothing.

It was the tattoo and the witches' mark that began to promise the hope of success. Not in relation to the missing children, but to other events that could be connected to each other and to the woman.

This route proved to be more fruitful. I found a link describing a report of a woman who had allegedly pushed a man from an underground station platform into the path of an oncoming train, resulting in his death. She had been captured on CCTV, but had escaped from the scene owing to the shocked inertia of witnesses. The newspaper reports spanned a couple of weeks until, no doubt, the editors became bored with the lack of progress on the case. The CCTV footage showed a tattoo that was indistinct, owing to her movement. It bore a resemblance to the shape of the Solomon's Knot; I was frustrated by the lack of detail. A Photofit picture showed a certain resemblance, again too imprecise to confirm it was Bella.

I continued to search for more evidence. It was by now late afternoon; I did not know what time the library was due to close. As the minutes went by, it was becoming increasingly difficult to stick to my task. The lack of further success resulted in too much distraction from interesting topics or items of news and knowledge that stimulated my curiosity. It was time to give up. I ought to refocus my efforts on deciding what to do with the information I had uncovered, rather than persevere with the same line of enquiry.

I was about to log out of the service when a headline caught my attention. 'Fire in university college kills seven. Students flee night-time blaze.'

I clicked on the article, from three years ago. I had a vague recollection of this incident. I remember the story running for a few days and the comments in the aftermath, lamenting the tragic loss of so many young people whose lives had shown great promise. I looked up articles from the subsequent days, describing the sad tales of the young lives cut short just after their final examinations. I read detailed accounts of their varied family backgrounds, the brothers, sisters and parents left behind; their unfulfilled ambitions to become leading figures in politics, sciences and the arts. There were stories of their kind and joyful personalities, how they combined the confidence that accompanies intellect and knowledge with humility and charitable acts, their consideration towards all of humankind.

The fire had started late evening in a college bar. The official closing time had passed, delayed by the inebriated, but good-natured, protests of those who wished to continue celebrating the completion of their finals. After several calm attempts by the porters to persuade the revellers to leave the hot basement room, the students had reluctantly agreed, only to find the exit door locked. It was later revealed that one of the celebrants had had the idea of locking them in, then throwing the key into the river. The students had at first seen this as an excuse to continue drinking. Loud cheers matched the aerial clinking of glasses. The porters telephoned the lodge for someone to find a spare key.

As the minutes passed, one girl grew anxious and began breathing heavily. Her boyfriend was alert to the possibility of her hyperventilating and panicking, something which had happened on more than one occasion.

He called to his friends to help get her out, raising her to her feet and ushering her towards the door, oblivious to the outstretched legs of a sleeping student lying on the floor, partly obscured by a battered old sofa.

The young man tripped and crashed onto a low table, knocking a candle onto the sofa, setting fire to a newspaper that burst into flames. No one in the bar knew that when the students had moved the sofa into the bar earlier that afternoon, it had not been thought to check its label to verify it was fire-resistant. Thick fumes quickly engulfed the surrounding space and began to spread through the room.

Someone shouted to everyone to get out of the room, to take the fire exit, quickly, and urged them to remain calm, while another person dialled the fire brigade.

Within seconds, some eighty students, lecturers and staff were grouped around the fire exit. It would not open. Through the wire-glass vertical windows, a chain could be seen, binding the handles together.

Within minutes the fire brigade arrived from their nearby station. They broke down the main door with an axe and released the occupants, at the same time extinguishing the blaze.

Had the fire station not been close, many more than the seven who died from the effects of smoke inhalation would have perished. No explanation could be found for the chained door. The college authorities were unaware of the obstruction, despite a cleaner claiming to have reported it to his supervisor.

The student who locked the main door was distraught. He killed himself a few days later.

I read the accounts over and over. At first, I paid little attention to the photographs accompanying the articles. When I eventually did, I was saddened by one, in particular, taken outside the building, showing flames and smoke rising, the fire engines hosing the blaze, and shocked onlookers, several of whom held their hands to their mouths.

It was then I noticed. A woman with her back to the

camera, illuminated by the flash. There was a mark on her arm. I knew immediately what it was.

What should I do? Ought I to report it to the police? What would I say? That they need to find a woman with an unusual tattoo, as she had undoubtedly chained the fire exit? The main cause of the deaths, after the accident of the upturned candle, was the smoke produced by the unauthorised sofa, compounded by the locking of the main door. These events would have been attributed to other individuals, easily identifiable.

Besides, I was now close to Durncot.

I had to use my time wisely, and there would be the matter of finding somewhere to stay for the night.

THE UNEXPECTED

I had taken the Monday off work to look after Adam, who was now four. Stephanie had been unwell over the weekend. It was nothing serious, but she had urgent work to do. Although she could do this from home, Adam's school had a prearranged non-pupil day. We had also agreed that Laura, the nanny, could take a day's holiday. She had been away to a friend's wedding and weekend trains were not running, and so she would be travelling home on the Monday.

I was looking forward to spending some quality time alone with Adam. He agreed with my plan to take him into town to buy some new shoes ('Boring!'), after which we would go for a pizza, to be followed by a visit to a bookshop and a toyshop, if there was time.

We drove into town and parked the car. On one side of the High Street workers were laying cables beneath the pavement. Several holes were fenced off, as were diversions into the road for pedestrians. I had forgotten from the days when I was Adam's age how interesting a deep hole could be. He wanted to know what all of the pipes and cables were for and why they were different colours, where they were going to and why they were laid so deep beneath street level. We had to look into each hole and spot the same number of pipes that we had seen in the previous one. There was no hurry; we had plenty of time and the incentive of the treats planned for later in the day made it easier to keep him moving.

As we neared the end of the line of holes, I gripped his hand and ushered him to the inside, away from the barrier with the road. I was startled, as were several other people, by the sound of an unseen motorcycle revving up and backfiring. From around the next corner the motorcycle, driven by a youth, turned quickly - too quickly for the busy location and conditions. He was forced to brake suddenly as a man stepped into the road. He stopped, briefly skidding, then momentarily lost his balance and rolled off the bike as it fell sideways to the ground.

A small crowd of about a dozen people stopped to stare. He began to shout abuse at the pedestrian, whom I would describe as being in the place between old and elderly, complaining that his machine was brand new and examining it for scratches.

I stepped in between them, holding Adam's hand to tow him to a position behind me.

An onlooker said he would call the police. The old person said nothing; I formed the conclusion not that he didn't care, but that he was oblivious to the alternative outcomes owing to the onset of a mild form of dementia.

'There's no need for that,' I called to the man reaching for his phone. 'It was an accident. No one's hurt. I'll talk to him.'

I stood between the old person and the teenager who, having brushed himself down, was continuing to inspect the bike for damage, striding around it in an emphatic, agitated way, while maintaining his gaze towards the machine, swearing under his breath.

'Take it easy. It's not his fault. He probably didn't hear you coming.'

'This bike's brand new. My dad will kill me if it's damaged!'

'Better that than risking injuring someone.' I refrained from using the word killing, not wishing to be provocative and aggravate the situation. 'It's an impressive bike and I can understand the pleasure it gives you. All the more reason to take care you don't risk losing your licence through an accident - it doesn't have to be your fault.'

I, too, felt a little angry. I tried to imagine what my reaction would be if he were my son.

'Just take a deep breath and think how much worse it could have been. You've both had a lucky escape.'

I sensed his tension ease. He turned to face me. 'It doesn't look as though there's any harm done.'

'Good. And no one's hurt. It all could have been so much worse. It's easy to forget that other people are less aware.'

'You're right; I'm sorry.'

His glance switched back and forth between me and his almost victim, his anger turning to embarrassment.

The onlookers began to disperse, muttering. The old man wandered off as if nothing had happened.

'Are you all right yourself?' I asked the youth. I thought that if I kept talking to him it would stop other people from intervening. The scene had calmed; normality was returning. Best to keep it that way.

'I think so. The bike's a bit more powerful than I'm used to.'

I took this as his way of excusing himself and making an apology. I was sure he had learned from the experience and no real harm had been done. I watched and waited until he drove off, cautiously.

Adam asked me lots of questions. He hadn't fully understood what had been going on. I explained that sometimes things happen that you don't expect, although they can turn out differently if you think beforehand about what might happen.

'Come on Adam! Let's buy these shoes, and then we can enjoy ourselves!'

With the shoe purchase completed, I described the short route to the bookshop. It was only a couple of minutes away. We walked down the road to the pedestrian crossing, where I took his hand.

'We have to wait for the Green Man.' I smiled to myself, in recognition of an association I hadn't thought of before.

The light changed; the Green Man duly appeared.

'There he is. We can cross now.'

'There's a car coming.'

'That's all right. They have to stop now that the lights have changed to let us across.'

I let go of his hand, confident that he would wait to cross with me. I was mistaken; he ran towards the other side.

The car did not stop. Time froze as he was knocked forward into the air by the speeding car, then hit the ground at the junction of his shoulder and head, before being run over and dragged along the ground. At last, the car braked, suddenly and too late. A woman screamed, a man shouted as though in pain. I dashed towards Adam and cradled him. He looked at me as if to ask, 'Why? Why did you not keep hold of me?' before closing his eyes.

My child was silent and would remain forever so.

The driver was arrested, bailed and sent for trial at the Crown Court. The inquest was to be delayed until after the proceedings. In the dock, the driver was distraught. A man in his late seventies, he had not immediately noticed the crossing light, let alone that it had changed. He told how, when he saw my son run into the road he immediately tried to brake, only to hit the accelerator of his automatic car.

The court heard evidence that there was no trace of alcohol and that in over fifty years of driving he had not committed a single offence. Medical tests had indicated the onset of the first signs of dementia; he had surrendered his driving licence without waiting for the court hearing.

Despite my unbearable loss, it was clear that he was tormented with remorse. He had had no intention of causing the accident and had not been negligent. If only he had seen the lights... He and I would be united in our unique forms of guilt and grief for the rest of our lives.

I tried to imagine myself in his position. He had killed a child through his actions, yet he had been unaware of the extent to which his mental abilities had deteriorated. He must surely be reliving the moment again and again. His remorse was unquestionably sincere. The court heard how his wife, too, was suffering from dementia, at a more advanced stage. He had struggled to keep her out of a home. They had no immediate family.

I was allowed to make a statement, in which I asked the judge to spare him from prison so that he could continue to support his wife. He was given a suspended sentence and banned from driving for life, a now irrelevant necessity.

The subsequent inquest was a formality. To our relief, both the trial and the inquest concluded quickly.

I kept the new shoes. They represented the final thing that Adam and I had done together.

*

This was to be the beginning of the lost years.

I returned to work two weeks after the accident, well before the trial, which had been formally delayed by the need for medical reports. Colleagues who knew me avoided eye contact. They would glance sympathetically at me, before directing their gaze sideways or towards the floor. Sometimes they would hurriedly make conversation with others, to avoid speaking with me.

I had to cope; Freya and Alex were ten and eleven. I became distant from Stephanie. She tried so hard, bless her, and I don't think that in her heart she blamed me.

Nothing could suppress my guilt, despite Stephanie's repeated reminders to me of the 'facts of the case' as stated at the driver's trial. I relived the accident day after day. At night I dreamed of it frequently, of different scenarios and outcomes. I would wake in sweats and panic. Sometimes, on waking I was able to convince myself that the true course of events was only a dream, that it was not real, only to be submerged by a wave of depression at the realisation of the truth of what had happened. I chided myself that I had disregarded a portent of death by dementia presented by the early motorcycle accident. Two accidents on the same day, in the same town, with a common theme.

The worst dreams were those in which I dreamed of saving him, of snatching him from the path of the vehicle and hugging him so hard that he would call out, 'Daddy, daddy, you're hurting me.'

Sometimes I would go to sleep and dream he was still alive: playing, smiling, usually out of doors in bright sunshine. I knew that for the rest of my life these moments would be the only times I could be happy.

I would open my eyes at the edge of dawn and try to hang on to the dream, to drift back into the bliss, shutting out the returning reality, yet knowing it was there, beneath the surface.

*

The grief never lets go. There are times when it feels more intense than when the event occurred (I found myself referring to it as 'the event' to avoid using the D-word).

'I'd like another child,' said Stephanie. 'I've been thinking, why don't we go on holiday, stay somewhere near a beach in France, like we used to before we had Adam?'

Her thought process was clear enough. She genuinely wanted another child. She also wanted me to 'move on' - a horrible expression that implies you can put the past behind you.

Stephanie had 'coped' - another horrible word - far better than me. Women seem to possess a greater inner strength in emotional crises. Perhaps it's because they are so often treated badly.

I felt a profound sense of guilt at any idea of 'getting over it'. I had been the only family member present when Adam was killed. I deserved to be punished for the rest of my life. I had no right to be happy.

All I wanted was for my own life to end, to rejoin him. It was not an option; we had other children who needed our support and a loving environment in which to grow up as normal as possible, to thrive and make the best of their talents and opportunities. If we had had more children, Freya and Alex would not have been so lonely. I was resigned to living a life of pretence, not to cover grief - it was essential to share that - but to demonstrate that life must go on.

'You have to do something, for the children's sake; a change of scenery will be good for them.'

It was true. Freya and Alex had lives of their own to lead. They could not and should not be expected to mourn forever. Somehow they needed to be able to put their baby brother in a virtual shrine, somewhere they could visit in their own minds' space and time, to be able to share their new experiences with him from time to time, then let him rest, while they lived and grew, to visit him again when the moment was right.

'You're right. We should do it. Let's start planning where we will go.'

I had to be supportive to Stephanie too. She was now bearing the greater share of the burden of bringing up the elder children in a positive fashion. I must no longer allow myself to be a burden to her.

I was unsure about having another child. There was no doubt that I would love and care for another in the same way. I was worried that a new member of the family would in some way cover up the loss and that this was in some way the intention. Since the accident, our love life had become infrequent and mechanical. I no longer had an interest in lovemaking, other than to go through the motions to prove to Stephanie that I cared for her, which I did. We developed a tacit understanding, a form of distance which acknowledged a past closeness and present regret.

And so Stephanie persuaded me. We would take a holiday that summer.

We agreed to go back to the South of France, to hire a villa in the back-country behind Bandol, an area we knew well, with good walking, clean beaches for the children and the prospect of good food and vineyard visits. A chance to get away from it all, whatever that is supposed to mean. It was 1995.

I had to make an effort, and did. We drove down, taking the Channel Tunnel, with overnight stops in Beaune and Orange, as we had done in earlier years. The journey provoked more sad memories, of how I used to joke that with each crossing we had one more child. Now of course...

After the best part of a day in the car, with frequent stops for snacks and to break up the journey, the hotel swimming pool was something to look forward to, followed by a long, slow family meal. It was difficult to keep up the pretence of having an enjoyable time. I kept thinking 'there is a child missing'. In the pool, I would suddenly be overcome with a sensation of panic when I looked for Adam and he wasn't there, believing for a split second that he had drowned. At our evening meals, it was wrong that we were seated at a table for four instead of a table for six with an empty chair. In my mind, there was always an invisible empty chair present at the table.

We arrived at the villa late afternoon, having stopped at a supermarket to stock up on essentials. The villa owners had kindly left us some fresh tomatoes, courgettes, apricots and a bottle of red wine. The next day we would go to the beach, for a day of doing nothing, to recuperate from the long drive.

We drove to Bandol early, to avoid the hassle of finding somewhere to park and to claim a place on the beach, close to the water's edge (where we could keep an eye on the children swimming), taking care not to sit too close to the water line for when the tide rose. I have to confess to having enjoyed the guilty pleasure of seeing those who have placed their mats in front of everyone else having to retreat when the water rises and encountering the refusal of the families behind them to move back and allow them room. It is a very French battle between the sense of superiority adopted by those who sit in the ideal spot and those who feel foolish, having misjudged the flow of the tide.

We were on the beach by ten-thirty. There was plenty of space to choose from as it slowly filled over the next hour. A family with three children, all under eleven, arrived and set themselves down a couple of metres from us, laying out their towels, their picnic boxes and beach toys around them.

I recognised the accent of the father as that of an Ulsterman, well-spoken with a calm and kindly voice. When I am in France I prefer to go native and, whenever I can, to speak in French. My French is quite good, although I cannot claim to speak it *couramment* and pass myself off as a local.

The family settled into their pitch and chatted for several minutes. I was not listening to the conversation. From the tone it sounded mundane - the kind of routine discussion families normally have. After several minutes, the father turned to me and asked whether I knew where the nearest decent sandwich bar was located.

'Pardon monsieur?' I replied, affecting to be French, as part of my going native pose.

'The nearest sandwich bar. I know you're English, you're wearing Marks and Spencer shorts.'

Stephanie giggled, amused at my failure to be convincingly French. The man had made his remark in a matter of fact way, to state his observation, without any hint of judgement. I felt sheepish, not to mention arrogant, even though that had not been my intention. I gave him directions to where we had bought ours, in a street nearby, parallel to the coast road. He thanked me, gracefully ignoring my earlier stupidity. He asked me how long we had been on holiday and our plans for outings. We all chatted for several minutes, comparing notes on the places we had visited and enjoyed on this (in his case) trip and previous visits.

'We come here every year, for the same two weeks. It's a sort of pilgrimage.'

'How do you mean?' I asked.

'We lost our little girl here, three years ago. She was the second child, seven at the time. She drowned here.'

This was not a conversation I expected to be having. I felt my throat constrict. Tears started to well. I had to take control. I had to appear brave in front of my family. A discussion was about to take place that they may prefer not to listen to. Should I send them off to swim? Stephanie put her arms around their shoulders, hugging them into her. She would decide what was best.

'It was a very unfortunate accident. We had been watching her enjoying herself in the water. She had only just learned how to swim, at school lessons. This was her first time in the sea without armbands. It was pretty packed and we thought she would be safe surrounded by so many people, regardless of the fact that we were watching her. We were distracted by someone nearby, who had been taken ill. A paramedic team arrived and people were gathered around staring, as they do. While this was going on, some children on an airbed pushed her out of her depth. It wasn't deliberate - they didn't notice until it was too late. It was only after she was recovered from the water that police interviewed other people who had seen her struggling to keep afloat. They had assumed she was playing and had taken no notice. She must have panicked at being out of her depth unexpectedly. All of a sudden we realised we hadn't been paying attention… It took a few minutes, with the help of others, including the lifeguard, who hadn't noticed, to find her. The paramedics were still on the beach. They tried frantically to revive her and continued to do so as she was carried to the ambulance, but it wasn't to be. Coming back here helps us to remember her and to let her know she's not forgotten.'

I was lost for words. Had they buried her here, rather than take her body home? I was annoyed at myself for having the thought, even though I didn't say anything immediately.

'We've lost a child too, our youngest one, earlier this year.' I nearly added that I knew how he felt, before stopping myself from making such a predictable and unhelpful remark. 'It's difficult to carry on, but we're doing our best. We have to help the others - our other children - to get on and lead their lives in the most positive way possible.'

I couldn't think straight. I wanted to add a message of comfort; I just couldn't find the right words. After all, there were three groups to consider: the other family's children, their parents and our children. Whatever I were to say could have an effect on the rest of their lives. Stephanie was less of a problem as she had heard every shade of outpouring from me and was unlikely to be shocked or surprised. Nevertheless, I wanted to be helpful, to offer some new words that may in some way provide the tiniest degree of sincere empathy and comfort.

'You know, one of the things I found most difficult was that while he was with us I was often accused of treating him as my favourite. Only jokingly, although I became quite sensitive to it. After all, it wasn't true. I was always telling all of them how they are all unique in their talents. I would say that there was no need for comparison, that they should celebrate their respective strengths and use them to help each other and other people, that they should avoid negative comments wherever possible. That's one of the things I learned from Americans. We went to Disney World and I watched how American parents handled their children when they did things they ought not. They would distract them by changing the subject. They would say "why don't you do this?" or "why don't we do that?" It seemed to work well.'

Stephanie pushed her fingers into my back. This was her familiar way of letting me know I was wittering. I should have stopped after my previous comment. I tried to wind up the conversation by switching it back.

'What I'm trying to say is that I believe it's important to keep looking forwards and try not to look back. It's impossible to change the past, however much I would like to. We all have some influence over our futures and those of our families: that's where the focus has to be. I find it helps for me, things are a little bit better that way.'

'I think you're probably right,' he replied.

One of his, their, children said something quietly to him.

'Excuse us, please. The children are getting hungry. It's been good to talk to you though. Very helpful,' he said, as he stood up. The children stood up too, followed by his wife. Neither of our partners had spoken until that moment, when Stephanie added, 'We're going soon, but we can look after your things if you like, while you go to buy your lunch.'

They thanked us and brushed the sand from their clothes before walking off towards the shops. I picked up on Stephanie's hint; she would find it upsetting to get into a detailed discussion of the families' losses. We would leave when they returned. I wish I could have been of more comfort to them.

*

Dreams, dreams; nothing but dreams. At first, I was afraid.

Now I am learning to accept them, to allow them a brief existence outside of sleep, before putting them to one side. I have a plan, of how to end it all, once I regain movement and speech. And experience a rare moment of clarity.

What happens when you're dead? If I can invent worlds as complex as I do, there must be something afterwards. That's not what stops me though. I can't just kill myself in the matter of fact, logical way that I would like to. I have to consider the effect of what I do on others: in particular on my children. And I would need to leave a note to my family, with a positive message, to say that there is no blame attaching to them, that I didn't want to let them down.

And then there is the fear. Not the fear of dying, it's the fear of messing it up. It has to be certain and final. I have looked at so many different methods. As yet I have found no clear-cut solution.

Shooting myself seemed to be the most logical way. It ought to be quick and painless. Blowing my brains out would mean I would have to take care to get the angle right - it should be possible, if I took enough time preparing and perhaps were to use mirrors. It's not the quickest thing to arrange though, as is true of many of the methods. There would be difficulties and the time-consuming process of obtaining a gun, legally or otherwise. I suspect that obtaining one illegally would be a waste of money, having to pay over the odds to some criminal. Assuming I could make contact with one, of course. I'm sure they would be wary of such an approach from a stranger and that they would suspect they were being set up or framed. It's possible that I would be arrested before even getting hold of it, or at least before using it. Even if I could obtain one, there's the mess. I would have to do it somewhere that I wouldn't be found by the family. And identification would be painful for them, especially if the injuries were disfiguring and widespread.

I thought about poison. The problem there is in

choosing the right product, let alone the difficulty of obtaining it in a large enough quantity. I would want something quick and painless, as indeed I would with any method. I have a low pain threshold; I would need to be sure I could bear it and not find myself in agony and to suffer the indignity of calling out for help.

The same problem applies to drugs. I suppose that poison and drugs are one and the same thing really. It must be possible to find something on the Internet and then source it, again, presumably from some disreputable person or company. Purchasing in that way you can never be sure what you are buying, which leaves you open to conmen. Even those US states where capital punishment is still legal can't source the drugs for lethal injections. I know that's partly because of other countries' reluctance to supply them, but all the same...

I could overdose on legally obtained drugs, prescribed, ideally, but then I would have to convince a doctor that I had a condition that demanded a particular drug and then build up a stockpile, which all takes time.

There are simple solutions, like paracetamol, in conjunction with large quantities of alcohol. It would involve going from shop to shop to accumulate a sufficient quantity; that's the least of the worries. It's not as quick as it might seem though. I've read that whereas you might fall asleep quickly, you are likely to recover consciousness. There is no cure: once the liver is damaged, death can be slow and painful.

In the good old days, people would gas themselves. They would just slowly fall asleep on their kitchen floor, with the oven door open and not wake up. Then someone decided we ought to replace the poisonous gas delivered to our homes, making an explosion a more likely probability. Attaching a hose to the car exhaust used to be popular too, if that's the word. Now that's no good owing to catalytic converters. I suppose I could buy an old car.

I read that a popular method of suicide in Asia is to

light a charcoal barbecue – in your bathroom, that is – with the doors and windows blocked, to prevent air circulation. The popularity of this method is allegedly due to the way you just gently fall asleep and don't wake up again, unless… Unless something goes wrong. There is the danger of interruption or the fire going out before death occurs. I discovered that in the worst case this could result in permanent brain damage from carbon monoxide poisoning.

I thought about electrocution, by jumping onto the track on the London Underground. I rejected this idea, as I would probably miss, cause myself a good deal of pain and have to suffer the far worse embarrassment of failure, as well as the consequences of severed limbs.

For a while, I considered finding an isolated section of train track and putting my head on the line. I thought that decapitation would be instant and painless. Until I watched a film about Spanish conquistadors, one of whom was beheaded by a sword and whose lips and eyes continued to twitch, in an agitated and distressed manner. So it may not be instant after all. Neither did it seem fair on others to have to sort out the mess.

Motor accidents are not a good idea. The outcome is uncertain and may result in killing or injuring other, innocent people.

I read that hypothermia leads to numbness and then eternal sleep. The trouble is, I just don't like the cold. In winter, I sit huddled indoors wearing layers of clothing and keep the heating on quite high.

Hanging is totally out of the question. Years ago, when I was quite young, my father showed me how to tie a hangman's knot. I've no idea why. I don't remember how to do it; I expect instructions can be easily found on the Internet. The consequences of a botched job, as a result of an inability to break the neck with an incorrect knot – jiggling around for ten minutes until you finally pass out through suffocation – do not bear thinking about. Getting the height of the drop wrong could lead to a messy discovery for my family.

Similarly, I quickly rejected haemorrhaging by cutting an artery. There would be pain and the need for perseverance, not to mention the possibility of discovery. Not something to do at home either, as the blood would congeal and block the drains, inconveniencing your heirs.
I know someone who knows someone who nearly drowned. The rescued person told them that, after the initial struggle, and the choking and water filling their lungs, the experience became quite dreamlike and serene. I'm not sure how you would manage to drown yourself deliberately, if you know how to swim. You probably have to select a good spot and attach weights. It had possibilities, but was not quite convincing.

Suffocation with a plastic bag seemed to be a possibility. I would have thought that breathing air with an increasingly higher carbon dioxide content would allow you to drop off to sleep peacefully. It should be easy to find a spot where you wouldn't be interrupted. This, though, was another example where I had seen a crime series in which someone suffocated in this way. The reality was quite different.

I looked up how high you would have to jump from a building, a bridge, or other tall place, to be certain of death. The consensus seemed to be one hundred and fifty feet over land (between ten and twelve stories) or two hundred and fifty feet over water. I'm not at all keen on heights. It's a long way to fall, too, and must be terrifying. There must also be a danger of instinctively trying to land on your feet, with the possibility not of death, but of painful permanent disablement. I suppose you could get very drunk, or drug yourself. I wondered whether that would relax the body too much, with similar, inconclusive results.

I thought about many other methods that would be out of the question: acid baths, drowning far out at sea, falling into an impenetrable crevasse or cave…

It's all very difficult.

Having considered many methods, I took a step back to think about my criteria for choosing the best way.

The most important thing is certainty: to avoid the eternal hell of disablement or dismemberment, being institutionalised and unable to make another attempt; having to suffer the misery of pain and a brain, with no bodily movement, dependence on others, the misery of strangers, the possibility of abuse by unsuitable or unsympathetic carers. It would be necessary to decide on a plan, once and for all and to carry it through at the first attempt, to avoid all risk of having to repeat the planning process, the indecision, the wavering, the execution.

And then there is pain. Although I am not afraid of death, I do have a fear of pain.

It would be uncomfortable to do it on a cold day (I've already said I don't like the cold). If death were not instant, it would be less unpleasant to fade into unconsciousness on a warm summer's day.

Avoiding discovery by loved ones is essential. The shock to someone loved would stay with them for the rest of their life. No, too selfish! I could not inflict that upon anyone.

Similarly, the need for identification has to be considered. It would be best for loved ones not to have to be concerned with this. I would imagine that in the case of a corpse charred beyond recognition in a fire, dental records would be used for identification. That would be one way of avoiding the problem. What happens with a partially burnt body though? I would not want to put my family through the distress of having to confirm recognition and identity of a mutilated corpse, especially with head or facial injuries, or damage inflicted by animals or birds. The chewed flesh, the pecked-out eyes… How can this be avoided? It would have to be carried out at a location where the body would not be discovered.

Is it better to leave open the possibility that I am not dead?

I must leave a note, and use a method that will result in my body being destroyed, but how?

Make it look like an accident!

THE TUNNEL

My encounters with the Green Man and his female associate had now reached a peak of distraction. On the one hand, I could reason that I was reading too much into the accumulation of contacts, events and tales. On the other hand, the number of occasions was beyond the bounds of statistical probability. I had begun to believe that I was being singled out for some purpose, as yet unknown to me. I could not continue with this near-paranoiac obsession with being a marked man. The problem was, what to do and whom could I turn to, to assist with my quest to find answers?

I needed advice, ideally from someone familiar with the Green Man, yet who would be impartial in their reasoning and judgement. Preferably someone with local knowledge, or specific insight of the events I had either witnessed or experienced. By now, in the present world, I could, of course, make more enquiries of my own on the Internet. Although I had already done a little research on the history of the Green Man, I did not have the appetite for spending days, weeks, sifting through enormous amounts of information to arrive at possibly erroneous judgements.

And besides, I was here, close to Durncot.

I don't know why it took me so long to find the answer, or rather where to turn for someone to ask my questions. I would go to Dymwold, the village near Durncot, where the young girl had disappeared, without trace or publicity. Once more I Googled both Durncot and Dymwold on my phone, in the vain hope of a different outcome. Could my memory be playing tricks on me? Was it possible that I had got the name wrong, or that I had imagined all of this? No, I had been to Durncot. I had seen the village sign and the name on the board outside the church. A stranger had mentioned it in the context of the missing girl, as a reference point, presumably a larger village than the nearby Dymwold. I was certain now, with the hill in sight, that after all these years I would be able to find it, albeit at the end of a much longer journey than that first time.

First I would visit the church to discuss my experiences and, with luck, the disappearance and possible connection with the vicar. I hoped that it would be the same man. There was a good possibility that, as he had been newly ordained, and had assisted the village in their time of extreme need, he would have remained in the position.

How could I be sure of getting a meeting? Briefly, I considered taking stock of my location and returning home to write to him to request an appointment. I laughed at this ridiculous thought: I could not write a letter or send an email to someone whose existence and address could not be traced online. Even if it were possible, the request for a meeting would likely be rejected.

It was odd that throughout the whole day, since arriving in this part of the country, I had been able to access the Internet intermittently on my phone, but location services had not been working. I had been unable to locate my position, either on paper or by using electronic maps.

I had to visit in person; to take him by surprise. I also needed a pretext to engage in discussion. The Green Man and 'The Old Religion' seemed the most promising opening gambits, without suggesting any reference to past local events, yet with the possibility of teasing out his expert knowledge. It was a long shot that I considered to be worth the effort. With it came the hope and prospect of satisfying my curiosity. There was also a chance that, if my growing conviction that I was known to the Green Man and his assistant was true, the probability of success should be high, especially if the vicar may in some way be connected to the two.

I made a mental note of the direction of the hill. There was no point in looking at the road atlas again; I was off the map. It looked to be about ten to fifteen miles away. For all I knew it could well be longer through the country roads.

As I approached, the setting sun disappeared behind the hill, allowing me sight of a group of houses set among the trees and above them the octagonal spire of a honey-coloured stone church, adjacent to a three-story building that promised to be the vicarage. Both church and vicarage nestled against the side of the wooded hill.

I drove at a snail's pace towards the church and confirmed from the sign on the wall of the next-door building that it was indeed 'The Old Vicarage'. I drove through the gate onto the raked gravel drive, reasoning that visitors to a church property, whether it be a religious building or a functional annexe, would be welcome or, at the least, expected. The door opened before I had time to pull the ancient metal bell, fixed to the wall beside the entrance.

'Good afternoon. Peter Shepherd – please call me Peter. I've been expecting you. Come into the study and take a seat.'

How he could have been expecting me I have no

idea. The man I met in the café must have alerted him. Why on earth would a stranger accost me, tell me a story involving someone I did not know, at a location I was unaware of, and then contact that person to say I was on my way to meet them? I had found the tale of the children's party engaging and mysterious; that didn't mean

I intended to follow it up immediately.

I returned his greeting and thanked him. I refrained from commenting on my 'expected arrival'. I had arrived; I was inside and welcome. There was nothing to gain from asking the question.

His study was as large as most people's living room, furnished with armchairs, two tables, a writing desk and a chaise longue. Each of the walls was lined, almost to ceiling height, with bookshelves and bookcases. He gestured to me to sit down in a leather armchair, one of a pair, while he took the other. Between us stood an occasional table bearing a small handbell. He raised and shook it as I continued talking.

'You have a lovely house. Thank you so much for inviting me in. I've come a long way, searching for information without much success. So far, I've found more questions than answers. I'm hoping you might be able to help me.'

'I'd be delighted to assist in any way I can. My housekeeper will bring us some tea. I know you shouldn't call employees by these old-fashioned names any more, but I can't quite manage to adapt to modern ways. At least it's not as bad as "maid", or worse still, "servant", and I wouldn't dream of addressing her by her first name.'

It was a word I hadn't heard for years. In fact, I couldn't recall ever having heard it spoken, other than in films and dramatisations. It brought to mind elderly bachelors, wearing woolly tweed suits, living alone. There again…

I heard the door open behind me. Peter looked over my shoulder. I didn't turn: it would have appeared impolite and too curious. And besides, I was distracted by a movement outside the window, as if someone were passing, close to the house.

'Would you please bring some tea for me and my guest? Thank you.'

There was no audible response; all I heard was the door close. I could imagine a curtsey, although this was just a fancy.

'So, what brings you here today?'

He seemed genuinely interested. I thought it best to start with the original reason for my journey, rather than to leap straight into asking about the children going under the hill. I told him how it all started, with a wave from a woman at a window thirty years ago, a memory that had been unexpectedly reawakened and had developed from curiosity to a mission and had now become an obsession.

'I had thought it would be a straightforward quest... a bit of sentimental nostalgia. Something to get out of my system. It started off simply enough: I decided to seek out the village where I'd originally seen her and to pay a visit to a traditional printing press and bookseller on the way. I'd been there before – to the press – the first time I came to this area. The trouble is that several new things have been added to the story during my journey here. And what I thought was a gap of thirty years... well, it's not quite like that.'

I've come to realise that certain things, incidents in my life, things that I've never given any significance to in the past, seem with hindsight to be connected, both to themselves, the waving woman, and the experiences I've encountered today. Everything seems to be coming together. Things are starting to unfold, to make sense in a way I would never have thought of before. There's a lot still unexplained, but it's as though I'm reaching the end of a journey.'

He smiled at me, adding, 'Well you could say that about most things in life. We seek answers and eventually they arrive by unexpected means – sometimes. Now, I understand why you might want to talk to a man of the cloth about the mysteries of life, but why me? Surely you wouldn't have come this far out of your way to talk to a rural priest?'

'When I arrived, you said you had been expecting me, so I think you may know the answer to that. I met a man earlier today, purely by chance – in fact, it was almost as though he had sought me out. We had a chat over a cup of tea. I mentioned my search for Durncot. He told me about the children, the ones that were led under the hill, one of whom didn't return. May I ask whether you were here at that time?'

'I certainly was. Is that what you have come to ask me about?'

'Not specifically although, if you are willing to spare me the time, I would be interested to hear your version of the story. It's just one more thing in the chain of events: things that appear to be related. But first, as you are a local person and a parish priest, I hope that you can assist me in explaining what is happening to me and to help me find answers.'

'Very well. So tell me about these connections you've made. What are the common elements?'

I hesitated and made an audible sigh.

'The most common thing is the Green Man. I assume you are familiar with him? And then there is a mysterious woman, with a tattoo in the form of a witches' mark. I was told it's known as a Solomon's Knot. The more she keeps cropping up, the more I'm coming to believe she's the woman I'm looking for. And the two seem to be connected in some way – the woman and the Green Man – not directly, but… I don't know – it's totally irrational – working together somehow.'

I told him about my encounters with the Green Man, real and imagined, starting with the face in the wall at Durncot, the strange performance of A Midsummer

Night's Dream and my weird dreams (I didn't mention Adam and the Green Man crossing. He would find that connection too far-fetched). I told him how strange it was that I had come across him more than once today in various guises: The Green Man pub, several instances in the garden and the tale of the children who had disappeared under the hill, one of whom was never to return.

I told him about Bella and the printing press, the woman at the Green Man pub and the representations in the garden, too.

He listened with interest, in silence, as though what I was telling him was normal. He waited patiently for me to finish before responding.

'Let's talk about the Green Man first. You may or may not know that the Green Man has a long and ancient history. The name is thought by some to be twentieth-century, although there are several references to him by name and description in sixteenth-century plays, which would indicate that he was a familiar figure to the general population at that time.

'The character himself can be traced back through history for thousands of years, through two routes of lineage. One possible source is the Sufi prophet Al-Khidr, The Green One, known throughout the Middle East and India. It's quite likely that the foliate heads we are familiar with today originate from the tales and images brought back from the crusades by the Templars.

'The Templars themselves used the image of the Green Man in their churches. There is one quite near here with a horned head. It sounds like an image of the Devil, I know, but it is not. Essentially the Green Man is benign, representing a reminder of the superiority of the force of nature over human endeavour. The connection with mysticism and pagan belief is there to see: he is usually adorned with oak or hawthorn leaves, the latter being connected with shamanism, as well as bearing male and female elements of blossom and berries respectively.

'The other source is the ancient pagan beliefs. Unfortunately, the Ancient Britons were illiterate and so we have no written history to consult, nor have we inherited a reliable oral tradition. It's important to remember that there are many common elements to what we think of as paganism in many countries. Trees and woodland play a significant part. The Tree of Life exists in many cultures and religions, stretching at least as far back as the Hindu eternal banyan tree. It occurs in all of what we regard as the major religions: Christianity, Islam, Buddhism as well as in Egyptian, Persian, Chinese and Jewish mythology. In the Norse myths, the Poetic and Prose Edda describe an enormous ash tree that connects the nine worlds of Norse cosmology and is where the Gods hold court each day.

'Then there are the beliefs in what we could call states of existence. The Anglo-Saxon Wyrd, or destiny, concerned with attunement into the "otherworlds". The Ancient Britons are alleged to have had a Shamanic cosmos consisting of three levels, underpinned by the Tree of Life: the Upper World, inhabited by ethereal spirit guides, the Middle World – where we live from day to day – and the Lower World, a place to be in touch with nature. So, while there is no documented proof, the numerous potential origins of the Green Man, a combination of local beliefs in nature and natural events, combined with influences brought in and spread over centuries are quite plausible.'

'I'd like to ask you about the Old Religion. I'm aware that many in these parts believe in it. I've been told that it's largely invented in the twentieth century. What's your view of it?'

'Indeed, the terminology is modern, but "The Old Religion" has always been here, within the fabric of the community. That's a whole subject in itself. It's about being in tune with the seasons, the crops and nature. A sense of nemesis. I prefer to think of it as a portmanteau term used to describe a unique combination of local beliefs and their following, or rather their alleged following, both here and in other parts of the country.'

'I was also told that it's a lot of nonsense, that it's a veneer placed onto selected ancient beliefs to give them respectability at best, at worst to render them harmless, a quaint pastime of people with no real purpose or direction in life.'

'Some would say that's what you are meant to think. I'm sure that many are sincere although, no doubt, other so-called adherents are just joining in the party out of boredom. There's not a lot in the way of entertainment around here.'

'So it does exist – I mean, it does have its followers. What do you feel about that? It must go against everything you stand for as a Christian.'

'You have to be pragmatic about these things. Over the centuries the Church has accommodated all sorts of existing beliefs. It had to, in order to recruit more souls. You can't just tell people to stop following things they have believed in for centuries, to ask them to discard their traditions. You have to find a way of absorbing them into the fabric, to enlarge the tapestry.'

'Even pagan beliefs?'

'It depends what you mean by pagan.' He stood up and walked to the bookshelf. 'Let's see what Chambers says.'

He opened the dictionary.

'Here we are. "Pagan: a person following a polytheistic religion; a person who is not a Christian, Jew or Muslim, regarded as uncultured or unenlightened, a heathen; more recently, someone who has no religion". Well, there are worse things than being uncultured or unenlightened. Those in themselves are subjective terms, implying a form of assumed superiority by those in established, conventional religions. We in the Christian

Church have to exercise tolerance – to be inclusive, welcoming. We need to recognise and respect the differences of others. Besides, their religion, if we are to recognise it as such, is as old as, if not older, than Christianity, Judaism or Islam. Being different doesn't necessarily imply being bad. All over the world, established religions and belief systems have accommodated earlier, dare I say, more primitive beliefs, which have grown organically from the soil, from nature itself, hence what I told you about the Green Man. Religion is underpinned by natural cycles, our so-called pagan roots.'

He returned to his seat.

'How does all this square with the established church, with Christianity,' I asked.

'Even in the British Isles, there are records of tolerance of so-called pagan activities as far back as the late Saxon period of the seventh and eighth centuries. The English Church elected to follow Rome rather than the Celtic tradition. In order to make this acceptable to all parties, facets of traditional beliefs and practices were not only tolerated, but absorbed into daily life and rituals. It was thought important to remind converts to Christianity of their former beliefs, or "superstitions" as they came to be regarded. You are probably aware that pagan rituals have been adopted into Christian celebrations. Pagan images were often incorporated into church buildings for this purpose, typically on the north, or "unholy" side of the building. This is where you will usually see the Green Man representations, although they also appear inside, as do other images of things the ordinary people were afraid of. That is why we see so many grotesque carvings, in wood and stone: on pews, for example. It all helped to convince the converts that they were being protected from their former fears. As I say, many church images, statues and carvings are based on things people were afraid of. By placing the things that troubled people in their daily lives into a "safe"' environment, it was believed that not only would people become accustomed to them and lose their fear, the images themselves would lose their power and therefore their influence, thus empowering the church. All of this was at its most evident in the ancient kingdom of Mercia, especially in the regions of its boundaries with other kingdoms and, in particular, those to the west and north.

'Let me quote you something from a book. This tolerance continued through the centuries. As late as 1617, King James I, in an attempt to resolve a dispute between Puritans and the gentry of Lancashire, who remained predominantly Roman Catholic, issued a Book of Sports, listing activities that could be indulged in legally on Sundays and Holy Days, so as to limit the killjoy restrictions that the Puritans wished to impose. Archery, dancing, and "leaping, vaulting, or any other such harmless recreations" were deemed to be acceptable. "May-games, Whitsun-Ales, Morris dancing and the setting up of May Poles" were also considered to be harmless.'

'This is the same King James who commissioned the Bible translation?'

'Indeed, it is. The King James Bible was designed to remove objections to earlier versions and to limit the influence of the Puritans, as perceived in earlier translations, notably the removal of marginal notes, which featured in the predecessor Geneva Bible. In common with most other translations of the period, the New Testament would be translated from the Greek, the Old Testament from the Hebrew and Aramaic, and the Apocrypha from Greek and Latin.'

'Why was it so important to limit the influence of the Puritans?'

'In part, at least, to ensure that the masses were on board. For hundreds of years, ordinary people had followed their hereditary, traditional beliefs, with a closeness to nature that they were not going to give up just because the ruling classes said they should. I've always been interested in what unites us as people. Once we understand this we can address what divides us.'

'So, what you are saying is that, despite the strength of Christianity, both the monarchy (and the Commonwealth, while they were in power) were aware of this and chose to live with it.'

'Precisely! There was a tacit agreement – an accommodation. In fact, it was more than that: there was a recognition that there existed forces, some dark, that governed human affairs and commanded acknowledgement and respect.'

'Is that what you believe?' I asked. 'And is the Green Man a part of what is meant by "The Old Religion"?'

'I don't have all the answers. You know, it's a strange thing: over the centuries, the image of the Green Man has changed. When he first started to appear widely, in the thirteenth century, his expression was represented as happy, smiling. In a way that's unsurprising. The lives of ordinary people were beginning to improve, without a significant detrimental impact on nature or the health of the planet. This is a generalisation but, with the increasing influence of Christianity, we see the Green Man's image change fairly markedly and consistently as the centuries pass. He moves from jovial to merry, to smiling; then serene, worried, distressed, and tormented, until eventually the common images become those of resignation, as if accepting fate, and finally calm.'

I heard the door open behind me. The housekeeper had returned with the tray of tea. As she placed it on the table her sleeve drew back. The mark on her wrist was clear and unmistakable.

I looked up at her. It was she, Bella.

I looked down and fixed my gaze on the tea tray. I could not continue to look her in the face. I said nothing, as she turned and left the room.

'Let me pour your tea. My goodness! You look as though you've seen a ghost. What is it? Are you unwell?'

'The mark, on her wrist. It's her – the woman I told you about. The Solomon's Knot! You must have known it was there: the witches' mark.'

I've no idea why I focussed on the mark and not the woman herself and the reason she was there. I took a few deep breaths to suppress the feelings of panic brought on as I made the connection between the housekeeper, Bella and the woman who abducted the child at Rachel's birthday party. The teller of the tale had mentioned that the young girl who returned first had noticed a funny mark on the wrist of the abductor.

'It's not quite what you think - the mark, I mean. It's a very ancient symbol. But if you recognise her, in that case, take care. Things are not always what they seem, as you will shortly discover.

He stood up and walked over to the bookcase once more.

'Here we are: Solomon's Knot. Let me read it to you. "The symbol is associated with magical powers, its name being derived from King Solomon and the pseudo-epigraphical work, The Testament of Solomon, a popular magical treatise incorporating Jewish, Christian, and Islamic elements. It was written in the Greek language, sometime in the early first millennium CE. It describes how Solomon was able to build his temple by commanding demons, using a magical ring that was given to him by the archangel Michael. An Ethiopian legend tells that the ring bore the symbol of the knot, engraved by God, which served as the most powerful device for subduing demons". So there you have it, it is a symbol of protection, rather than one of evil implied by the term "witches' mark". It signifies good intentions, not bad.'

Up until now, I had been careful in my questioning, in case Peter asked me to leave. I now needed answers more than ever.

'I'd like to ask you about the little girl that disappeared, if I may. The man who told me the story described the woman who was with Jack in the Green, who led the children off with him and the drummer, as having a mark on her wrist. I realise that it could just be a coincidence...'

'I know what you are going to ask,' he interrupted. 'I can't say now but, believe me, I can promise you the answers to all of your questions. It will not be long now.'

'You have been expecting me, haven't you? What's going on here? I don't understand what's happening.'

'Yes, it's true. We have been expecting you.'

'Why have you been expecting me? And why is it happening now?'

I was becoming more and more anxious; Peter remained calm, rational and friendly.

'Try to think of it as destiny, as something that has been mapped out, not necessarily from birth, perhaps triggered by a certain event or series of events. Let me phrase it another way: there is an anniversary that occurs in everyone's life, the date of which they are unaware.'

He looked at me, still smiling, as if I should know what he meant.

'No, I'm sorry. You'll have to explain.'

'It's the day of the year on which they will die.'

Without waiting for me to respond or to gauge my reaction, he stood up and rang the handbell to summon the housekeeper back to the room.

'Come. I'd like to show you our underground chapel. Where the new meets the old, and the established church meets its precursor.'

I chose to disregard Peter's comment about the anniversary. I thought it strange that he should make such an observation, vaguely menacing and apparently unconnected with our discussion. He may have intended it as an analogy for destiny. I reasoned that I was in a vicarage, a safe place, a place of refuge, yet I remained alert to possible danger. I was alone with two strangers, one of whom appeared to have unexplained powers. I had secretly checked my phone; there was still no signal. No one knew I was here, in a remote location, with no means of communication with the wider world. Despite my fears, I was determined to appear to my hosts as sane and positive. I was looking forward to the description and historical background that Peter was about to deliver, and to his promise of answers to my questions.

The housekeeper returned. I was now certain that she was the woman from thirty years ago. I still could not look her in the eye. Peter had not given her a name. He was my host and I was unsure whether I would be considered impolite if I asked.

Peter led us through the house to a door that opened into the vestry. He ushered us towards another door in the far corner.

'You can't be too careful,' he said, as he took a bunch of keys from his pocket and selected three, to open locks at the top, middle and base of the solid oak door to reveal a square brick landing at the head of a spiral stone staircase with an ornate iron balustrade. He turned a switch in the vestry to illuminate the descent.

'I wish you peace,' said Peter, holding the door open and sweeping his arm towards the opening.
'Are you not coming with me?' I asked.

'You will find my housekeeper is all the company you will require. She will provide any explanations you may ask of her. You could not possibly want for more.'

The light was fading within the study. I turned to see Peter silhouetted against the window. His tousled grey hair shaped his head in a familiar way. I felt tired, drowsy. I continued to stare. His face was dark in the dimmed light. And then it became clearer, changing shape until, although still shaded, the outline of the Green Man was unmistakable.

As I passed under the lintel, I read the wooden inscription carved into it: Wise toad, tell me this… What are the secrets I must learn, to gain entry to this hidden world?

It was not a quote that I was familiar with.

I stepped into the unknown. The housekeeper followed. I heard Peter close the door behind us, followed by the sound of the keys turning in the locks. I remembered the words of Mr Wyrdstaff: 'no one ever returns to the garden; it's not possible.'

RESIGNATION

'I'm leaving.'

Stephanie had had enough. I couldn't blame her. Freya and Alex were through university and had been fortunate enough to find jobs. Both were looking for flats closer to their work. This was before Alex moved abroad. I was adding nothing to Stephanie's life.

We met with the children and explained, as best we could. We hadn't so much drifted apart: it was more that the accident had driven a rift between us. Stephanie was desperate to create a new life, ideally as a grown-up family, taking turns to visit or receive visits from our now adult children. I was the obstacle to this. I had absorbed myself in work. It was the only thing that kept me sane. The more engrossed I became, the less time I had to allow the memories to haunt me. It was no exaggeration to say that I relived the scene several times a day.

Every night I would dream of Adam, in imagined worlds created by my sleeping mind. Worlds in which we played joyfully, shared our lives and embarked on new experiences. The dreams were different from those immediately after the accident. These had an organic life of their own, twisting, turning, as though exploring ways in which we could all be together and happy again. In my waking hours, I knew this was not to be; I was grateful for the night-time illusion, as an opiate.

There were many times when, on the verge of waking, I clung to the dream, unwilling to let go, knowing that the world I was about to leave was one in which I would give anything to remain. I was unable to force myself to focus on the living. It was as if, by constant thought and willpower, I could bring him back or, failing that, we could share another life, a happy life, together, in dreams.

The house sold quickly. By the date of the move, Stephanie was already established in her own home in the city, where she had taken a new position. The day that she left and closed the front door of the family home for the final time, she did not look back. So many happy memories had been wiped out by Adam's death and its effect on me.

A year after Stephanie left, I learned from Freya that her mother had met someone new and that she would be moving abroad with him. She would remain in contact with Freya and Alex and invite them to visit her whenever they wished. I was pleased that Freya had been in regular contact with Stephanie; I was worried that they may lose touch, which would not have been good for either of them. I was the cause of the split and it would have been better had I have been the one to move away, or to disappear completely. I was not sufficiently detached; I had lost one child and could not bear to be away from Freya and Alex. Not for my own sake – I thought that I could get myself together and be more supportive to them. It did not turn out that way.

Stephanie and I arranged to meet to discuss divorce. We only needed the one meeting. It was to be 'amicable' (another horrible word). I would have readily agreed to any terms to help Stephanie 'move on'. If anything she was too generous towards me in the agreed settlement.

I took out a new mortgage on the house to buy her share. Neither of us had any strong views on possessions.

I did not want to downsize. I wanted to retain the space for the children to visit whenever they wanted... No, that is not the real reason; I could not bear to leave the house that cradled Adam's room. To do so would be to abandon his spirit and betray his memory. I felt his presence there. Sometimes I thought I heard his voice and believed that he was trying to communicate with me, that he had something he needed to say to me. And I needed him to talk to.

Why is it always too late to do the right thing?

In a deep down part of my mind, I clung to the possibility, not consciously, that one day Stephanie might come back. I knew in my heart that this would not happen. I took some small comfort from leaving the door open, a door that finally closed two years later when Stephanie was killed in a sailing accident.

I wanted to attend her funeral, to be close to her one last time, to say goodbye. It was not to be. The cremation had taken place quickly. She had always liked to be close to the sea. Freya told me that she had stipulated that her ashes were to be scattered out of sight of the shore. We were now parted in death, as well as life.

Our separation had not diminished my feeling of loss. I had continued to love her, possibly more than ever before. I now had to make an effort to live beyond mourning Adam. I discovered that having two objects of intense grief does not double the distress; each inhabits its own dark corner of the same room.

Not long after Stephanie's passing, something happened to me. I don't know what it was. There is a gap in my memory... Everything is different now.

I don't understand.

Part 3: Things Fall Apart

POINT OF NO RETURN

'No, Simon. There is no way I will ever agree to that,' said Freya. 'Not while there is the remotest hope that he could recover.'

'I understand how you feel. He is your father, after all. But it's been two years now and there's been no change in his condition. He's totally unresponsive to external stimuli, even binary choices. If he could just let us know he can understand that we are trying to make contact. He could live for years, decades, like this. It would be kinder to end it all, rather than for him to be enduring this lingering death.'

'And so what? What if he does live for many more years like this? He may be in a coma, but there's nothing to suggest he's suffering.'

'It's about quality of life. Look, there are two alternatives: either he knows nothing of his condition and is unable to think, or he is aware that he is a prisoner in his own body, dependent on other people for every aspect of his care. He has to be fed and medicated intravenously, his hygiene managed… in either case, he has no control over anything. There is no joy in his life, no purpose. If we were able to ask him now, whether he would prefer to continue in that way or have an end put to his suffering, what do you think he would say?'

'Simon, when I agreed to get back together again, eighteen months ago, he was already in this condition. Nothing's changed.'

'That's the whole point...'

'Let me finish. You knew what you were taking on then and you seemed happy enough to accept and share the responsibility for caring for him. Nothing's changed.'

'Exactly! Nothing's changed. I thought, and I believe you did too, that either he would recover, or show signs of recovery, or that nature would take its course. Can you imagine: if he is aware – and I don't believe he is – of what life is like for him, unable to move, talk, or even open his eyes to see what's happening around him? Just think how long his days must be.'

'Do you think I haven't considered that, many times? Of course I'm concerned about his condition and what he feels. If I thought there was no hope, then I might agree with you. There's no way I would want to prolong a hopeless life, but things could change.'

'If there's been no change in the two years since it happened, when he took the overdose, it's unlikely there ever will be. Okay, his eyes open, but he only stares ahead. He can't follow an object in front of his eyes and there's no sign of any emotional response. Freya, I know it's hard to accept, but, at some point, you need to come to terms with it. Surely, deep down, you must know this is true. How could things possibly change?'

'In two ways. Firstly, he could recover. There are times when I'm alone with him, talking to him, that I sense he understands some of what I say – fragments of what I tell him seem to resound, to click into whatever thought processes he has. I sometimes think I see a flicker of movement beneath his eyelids when they're closed, as though he wants, is trying, to communicate.'

'Well, no one else has noticed this.'

'Simon, I spend much more time with him than anyone else, including the medical staff. I have pointed out to them that the graph measuring his mental activity shows small changes during these periods.'

'Freya, darling… We've discussed this with the doctors. They think the variations are too small to indicate anything significant.'

'That's just the first thing. Medical science is progressing so rapidly. So many advances are being made in understanding how the brain works and the treatment of conditions previously thought to be untreatable. At the moment he's in a halfway place between a coma and a vegetative state. It could all change. If he were allowed to die and a cure were found shortly after, it would be unbearable. In the meantime, I'm happy to visit him daily, to cut his nails and hair, to stroke his hand and talk to him about the good times we shared.'

'Look, I don't like to remind you of this, the reason he's in this state is because of what he did. He wanted to die, from what you told me.'

'I never said that and I don't believe he tried to kill himself. It's what you've read into it. He was depressed after mum's death. It was too much for him, having lost one child and then to lose all hope of reconciliation with her.'

'You told me he took an overdose.'

'Yes, I did, but there was more to it than that. He'd taken some sleeping tablets. It seems he'd taken several – I've no idea of how many – and then had a few glasses of wine. He then tripped over something and hit his head. It was fortunate that I was staying with friends close by. When he didn't answer the phone I used my key to get into the house. I'd been worried about him. I found him lying on the floor and called an ambulance.'

'Why don't you think it was an attempt to end it all?'

'When I went back to the house, I found he had a hidden stash of tablets that he had been prescribed from the time of Adam's accident. He must have been putting them aside instead of taking them. If he'd have wanted to kill himself he could have taken all of them and then drunk a lot more alcohol. If he'd have been trying, he would have taken them lying down in bed, where he could expect to fall asleep peacefully, rather than in the living room. It was the brain injury from the fall that caused the coma and necessitated putting him on a ventilator, not the tablets.'

'What do you think will happen, the longer it goes on? Do you think the hospital will move him to a care home?'

Freya stood up. She strode over to face Simon, looking up at him.

'That's what really worries you, isn't it? Do you know what I think, Simon? I think that what really worries you is the prospect of it costing you money: the thought of us or me having to pay for his care! It's not about him, is it? It's about you. You're so much in debt from this latest stupid business venture of yours that you're afraid of responsibility for anything. And this, after he lent you money to try to help get you out of one set of problems...'

'I would have been totally out of those problems if he had lent me the full amount I asked him for originally. I would have had a majority stake in the business and could have taken different decisions without having to please other people.'

'Well, it's just as well he didn't. You have such a lack of business acumen that the whole thing would have collapsed sooner and even more of his and mum's money would have been down the drain. And to think that now, all you worry about is how much it will cost you, after you nearly bankrupted the family with your schemes.'

'Well, that's rich. You're the one who's going to bankrupt us by keeping an incurable invalid alive while letting him suffer.'

'The one good thing that's come out of this is that I can see how selfish and self-centred you really are. All you think about is money. Thank goodness we don't have children. I should never have taken you back. We're finished! And you needn't worry about me; I can support myself, and my father.'

Simon turned and left the room. Freya ran her hands through her hair and returned to her father's bedside, taking hold of his hand.

'You were right, dad. He's no good. Don't worry; I'll look after you. I have a plan. I'll talk to Alex about it. Thank goodness he will be flying back soon.'

Simon left the clinic, alone. Freya would only ever see him once more, in court. She arranged for a friend to be at the house to allow him access to collect his personal possessions.

The divorce would not be contested.

TAKING THE SOLUTION INTO HER OWN HANDS

'Alex, how was your flight?' Freya embraced her brother and kissed him on the cheek.

'Yes, good, thank you. You're looking good, considering all you've been going through.'

'It's not been easy, but there's no one else to do it. Let's not talk about me. Come in, put your bags down. It's been so long since I've seen you. The girls must be growing up. It's a shame you couldn't all come over.'

'Yes, you know how it is – school term time; and Angela's about to go back to work. We hope to come again… if things work out as we've planned.'

'Come through. I'll make some tea.'

Alex placed his bags in the corner of the hallway. Freya smiled, recalling how, since Alex was a child, he had always been a tidy person. He opened one door, then another.

'It's in there,' said Freya.

Alex looked at her quizzically.

'The bathroom. I assume that's what you're looking for.'

Alex smiled in recognition. Freya put the kettle on, then rearranged the cushions on the living room sofa and tidied the coffee table while waiting for Alex to return.

'So how is he?'

'He's deteriorated. The hospital gave him six months originally. Now they're saying they don't expect him to live for longer than a month. I live in hope, as you know. Which is why I wanted to talk to you. And as nice as it would have been to catch up with all of your family, it will be easier to talk between ourselves.'

'I agree. I talked it through with Angela, when you invited me over. She understands,' said Alex. 'We're both concerned, too, that you've looked after him for so long now. We really do appreciate the burden it places on you. Is there absolutely no possibility that he will ever get better?'

'Definitely not, barring a miracle. You don't need to worry about me. I don't see it as a burden. It's more a labour of love – to visit him in the hospital, to talk to him, to tell him my news. Only the good things, mind.'

'I know how much you love him. We both do. He's always had a special spot for you. But I really think you have to come to terms with the fact that he's never going to improve. Not to the extent of leading a normal life. Tell me, are you thinking of…'

Freya raised her palm.

'I know what you're going to say. No, I'm not going to ask them to turn off the life support system. You know that he made a living will many years ago, to allow me, as the eldest child, to take any difficult decisions regarding his care. Believe me when I say that I wouldn't do that without discussing it with you first.'

'Of course not. Although it's the quality of life that's important, I'm not sure I'd want to be kept alive in the same way.'

'The truth is we don't have any idea what his quality of life is like. It'll probably help if I tell you what I know. The doctors agreed that there are no signs of physical pain. If there were, I'd have no hesitation in pulling the plug.

The significant thing is that he has phases of evident brain activity: eye movement, even though they remain closed; and his lips twitch.'

'That sounds positive. Do you think he could be trying to show that he's still with us?'

'That's what I think, but the doctors also say that there's no sign that these things indicate attempts to communicate; it's all internal thoughts or dreams. No one knows what's going on in his head. For all we know he could be living through some dreadful nightmare – reliving Adam's accident or just thinking about being trapped without hope. I wish I knew. It would make life so much easier.'

'You're right not to give up hope. You know him much better than the doctors. What they see is a patient; what you see is someone whose habits and gestures you are familiar with. Signs that people who don't know him wouldn't recognise.'

'Alex, there's a particular reason I wanted to talk to you face to face. I've been doing some research and I think I've found a way forward, something that will make a difference.'

'That sounds interesting. I hope it's not some sort of faith healing or other quackery. You know what I mean: people who claim to have invented a wonder drug or therapy designed to take money off desperate and gullible people... Sorry, I'm not suggesting you are either of those. I'm worried that you could be taken advantage of... Please, tell me about it.'

'You don't need to be sorry. I'm quite capable of distinguishing the genuine from the hoaxers. Have you heard of cryonics?'

'Yes, I have. I don't claim to know a lot about it, other than it's to do with preserving bodies after death, in the hope that they can be revived once science has advanced to the stage where it can offer a cure to whatever the person died from. Is that a good route to follow? It seems a bit too long-term and probably very expensive.'

'They've been working for years on preserving bodies in the hope of finding cures in the future – cures for the diseases that killed people, typically cancers which are incurable now, but may be in the future. Cryonics is more than just preserving the body. It's concerned with maintaining the cell structures and chemistry to keep the body functioning without the deterioration that would make it impossible to revive the patient; patient being the key word.'

'Stop there – he doesn't have cancer, he has terrible brain injuries that will never lend themselves to a cure. Freya, we've been through all this before – so many times. I thought we'd agreed that there are only two options: to leave him as he is, in hospital on the life support system, or to allow them to turn it off. We know he's never going to recover...'

'No, wait! That's not where I'm coming from, although theoretically even the most devastating injuries could be reversed in the future, by repair, stem cell treatment, or even some new process. This is only a part of what I've been looking into. What I've discovered is a means of improving the quality of his present life, way beyond recognition.'

'How can you possibly improve the quality of life of someone who is unconscious, unable to move anything below the neck and unable to communicate?'

'That's what I'm about to explain. Will you please let me continue?'

'I know how distressing this is for you and that you need to cling on to hope.'

'It's not about hope! It's about making a real change. Believe me, once I explain you will understand. Just give me a chance.'

'Very well, I'm sorry. I'll do my best. Tell me Freya, how far have you taken your research? A long way, I would imagine, if you are thinking of doing something now, when dad may only live another month.'

'I've had discussions with an expert in the field. Don't worry, he isn't a money-grabbing quack. Dr Kristal has been working with the cryonics people on and off for years and has impeccable credentials and endorsements. He explained that the cryonics companies – and there are several – don't pretend to provide solutions, only to preserve bodies in the short time between legal death, when the heart ceases to beat and real death, which occurs shortly after, when the body's tissues begin to decay irreversibly. What he's been working on most recently is transhumanism, the ability to develop the human organism beyond its present capabilities, in particular, the brain. By putting these two concepts together, he's come up with the promise of new and innovative solutions. I have some brochures that I downloaded from Dr Kristal's website. I'll fetch them.'

Freya brought a small pile of leaflets and scientific papers and placed them on the coffee table. Alex picked them up and flicked through them one by one, stopping every now and then to read a short section. His frown and hint of a pout betrayed his scepticism.

'Sounds like science fiction to me.'

'Yes, it has been until recently and now it's becoming real. He says they have the ability, in layman's terms, to upload the brain to computers and to model its activity, including thought processes, within the computer's processing systems. Effectively, they can upload the brain from the body into a computer and eliminate the need for the bodily functions that support it in normal everyday life. Apparently, there are lots of universities and research organisations working in this area. As you would imagine, there is no shortage of funding for their work.'

'So, are you telling me that the person lives on, as a brain, a mind, but without a body?'

'Yes, in a way. It's really no different from how he lives now – entirely within his head.'

'We have no idea what's going on in his head. It's quite possible that he's aware of his body, or at least the lack of a working body. I can't imagine how awful that must be, to know that it's there, but doesn't work and quite likely to be conscious to some small extent of what's going on around him, yet be unable to communicate.'

'Yes, and that's where the benefit lies. Preserving the body is only part of the solution. Keeping the brain operational allows the patient to continue living a meaningful life while any previous pain and suffering is suppressed, managed.'

'What you describe doesn't convey any sort of quality of life. It sounds more like a dreadful form of disability, where you can think, but have no physical capability to do anything.'

'Don't you think I haven't thought about that? Endlessly! But on the positive side, I recognise the possibility that for at least some of the time he could be reliving happy memories. And that's where the exciting bit comes in. What I've just described is the full package, based on preserving the brain after conventional death. However, what Dr Kristal has been working on is to capture not only thoughts but also dreams, while the patient is still alive. And there's more, they can monitor the brain's reactions to thoughts and measure emotional responses. Using that information, it's possible to push pleasurable thoughts and sensations to the fore, so that he could relive all the best experiences and memories of his life over and over again. It's a bit like playing a grandmaster at chess: every new move is analysed and played through to arrive at the ideal response. The potential is enormous. Imagine, if this were to be offered to the old and frail, to people with various forms of dementia, as well as those in situations like dad's, so many lives could be improved, or made bearable.'

'If this could really be possible, it must cost a fortune. There's no way we could afford it. The preservation costs alone must be enormous, let alone all this cutting edge technology. And he could live for years in that state.'

'No. Dr Kristal is prepared to provide the care free of charge. He sincerely believes it is the way forward in so many cases and wants to demonstrate the benefit and that it works. Remember, I said there's no shortage of investors for this research. He's offered to do this on two conditions. Firstly, that we, I, sign some form of confidentiality agreement.'

'Why should he ask for that? Is what he's doing legal?'

'Yes, it's perfectly legal. He doesn't want to attract attention or publicity until he's put it into practice. He's concerned that others will resort to espionage, to steal his ideas, by bribing his team or by more desperate means. The second condition is that we agree to cooperate with publicity at a time of his choosing.'

'So he can make his fortune, I imagine.'

'I expect that's one aspect. I don't have a problem with that if we get dad back. I think he's more interested in the prospect of a Nobel Prize and the acclaim that goes with it.'

'I'm not sure. This is an experimental approach. What if it goes wrong?'

'Dad will be in no worse position than he is now. The options will still be there to sustain him as he is, for as long as he has left, or to turn off the life support system if it doesn't, or if he begins to suffer.'

'You make it sound as though there's nothing to lose. I must say I'm not entirely convinced.'

'I've made up my mind and I would like you to agree. It isn't fair to let him go on existing in that living limbo, partly aware of what is going on around him, yet powerless to communicate, when we could be doing something.'

'Freya, I can understand the benefits, if it works. Part of me says, yes, let's go ahead. Another part is concerned about what might go wrong. I need time to think it through.'

'Time is one thing we don't have. Dr Kristal will only perform this procedure on someone who is terminally ill, who has been confirmed as having had only a limited time left to live, in the usual sense.'

'Why is that? If something as promising as this is proven to work, every family with a relative in a coma would want it.'

'Exactly. It's because it's not been performed on a human patient before and there is a remote possibility of unexpected outcomes. The risks are minimised by restricting it to those who are close to the point of their death, using it as a palliative measure.'

'So if it is successful, what happens when he does finally pass away?'

'To put it into simple terms – and these are the only ones I understand – we will be given the option to upload his brain, as an enormous dataset, to a computer, Once that process is complete, his bodily life support systems will be turned off and he will be allowed to die. There's still a further option to freeze and store his complete body and brain cryogenically for possible future revival. Dr Kristal has offered to do this free of cost too.'

'So, in effect, dad gets the benefit of being an early adopter.'

'You could put it that way. I know that's not always good news with technology and science. Nevertheless, it's the best, almost the only positive option open to us. It would mean that he lives out his final days in peace and happiness.'

'It does have an appeal. I'm not disagreeing. This has all come as a bit of a surprise. I have to ask myself, what does it mean to be a human being? If I were to be in his position and were able to choose to go through with it, would it still be me?'

'What I'd like to do is to take you to meet Dr Kristal. He's come over especially to see me. I've taken the liberty of arranging an appointment for us both to meet him the day after tomorrow. He will be in overall charge of dad's care, from further tests to supervising the treatment, making fine-tuning adjustments and ongoing monitoring.'

'Yes, I'd like to meet him.'

'Good. Thank you. Then that's what we will do. I'll meet you at the clinic. We can have a cup of coffee first, to go over our questions so that we make the best use of his time.'

'Thanks for the coffee, Alex. We've got about fifteen minutes before our appointment.'

'So Dr Kristal is American. Will that mean dad will have to travel to the US?'

Alex could not believe he had not asked the question before. There had been too much new information to take in from Freya's account.

'Yes, it's all part of the package. There's no additional cost involved. I've applied for a visitor visa. It should be approved any day now. I'll be able to visit him regularly.'

'I'd like to join you from time to time, when work allows. I wish I could do more to help.'

'Here's Dr Kristal now: he's early. Allow me to introduce you. Dr Kristal, this is my brother Alex. Thank you so much for agreeing to see us both.'

'It's my pleasure,' said Dr Kristal. 'Delighted to meet you Alex. I've booked a meeting room. Please come with me.'

Freya and Alex were led to the lift and taken to a glass-walled room, one of several identical spaces, located on an upper floor. A woman sat on the far side of the table, a laptop open in front of her.

'I should have mentioned, this is my colleague Donna. She's here to record our discussion. That is her only role here today. I'm sure you will understand that we have to document all discussions with patients and their relatives. I apologise for these formalities. I hope you will understand. I am happy to send you copies of the

243

recordings. Are you OK with this?'

'Yes, fine,' said Freya. There would be little point in refusing.

'Excuse me one moment,' said Dr Kristal. 'Donna, please start the recording.'

He dictated a brief statement of the date and time, the location, the persons present, and the case to be discussed.

'What I would like to do is to summarise your father's condition, the options available and then describe the procedure he will undergo and his ongoing care. We will then turn our meeting into a more informal discussion entirely for your benefit.'

Dr Kristal confirmed the details of their father's diagnosis in medical terms and then in layperson's language, together with the prognosis. Freya and Alex confirmed that they understood. He went on to describe how their father's thoughts and dreams would be monitored, recorded and played back to him.

'As of today we can upload thoughts, introduce new connections and download these to the physical brain. We are almost at the point where we can upload a complete brain as data and turn off the physical body and brain, thus creating a virtual person. Of course, it's one thing to upload a complete brain as pure data; there is then the issue of what you do with it. Some scientists like to think of our brains as software running on the hardware of our bodies. It's true that emulating the brain is concerned with the liberation from matter; nevertheless, it's not quite as straightforward as that. The human brain and a computer work in different ways. I will try to describe some of the differences.

'You may have heard of Moravec's paradox – I keep a copy framed on the wall over there. It says, "It is comparatively easy to make computers exhibit adult level performance on intelligence tests or playing checkers, and difficult or impossible to give them the skills of a one-year-old when it comes to perception and mobility". The control systems of a human brain bear less resemblance to a laptop than with other complex systems that occur in nature, such as shoals of fish and flocks of birds, where individual creatures interact and come together to behave as a single entity, whose movements are both magnificent and unpredictable. In a human context, the same could be said, to some extent, about stock market behaviour. One of the challenges for AI is to implement hierarchical decision-making in computers. This is a key component of human intelligence – to be able to think in terms of the big picture.

'Yet if we take other analogies of speed and size of brainpower compared with computers, the latter are far faster. Neurons fire at 200 hertz a second, whereas transistor speeds are measured at the level of gigahertz. Signals travel through our central nervous systems at about one hundred metres a second; computer signals travel at the speed of light. Our brains are limited in size and housing by our cranium, whereas computer arrays can fill entire warehouses.

'In many ways, the human brain is a highly efficient device, although it is prone to frequent miscalculation, errors. Often, it does not take the direct path towards its planned or intended goals, and may indeed abandon them. It's important to remember the distinction between computer science and biological science. Computers involve bits and reversible processes, whereas biology is concerned with flesh and seemingly irreversible processes. We are working towards a world in which computational power will be brought increasingly to bear on the field of biology, permitting us to reverse human ailments in the same way that we can fix the bugs of a computer program.'

Alex shook his head from side to side and sighed.

'I can see you're confused. Don't worry, I'll try to make it simpler. One of the challenges we have had to overcome to develop the process your father will undergo is to make machines that use language, form abstractions and concepts to solve problems that have historically been the preserve of humans. But we have had to go further and to program the computers to learn and to improve themselves – to create constantly evolving machine thoughts.

'Brains continuously reorganise themselves as a result of experience. The characteristics that define such a complex evolving system are the ones that make its behaviour so difficult to predict. However, generally, there is a consensus that all that I am describing could be translated into data. What we are doing is giving progress a nudge. I wouldn't claim we've solved the entire problem; what we have achieved is to develop an interim solution that works and which will provide an enormous improvement in your father's remaining life and the lives of others. We have succeeded to the extent that we can analyse certain thoughts and memories, compare them with others, recognise emotional attributes and then suggest further logical thoughts. There is a long way to go, but we are able to use our knowledge to deliver this process now, as a practical reality.'

'And this is what you are proposing for our father?' asked Alex.

'Indeed. One way to describe it would be to compare it to a form of virtual reality. We will use our technology to capture and analyse his memories. What we can do is to screen and filter them to select the most pleasant and enjoyable ones and to ignore or block the unpleasant and the stressful.'

'How can you possibly do that?' asked Alex.

'By stimulating them and at the same time measuring his physical, bodily responses. We then associate them with other memories and thoughts and play those back to him, creating a form of dialogue, which he experiences as reality. Everything will appear real, to the extent that he will experience new scenarios that he has never encountered before: new outcomes. Think of it as being like a game of virtual tennis. A thought is struck over the net to our process; it's batted back to a position that cannot always be predicted and returned once more. The game proceeds in this way, developing in response to what stroke each player offers. And the fact that it can process and communicate information far faster than the brain means that the responses to the patient's thoughts are instantaneous.'

'What concerns me, Dr Kristal, is that this is a new technology with unpredictable results. I say unpredictable, because that seems to me, as a layman, how thought processes work. Are you sure he can come to no harm from this? What have you done to prove this to be the case?'

'That's a good question. As I have said, there are several agencies working in this area. We have shared our findings with a peer group: a small group of trusted collaborators, sworn to secrecy, for obvious reasons. They have unanimously concurred with our findings that it is safe. There is also the long stop that we have agreed only to trial the procedure on patients with a confirmed diagnosis of a very limited life span. This gives us both the option to discontinue the treatment and to limit the time frame from any bad reactions occurring either while it is in progress or after it has ceased. We will also only offer it where the patient has consented or, if he or she is unable to consent, the agreement of relatives has been secured.'

'And you really are convinced that it will provide an improved quality of life?' asked Alex.

'At the end of the day, there is no way of measuring "consciousness". What we can do is to monitor the patient's emotional and physical responses and to fine-tune them. In answer to your question, yes, I believe that, for your father, this will mark the end of his ordeal. And in the longer term, we will be liberating men and women from the captivity of flesh by enhancing bodies and brains with technology. You know, Greeks, Hindus and Buddhists are close to the Gnostic tradition that regards the human spirit as living 'in' a body. There will eventually be no distinction between human and machine, or between physical and virtual reality. Death will no longer be a mystery; it will become a solvable problem. In the meantime, you have an option that does not commit you to the future. You can take the short term solution and decide later whether to proceed with the cryogenics and/or whole brain upload.'

'Do you feel any happier, Alex?' asked Freya.

'A little. As you say, the short-term decision is urgent; there is little time left,' said Alex. 'Let's go ahead.'

'That's great. I believe you've made the best decision. You won't regret it,' said Dr Kristal. 'The first thing is to arrange for him to be moved to Arizona, to be in the right place, in case he suddenly takes a turn for the worse. And remember, what we regard as death today may not be considered as such in years to come. Death implies finality. If you can restore the person to health in the future then by definition they are not dead in the first place.'

'Alex, I've decided I'm going to move to America, to be with him. At least for the time being. My visa's through now. I've arranged to put the house on the market. The agent expects it to sell quickly and I'll rent when I return, at least in the short term. The few things I want to keep I'll put into storage. That's another good thing about splitting with Simon – I don't have to think about anyone else.'

'How's the divorce going? Is it any nearer to being finalised?'

'Not really. It's at a bit of a standstill. Money's the problem, as is so often the case. Fortunately, dad's assets are ring-fenced towards his care, if and when he leaves hospital. As you know, I've been talking about setting up a trust to pay for ongoing costs, such as my travel and accommodation expenses, on top of any future call on his assets. That's what Simon has an issue with. I haven't told him about Dr Kristal's offer. I believe that I should be entitled to put a share of the house sale into the trust before we split the remainder of the proceeds. After all, mum and dad gave you and me a substantial sum towards the deposit on our houses. It seems only fair to repay it after the sale. It's not as though we can't afford it. I'll be able to manage and I'm not an extravagant person. Unfortunately, Simon doesn't see things that way. He thinks dad is going to be a drain on him personally until… So he's trying to grab as much as he can now. No doubt to throw at another of his ridiculous business schemes.'

'Well, I wish you luck with that. And I do wish I could come with you, but I have family commitments now. I'll be able to visit regularly – every couple of months or so.'

'Yes, that would be good.'

'When will you be leaving?'

'As soon as possible. Simon and I have exchanged contracts on the house sale. He didn't object to that, on the understanding that he could get hold of his share, less the disputed sum being held back. You know, I'm surprised he agreed to that. It makes me think he's already in big financial trouble and that he's desperate for cash.'

'Will you travel out with dad?'

'No, he'll be going first. They want to do some more tests and some sort of due diligence procedure to justify everything as legal. They suggested I follow on a week later. It suits me really: to be able to wind things up here.'

'OK. I'm flying back tomorrow. Please keep in touch regarding what's happening and if there are any problems, anything I can help with.'

'I will do. And thank you, both for coming and for understanding. It means a lot to me.'

'Good evening, Alex here. Who's calling please?'

'Alex, it's Freya.'

'Oh hi, Freya. You came up as an unidentified caller. Where are you?'

'I'm in Phoenix, in a hotel. How are you?'

'I'm fine. It's good to hear from you. What's happening there?'

'Well, I hope you're prepared for this. Events are taking the expected course. It's good news, though, under the circumstances. It seems we got him here just in time. He had been in the clinic for forty-eight hours when his heart stopped beating. At that stage, things could have gone one of two ways. If he couldn't have been revived, they would have offered to go into the cryonics procedures, either for the full body or the neuro option, where they preserve just the head, after first declaring him legally dead. They would stabilise his brain to protect it from damage and then embark on the freezing process.'

'Is that what happened?'

'No, fortunately they revived him, but it prompted the urgency to embark on our option. As we speak, they are uploading his brain, or rather the data representing his thoughts and mind processes, to their computer systems. It takes a while, as you would expect, to upload it then validate it.'

'What will happen next, after they've finished that?'

'He will be under way. Having mapped his brain electronically, they will use their systems to interact with his memories, not to alter them in any way, but to use them to generate new thoughts: new links, like dreams, to create a new life.'

'I have to say, Freya, that I'm still not entirely convinced by this, but I can see it is the one ray of hope for someone who is about to die, in the conventional sense of the word.'

'He's at peace now. If dreams can be made sufficiently lifelike and authentic, then living forever becomes an almost realistic and attractive prospect. There is no longer a need to worry about whether he's in pain: they can dull the receptors. He will just live in the stream of experience of his memories, adapted by a multitude of options controlled by the brain, steering thoughts and dreams in conjunction with the system, at will, through each junction, while other systems support essential bodily functions. Then once he passes away, with your agreement, we can sign up to the cryonics process. And in the very long term, possibly beyond our own lifetimes, if there is ultimately no hope of repairing his body, for whatever reason, there's the prospect of turning off just the physical body and letting him live on as a disembodied mind. Or alternatively for his brain to be implanted into a new host – either the physical brain or the electronic copy.'

'I'm pleased his journey's begun. Are you sure you are all right there, on your own?'

'Yes, there was just one spooky moment.'

'What was that?'

'Before I left for the US, I had a call from Simon. The usual aggressive thing, about divorce matters. Nothing I can't handle. I made a mistake and told him about our plans for dad. He was none too happy about it, but I don't see that it's any of his business. Anyway, a couple of days ago I was in a downtown area – it was quite crowded, unusually so, although it is almost Thanksgiving – and I thought I caught sight of Simon. It was just a glimpse and I'm sure I was mistaken. it really shook me.'

'It's just stress, playing tricks on your mind. There's no reason he should go there, particularly if you've argued over the subject. I'm glad you're able to put it behind you.'

'The other thing I was going to ask is whether you are going to be able to come over for dad's final moments. I know it's difficult, what with the unpredictability.'

'I certainly plan to. I've made arrangements at work to take a week off at short notice. I can be with you within two days of you letting me know.'

'I'm so pleased. It will mean a lot to me and I would like to think he could possibly be aware of your presence at the end. I know that's a little fanciful, but it does no harm.'

Part 4: Before Finally Coming Together

WHY HAS IT TAKEN SO LONG?

The door closed behind me. I heard keys turn in the three locks. I stood with the housekeeper on the square landing. There was only one way to go: to descend the spiral stone staircase. A single pendant light hung over the centre of the stairwell. I peered over the balustrade. More light was visible at the foot of the stairs, its source as yet unseen.

The housekeeper stepped in front of me and led the way down.

'Please follow me.'

I felt happier with her walking ahead of me. I did not have to see or feel her gaze. And it gave me the chance to study her from behind as she descended with grace and elegance.

We reached the foot of the stairs, some two floors down from our starting point. She led me along a narrow hallway leading to a doorway to the right, opening onto a series of identical vaulted rooms. The design was unusual in that the walls sloped slightly inwards towards the ceiling. Stone arches linked the rooms to form a long, segmented passageway. I recognised something familiar in the design. Although constructed in stone, it reminded me of the rose tunnel in the eighth room of the garden I had visited earlier. The similarity did not end there. Here too, at the far end, through the doorway, I could see bright shafts of light radiating from an elevated point.

She led me through the vaulted chambers until we reached the opening to the much longer, penultimate one. By now the light at the end had become so bright that I could neither stare into it, nor could I see beyond. She turned to face me. Her expression had softened to a Madonna-like smile. Her eyes... no, I will not describe them. There is no satisfactory way to describe the eyes of a woman with whom you are obsessed, that create such depth of feeling you alone experience. I no longer had any doubt of her identity.

'We will wait here for a while, until they are ready for you,' she said, in a warm, calm voice. At that moment it did not occur to me to ask what she meant. I was thinking of Edmund Wyrdstaff's description of the nine rooms of his garden, representing stages of my life, past, present and future, terminating at the centre, terminating...

'Where are we?' I asked.

'Can't you guess? We are under the hill.'

I sensed she saw the fear in my eyes.

'Don't be afraid. It won't be long now. All your grief is behind you. You have nothing to fear, I promise you.'

'I don't know your name,' I said, lost for words and failing to speak in the confident manner I thought appropriate to a first spoken exchange. I could tell that she knew I was trying to deflect my thoughts from whatever might be about to happen.

'Names are not important,' she replied. 'You can call me Bella if it helps.'

She smiled, mischievously.

'Bella, forgive me, I must ask – do you know me, do you remember me from anywhere?'

'I do, I remember you well. It was thirty years ago, on a sunny, slightly misty spring morning that you came to the village, by accident or so you thought. You had lost your way. You stopped and walked around until you came across the house where I lived. I was upstairs in my room. The window was open, overlooking the garden, with its stone wall adjacent to the lane. I glanced outside and saw you leaning on the wall, your camera in your hand. I could see your beautiful eyes, even at a distance. You had a look of yearning about you, as though you'd found something you'd been seeking for a long time. I knew instantly that you were the one. It had been your destiny to arrive in the village, in Durncot. I came over to the window, smiled and waved to you. I wanted to let you know you were in a place that you should find familiar, even though you had never been there before; a place that you would remember, somewhere you would want to return to.

'You seemed surprised, off guard, perhaps embarrassed at having being caught looking over the wall and towards the window. You turned, almost casually, not enough to hide your awkwardness, and walked away. I had expected you to realise that you had found a special place and that you would return within a day or two, but you didn't. For days, months, I looked out of the window at exactly the same time of day, hoping to see you. Eventually, I had to find a new way of communicating with you, to enter your consciousness and to reawaken the memory, to arouse your desire to find me.

'That's how it was: you looked, you saw me, I waved. You remembered this, deep down, for thirty years, and after all that time you felt the need to find me, as though you were seeking a truth, searching for answers to a question you could not define, hidden within you. Many others would not have given it a second thought.'

'Are you saying that it was no accident, my stumbling across the village? That I was being tested in some way? Was I the only one, or were there others, like me?'

'It was certainly no accident. Neither was it a test, as such. We were letting you know we were there, you might say, placing a suggestion in your unconscious mind.'

'So does this mean you've been watching over me in some way? Controlling my life?'

'Watching over you, yes. How many times in your life has something happened and you have thought that someone is keeping an eye on you, protecting you? Helping you in difficult times, when things seemed hopeless. I am sure you can think of many such instances. This does not mean to say we were influencing you in any way. You have enjoyed complete freedom of choice and control over your actions. And no, you are not the only one. You are one of a select band, singled out for your unique qualities, as you will shortly discover.'

'You're right. There have been so many times when I've felt depressed, low, hopeless, with no apparent way out or desire to carry on. Yet often, when I've felt at my lowest point, something good has happened that has seemed like a sign: a sign that things will not always be that way, that things will get better and that someone or something cares about me. Except for that one time… And all this began thirty years ago. How can that be?'

'In linear time, yes. Time is of no importance; it is the connection of events that matters. And now you are here.'

'I don't understand: "linear time", what do you mean by that?'

'You have been brought up to believe that events happen in a straight line, that one thing follows another and is a consequence of another, rather like holding a book and reading the individual pages in turn. What is really happening is that the book of your life is closed, in more ways than one. When you look at a closed book, lying on a table, the pages are stacked on top of each other. If you turn it on its side, or upside down, the sequence changes. Time and the sequence of the pages have no meaning; time is a perception of the human mind, an ordering, a sorting of facts and events, in order to make sense of them.'

'Well, that doesn't make sense. If I hadn't have seen

you that first time, all those years ago, I wouldn't have sought you out – I wouldn't be here now. But I did and one thing led to another. The encounters were a consequence of that first occasion.'

'I can understand that it helps you to think in that way, to justify why things happen. Look at it another way. You are a perceptive person. When presented with a situation, whether in waking life or in a dream, you often instantly see the potential connections and consequences of that situation. You don't think of them as a series of events; they are presented as a whole, like a snapshot, with no time delimitation between them. That is how things work.'

'Surely, every event in life, or most of them, involves other people, an interaction with them and their lives. If my life were to be laid down in the way you describe, with no regard to time, it would impact differently upon the definition of the lives of those people.'

'You are making the same mistake again: thinking in terms of time as a straight line. That's understandable; it's part of your upbringing and conditioning, which repeats that of your parents and educators. It's hardwired into your brain. It may be a cliché, but time is an illusion.'

'So what are you saying, that life is predestined? That our lives are all programmed to be intertwined, that our destiny is predetermined, with limited choice?'

'I have a problem with the word "destiny". Two problems in fact. Firstly, the concept of time, again. Destiny implies the passing of time, one-dimensionally, in a straight line, rather than as, say, a carpet rolled out before you with many options of where to tread. Secondly, it implies that outcomes are unavoidable, that you cannot change anything. The reality is much more fluid. Let me give you an analogy that might help to make it clearer.'

She thought for a few moments.

'All right, think of the sum of human experience, across the whole of history – yes, I know that describes time – as a giant gaseous ball. It is denser towards the centre and thinner towards the edges of the sphere – in fact, there are no edges and there is no boundary to the sphere – I hope that makes sense. What lies near the centre is more certain, whereas towards the outside the gasses mingle, searching for something to bind with. Now think of a balloon. If you squeeze it at one point, it expands at another, or rather across its whole volume. It has the same total mass, it is the same thing, but in a different form. And that's how it is with human life and experience, with this added layer, so incomprehensible to you – and I do understand that – of the illusion of time. When you, or another person, does something or changes something, every interaction changes.'

'I'm familiar with the butterfly effect. That doesn't explain why I was destined to meet you years ago and again, today. I didn't choose to do so.'

'Choice depends on so many things too. A conscious decision is the product of external events – external to you, that is – tempered by your own reasoning and instinctive reactions, together with consideration of what you believe to be the most likely probable outcomes and the moral consequences.'

'I still find this difficult. The "external events" are just coincidences: things that happen, which by chance I am involved in.'

'I'm glad you mentioned coincidences. Think back over what you have experienced, both in the past and on your journey to arrive here today; your encounters with me and the Green Man. Can you see the connections?'

'The first time you saw me, at Durncot, you noticed people at the school putting up a maypole.'

'How on earth do you know that?'

'It's not important. At the printing press, you saw the photographs of their Open Day, held on the first of May.'

'This is impossible! You couldn't possibly…'

'The children's birthday party, the loss of your child,

your accident… I could go on. It's all part of the same thing. And now you are here.'

'I don't know what to say. If you really have been watching over me, then why didn't you intervene to stop all those dreadful things happening?'

'We have been watching you, yes, but we tread lightly, softly. We knew you would find me, us, again. It was destined to be that way, as you would say. You just needed a little nudge. When you looked up at me through the open window, from behind the garden wall, the germ of a connection was implanted in you, a seed that would slowly grow, to create an itch that eventually you would have to scratch.'

The words 'tread softly' were familiar. I thought of Yeats: 'Tread softly because you tread on my dreams'.

'Well, I ought to say that I've been watching, or rather investigating you too, or the multiple people I think are you. It could be a coincidence that someone with the same description and appearance, with the witches' mark… Forgive me if I am mistaken…'

'Say it. Say what you are thinking.'

'It looks to me that you are responsible for, or at least connected in some way, to a large number of deaths.'

'Would you like to give me some examples? Tell me what you think you have learned and I will respond truthfully. I should add that not everything is as it seems.'

I explained that I had no direct proof of the connections. I had made associations based upon the apparent presence of Bella, the woman who stood with me now, or someone who very much resembled her. At last, I had an opportunity to put mind my mind at rest.

'There was the fire, at a university three years ago. Seven young people were killed as a result of the fire exit to a bar being blocked when the fire broke out.'

I described the newspaper account I had read of the fire and the photograph. Her response shocked me.

'If the seven had survived, they would have gone on

to commit terrible acts. Not all would have been intentional or foreseeable to the individuals. The effects, nevertheless, would have been catastrophic. One was the son of a head of state, a dictator who would have passed his power on to his son with no free elections. The son would have ruled through terror and committed war crimes against thousands of the nation's people, resulting in deaths, famine and displacement. By removing him the family line was at an end. A brief revolution in the future will result in more loss of life on the way to restoring democracy. The number of deaths will be far fewer than would otherwise have been the case. Another would have committed a heinous crime, beyond imagination.'

'That sounds more like a form of mental illness that should be treated, rather than a crime to be punished.'

'You are quite right, of course. If that had been the case we would have acted differently. Unfortunately, it was not and we had to intervene.'

'What about the others?'

'One would have gone on to use his scientific genius to invent a radical new weapon, easily copied and manufactured, that would be used by warring states to kill on an enormous scale. Once you have invented something and the knowledge is shared, you cannot uninvent it. Another would have become an influential politician and national leader whose policies would accelerate global warming to the point where it became irreversible. The others would have caused more death and chaos in various ways. Sadly for them all, the world will be a better place without them.'

'How many other people have you killed or caused to disappear?'

'Who do you mean?'

'Well, there are those children, for a start, at the party near here. The ones you led off under the hill, with the Green Man.'

'They all came back, except for one.'

'What happened to her?'

'We saved her from a real kidnapping that would have taken place later. She would have been taken and tortured, subjected to every imaginable type of abuse and then left to die alone in pain and misery.'

'These are serious interventions, not cases of treading softly. I can understand that in the overall scheme of things they are better than the alternatives. So are you saying that you can change the future?'

'You are talking about time again. There are instances when the system goes wrong and has to be put right. We are like a maintenance team that identifies these problems and then steps everything back to just before. Rather like reversing a train back to a junction, then switching the points to take a different track.'

'I don't understand why you are so selective. Why do you intervene in some cases and not others? Sometimes you kill people; sometimes you appear reliant on other people to influence matters. Is it because you don't see everything, that some things slip under your radar? If you do, then why don't you eradicate all evil in the world and make it a better and happier place?'

'We use our influence to ensure things don't get out of hand, that they remain under control or, at worst, are contained and their limits understood within society. Free will must be allowed to rule, wherever possible. Humankind is defined by its actions. When individuals perform benevolent acts that radiate to those they come into contact with, their deeds will take them forward to a higher level in future lives. Other deeds will set them back, although the subjects of their actions may become stronger in adversity. It is only in extreme circumstances, where there are serious consequent effects, that we seek to change the course of events.'

'So what about wars, famines, extreme poverty and other gross injustices? Why do so many people have to suffer?'

'The undeserving victims will be compensated in their later or future lives. Some good can come from the most dreadful events. Remember, that while they suffer, they create a response in observers, which often brings out the good in people, through direct or indirect acts of charity, assistance or aid, and drives the momentum for change.'

'Are you saying that suffering is a good thing: that it should be tolerated to test the response?'

'Not at all. These tragic events occur through a combination of circumstances that the victims, in most cases, cannot control. It is our task to create the conditions to alleviate and eliminate such suffering, both in the short and long term. To answer your earlier question, we intervene to undertake tasks no normal person would do, or would be capable of doing. We are not accountable or traceable in the same way as ordinary people.'

'And all of this is connected to The Old Religion, not superstition or witchcraft, or any other mumbo-jumbo. And where does the Green Man fit in?'

'There is where the problem exists, with the words. Words can be emotive and have their own baggage that colours judgement in communication. They are just labels and are used to disguise the reality. Try not to think in terms of The Old Religion and witchcraft. There is one layer of universal truth that applies to everyone's lives. Religions and belief sets help to explain and comfort their followers, but they do not alter the underlying principles. Take the so-called witches' mark for example. Its origins can be traced back to Roman and even African societies. It represents weaving spindles. That in itself tells you a lot. Weaving is about combining threads to make a harmonious object, with the vertical and horizontal elements coming together to make a strong, unified cloth or material. The threads in one direction depend upon those in the other for their strength. On a symbolic level, it represents the interlinking of cause and effect. And as for the Green Man, he is a symbol of being in tune with nature. A spirit, not a god.'

'You really believe your intentions are good, then.'

'It's about balance and harmony; keeping things in an ecological equilibrium.'

'So why do all these terrible things happen? And why have so many things gone wrong in my life, over such a long period of time, when I've tried so hard to do the right thing? It doesn't make any sense. Everything I touch is doomed to failure. I've let everyone down and I'm responsible for the death of my son. There's nothing special about me.'

'Oh, believe me, there is. You are a very special person. You have undertaken many things that have benefitted others. You have changed many people's lives for the better.'

'Well, I can't think of anything. Tell me… Please.'

'There are so many – where shall I begin? There was the woman you met in the street, expecting a child, and upset because her husband threatened to leave her as he didn't want children. You helped her to have confidence and to be resolute in deciding her own future. She stood her ground and had the child. Her husband stayed with her and now they have another. You didn't tell her what to do; you gave her the strength to consider her options and to become mindful in her thinking.

'The dropped letter that you posted when you collected Freya from school. The parent who dropped it was distraught that he couldn't find it and had no idea where he had lost it. It contained a detailed response to tender for an important contract for his business. It had taken him days to prepare and he didn't have a copy, or the time to reproduce it, owing to the detailed drawings and correspondence attachments included. He was overjoyed to find an acknowledgement drop through his letterbox the following week. He won the contract and, based on the quality of his work, was offered further contracts allowing him to expand his business and make his family more secure. Remember when you gave someone the directions to a job interview?'

'Yes, but that couldn't have been significant. It was a Sunday morning, so it was presumably only for some sort of domestic employment. Not that there's anything wrong with that.'

'It was, but the woman you helped was applying for a position looking after the children of a human rights lawyer. The woman, the lawyer, that is, had been looking for someone for weeks, to live in, but without success, as her house was difficult to reach, particularly in winter. You will know this, as you were living nearby at the time. Finding someone quickly allowed the lawyer to take on more high-profile international cases and to achieve a significant rate of success, resulting in the freeing of a number of political prisoners who had been unjustly treated.'

'That's a very distant consequence. I couldn't possibly be credited with that.'

'Yes, you can. Even small deeds lead to different outcomes. Your considerate actions have changed the course of people's lives. And what about the money you refused to lend to Freya's husband Simon? You saw the problem and didn't give in to pressure. You made the right decision for both of them.'

'That's not how he saw it.'

'That isn't important. It was your intention and it's the bigger picture that counts. Even little things you have done have made a big difference. Like the occasion when you gave a small sum to an appeal for aid and were fretting that it was too small and that you had not been generous enough. You needed Stephanie to remind you that at least you had given something, which was more than many others had done. Your donation made all the difference.'

'How could that be? It was such a small amount.'

'Your modest donation, several weeks after the event, tipped the total balance over the threshold at which the

Government had offered to match donations from the public. So, effectively you are responsible for fifty per cent of the relief fund.'

'Oh that's nonsense; it's too far-fetched!'

'It's perfectly true. The bulls' field… On your family walk, you took the trouble to ensure that a broken gate was properly closed. Had you not done so, the animals would have escaped into the lower field and trampled a small child of a family that you did not know were behind you, who were following the same route. And remember how you defused an unpleasant situation with the aggressive motorcycle rider. Not only did you stop the crowd from getting out of control, you also helped the young man see the error of his ways. After that, he became more considerate of other people and the effects of his actions. If you had not done that he would have declined into delinquency.'

'You really have been watching over me, haven't you?'

'Yes, in all aspects of your life. At work, you exercised your responsibilities in the way that a religious leader might go about pastoral care. When you were asked to make all those people redundant, you took the trouble to examine not only their value and contributions to the workplace, you took into account their personal circumstances.'

'I failed miserably there too. I couldn't find reasons to keep all of them.'

'The impact you had on those people's lives was enormous. You saved some jobs (and in some cases their marriages), and those you couldn't went on to other, in some cases more suitable, employment.'

'I still feel I am a failure, that I've let people down, that I could and should have done so much more.'

Bella turned her head to one side. She looked to be on the verge of smiling, a kindly smile that did not quite materialise.

'Oliver,' It was the first time she had spoken my

name. 'You are a good person. You have demonstrated that you are capable of improving the human condition. You have done so much good in the world, even though you think you haven't. What you regard as minor deeds have changed and inspired the lives of others. You have helped them to become better people. They in turn have and will continue to spread goodwill and, between them, all will do enormous good for humanity in many spheres. You have demonstrated compassion and humility in selfless, non-political ways and, without knowing it, you have shown yourself to be capable of mentoring others. Now, I know that there is one more question you want to ask. You've been holding back, haven't you?'

I had. If the lives of others were subject to intervention in extreme cases, and my own life had been watched over for so many years, what had happened to Adam? Was it possible that his death had not been an accident? I wanted to know, yet I was afraid; afraid of discovering a truth so unbearable that it would eclipse the grief I had already suffered and continued to endure. It was no good. I could no longer hide. I had to ask.

'I have. What are you able to tell me about Adam? Was it a genuine accident? I can't believe he was going to grow up to become a bad person.'

'No, he was never going to turn out to be anything other than good, in the image of his parents. I will tell you what you want to know. Are you sure you are prepared for this?'

'As prepared as I ever will be. It's my only chance to find out.'

'It's very sad. He was going to suffer a painful, debilitating illness, a rare form of progressive, untreatable cancer, with no hope of a cure. We couldn't let that happen to him or to you or your family. You are the type of person who never gives up hope. You would have researched all of the options, weighed up the remotest of possibilities of saving him, whether through conventional, available medicine or experimental treatments. That would have left you open to the quacks and charlatans who would have had no hesitation in bankrupting the family, both financially and emotionally, by offering a future that could not be delivered. A quick, painless death, after a brief life in a loving family, was a far preferable outcome.'

I was shocked. One part of me disbelieved what Bella was saying. I wanted to dismiss it as speculation, to cling to an illusion that she could, to use her earlier analogy, roll back the train and take a different track. Another part felt relief that, after all these years of grief, Adam had been spared a far worse fate.

'That seems unfair - to others, I mean. The old man who was driving the car and his family; they were made to suffer.'

'As you know, the driver surrendered his licence following the accident. Had he not done so, he would have caused another fatal accident, involving more than one person. Your son's accident saved several other lives.'

If only Adam could have known and understood this. He would have been too young.

'Come, it is time to go now. We have something to show you. Everything will begin to make sense.'

As we approached the opening to the next room the brightness of the light became intense. I could not see the source, nor could I see into the room, beyond the beginning of the path before me. It was as if the sun were shining through a mist, or clouds of white dust, with a brilliance that obscured everything beyond the immediate foreground.

'Where am I? Why am I here?'

'You are in a very special place. It is your destiny.'

'Why am I the only one?'

'Everyone comes here eventually, in their own time, each taking their own route. Not just through the vicarage: there are many portals, all over the world, to which people are led in the final moments of their present lives to the

White Room. Soon, all will become clear to you.'

A cool, calm chill flowed over me. It was not an unpleasant sensation. I had recognised and begun to accept what had been coming together within my mind. Still, questions remained.

'In the end, you say. Does that mean you are going to kill me? Am I going to be sacrificed, as part of some Old Religion ritual?'

'No, not at all. And besides, there is no need for that. You have already passed away, to use the everyday term. Your familiar life has come to its irreversible end; there will be no going back.'

Curiously, I felt no fear. Somehow it made sense. I would no longer be troubled by the doubts and responsibilities that had troubled me for so long.

'What are you saying? That I am in some form of afterlife? That I am in heaven, or perhaps hell?'

'Neither. Try to think of it as being in a waiting room. A place of assessment and reflection, where your credentials for the next stage are to be reviewed.'

'Like purgatory, you mean?'

'Purgatory is a place of agony. That is not the purpose. Think of it as being a process of weighing up and offsetting of good and bad intent and deed.'

'A place of judgement then. I am to be assessed for where I go next.'

'We don't judge. There is no need. The conditions of right and wrong are not matters of judgement but of fact. They are absolute truths.'

'Surely nothing's that black and white?'

'Please, let me continue... Absolute truths that take into account circumstances and motives. Your next stage will be determined by the totality of how you have led your expiring life. You are here now for reasons of transparency and to help you to understand where you are on your journey.'

'You say that everyone comes here. Does that mean

that you, personally, meet every person in this way?'

'That's not how it works. The underlying process is the same for everyone, but the circumstances of this preparation, this taking stock, will be different. People live different lives, at different steps on the spiritual ladder. Each individual will be presented with a summary of where they are in a form they can understand and identify with. It is for the best, to help them to recognise how things could have been different in the past and how to live better future lives.'

For perhaps the first time in my life, I felt truly serene. I have never been afraid of death, only of pain in dying, and the wish not to leave unfinished business that would harm or inconvenience others. And now, confirmation of death was being ameliorated by the prospect of some form of reincarnation, with the chance to do better in a future life. This was not death as I had always considered it, as the one alternative to living. It was more like passing through the life stages of insects: egg, larva, pupa, imago.

'Well, I don't remember any of this happening before, at the end of previous lives. Does this mean I'm on the bottom rung of the ladder, or rather one above the bottom rung: a small step above the animal kingdom?'

'You should not consider human lives as superior to animal lives. They are just different. You do not progress from being an amoeba to a woodlouse, to a shark, a bird, a chimpanzee and on to a human form.

'And you will not remember your expiring life, in the same way that you do not remember earlier, previous lives, except for flashes in dreams that seem real. The dreams where you encounter people and places you believe you have never met or seen before. Dreams so vivid that you have to tell a close friend or partner about how extraordinary they are. And you will not remember being here, even when you return the next time.'

'What advice can you give me, so that I can lead a

better life the next time around?'

'You must judge that for yourself. What we have discussed here will, though, influence your journey, for the better, I hope, although there is always the possibility of regression in moments of weakness and selfishness.'

'Yet you say that everyone has a unique experience.' Oliver shrugged his shoulders, uncertain of the question he wanted to ask.

'I will say what I can. As I have said already, your memory of this will be completely erased. Some aspects you will identify with – you have already made the connection.

'To answer your earlier question, your experience was unique, as is everyone's. Every person is given a sign that they are being watched over, in a way that is most appropriate to the individual's character, the stage they have reached in their spiritual evolutionary cycle and their sensitivity. Everyone is given an equal opportunity. It is up to the individual how they respond.'

'I don't understand how, if everyone is treated in the same way, some people end up good and others bad, so to speak.'

'Firstly, choice. Secondly, not everyone you meet is a real person.'

'May I ask what is your role here? Where do you stand on the spiritual ladder?'

'Think of me as a messenger and a sort of facilitator. Along with many others, I am working my time, as a trusted person. You could say that I am near the top of the ladder, but I would not dare to be so presumptuous.'

'Will you be coming with me?'

'No. We may meet again in another life, but now I have other work to do. They are ready for you. It is time for you to enter. I wish you well on your journey.'

FREYA'S DECISION

Freya took her seat on the Valley Metro Rail, as she had done every day since her arrival in Arizona. There would not be many more such journeys; each new day could bring the last. She was not one to pass her time idly and would in normal circumstances have passed the journey reading a book. She had resigned herself to accepting her inability to focus on anything other than her father's plight. There would be plenty of time in the months to come to immerse herself in her chosen activities. She had resolved, when the time arrived, to put the past behind her and to build a new life.

The carriage was less than half full. All of the passengers around her were embarked on individual journeys, travelling alone. As the train pulled into the next station, two women in their fifties, deep in conversation, stepped inside and took seats a short distance from Freya. Both carried copies of the same newspaper, which they began to read, commenting on the articles as they turned the pages. Still focussed on her own thoughts, Freya paid them little attention, until a snatch of their dialogue caught her ear.

'Have you seen this? Another drone attack on terrorists in the Middle East. A whole bunch taken out. It's amazing what they can do these days, remotely. I've heard that a lot of these strikes are controlled and executed from offices in downtown LA. I find it incredible what they can do from so far away to manipulate these machines.'

Her friend agreed.

'It is. They can do it without ever seeing the enemy face to face or the enemy knowing they are there. Total detachment and focus on the job!'

Freya felt troubled by what she had overheard; she was unsure why. There was nothing she had heard that she disagreed with. She had worried, on previous such occasions, what steps had been taken to avoid 'collateral damage', an expression she abhorred as being devoid of humanity. This vague, anxious feeling persisted after she left the train and as she walked through a shopping mall, irritating her in the way a partially-formed thought or an irretrievable memory would. She passed a store with an array of large television screens displayed a little way back from the window. She was surprised to see multiple images of Dr Kristal on several of the screens, in discussion with an interviewer and another person, described in the screen text as something to do with human rights - Freya did not catch his exact title. Curious, she entered the store and walked over to discover what he was talking about.

She stepped close to one of the screens. The volume had been set at a low level, so as not to distract shoppers. The two interviewees were debating Dr Kristal's work, prompted by the interviewer's probing questions.

Dr Kristal appeared to be extolling the advantages of uploading human brains, once this became possible.

'If we live in a world where brains are uploaded and translated into data, we will introduce a new order in society. There will be the enhanced brains, with the processing power of supercomputers, far faster than a human brain. These brains will be dependent on the humans to perform or create environments for physical tasks. The humans, in turn, will be dependent on the brains in the way we have become dependent on the machines we now take for granted in our daily lives. Everyone will benefit.'

The interviewer challenged the assertion.

'Will this not create a form of slavery, whereby the humans will control the thoughts of uploaded former humans, with the risk that they will be subjected to torture and abuse?'

'Not true at all,' said Dr Kristal. 'This is the goal of science: to use technology to enhance the human condition, to perform tasks quicker and more efficiently. Containment and control is key to the whole process.'

'I have to interrupt you there,' said the other interviewee. 'We're not just talking about technology. These are captive human brains. It's widely known that it's possible to control the movements of rats from a laptop, using electrodes implanted in their medial forebrains. What's to say that these imprisoned minds could not be manipulated, tortured even, by the people paid to care for them? We regularly hear of abuse of vulnerable people in care homes. Those whose brains are preserved using the methods you describe will be much more vulnerable. They don't have a voice; they have no one to complain to.'

'There will be controls in place to stop this sort of thing happening,' said Doctor Kristal.

'What sort of controls?' interrupted the interviewer. 'It doesn't seem to work in ordinary medical and social care. Abuse is often only detected when relatives place secret cameras in the patient's room. You can hardly do that with a remotely-controlled brain! It won't be long before the people controlling the brains are the same people who take out terrorists using drones from offices in LA.'

Freya had heard enough. She walked away. Her unformed thought from the earlier overheard conversation had been articulated and new doubts had been implanted in her mind.

In an instant, she recognised so many possibilities she had not thought of before. If it were to happen that her father's supercharged uploaded brain was under the control of others, could it be manipulated in unpleasant ways? Could the machine assimilate his experiences and thoughts and emotions: to augment, to grow its own intelligence in the way a social media platform does and to implant them in the minds of others that it controls or is linked to? Would the artificial intelligence develop the capability to exchange information with her father's brain to the extent that it could create new, false memories and remembered experiences, some horrific, at a point in his potentially infinite lifetime years, decades, even centuries into the future, when all who knew or cared for him would be long dead?

She remembered, too, an article she had read a long while ago, describing how a concert pianist, playing beautiful, moving music on an antique instrument, was unaware of the destruction caused in the manufacture of the instrument: how elephants had been shot for the ivory, rare trees destroyed to make the frame and both gathered using the labour of slaves. Could it be that a machine could decide to break up and use constituent parts of her father's thoughts, intelligence and memory to produce something new and even hostile to his own beliefs? Something that might bring harm both to him and to others?

She had been naïve. She had inferred that the plan was for her father's mind to be uploaded to an individual, stand-alone computer. Why had it not occurred to her that it would be stored in the Cloud? It was now so obvious. The medical pioneers, who had been sharing and validating peer research would be looking to monetarise the value of their investment. Dr Kristal's offer to provide the treatment, the service, was not an act of altruism; it was a commercial investment. Not only would her father's mind be sharing virtual space with hundreds, thousands, eventually millions of others, it would become a collection of fragments that could be merged with fragments of other minds to create something new, something obscene.

The aggregated minds would become the property of a new breed of digital services company, which the patients' relatives would regard as a free service, not comprehending that, as with other, existing digital services providers they, the patients, or their minds, were no more than data: they were the product, a collection of components with which to build more products.

She knew she had to stop the process.

She would ask for the life support system to be turned off and to let her father die, naturally, and to arrange for him to be cremated. Would Dr Kristal allow it, she asked herself? She was sure he would have no objection to letting him die, but what if he insisted on freezing or uploading her father's brain? He had invested so much time and expense... Freya could not recall the terms of the consent form she had signed. There would not be time to consult a lawyer.

She had decided. It was her duty to do the right thing, regardless of the consequences.

Freya arrived at the clinic to discover a scene of turmoil. Police cars, their lights flashing, were parked at angles outside the main entrance. Inside, a group of police officers stood in a corner of the lobby, talking quietly, some taking notes. Freya announced herself at the front desk.

'I won't keep you a moment. I'll tell my colleague you are here. Please take a seat.'

The receptionist spoke to her colleague, who walked over to the police.

'Is there a problem here?' Freya asked the receptionist.

Before she could respond, one of the policemen

introduced himself and asked her to follow him. He gestured with his head to the group, two of whom joined them.

'What's happened? Where are we going?'

Freya was led into a room off the corridor and asked to sit down.

'We have some bad news for you, Mrs…'

'What's happened? Is it my father?'

'We've arrested your husband. He entered the premises and gained access to your father's room. We believe he then turned off your father's life support system and tried to run out from the premises. The security personnel apprehended him and we were called. I'm very sorry ma'am. We will need to take a statement from you and ask you to attend the court hearing when it's set.'

'I'm shocked. Are you sure it was him? Could it have been an accident - disconnecting the system - tripping over a wire or something? We're in the process of divorcing, but I can't believe he would do such a thing.'

'We have CCTV footage and he's admitted to it. The alarm was set off, but he was able to block the door for long enough to make it impossible to revive the patient.'

'I'd no idea he would come here. He wasn't supposed to be in the country. I thought I saw him the other day, but put it down to my imagination. Did he say anything - about why he did it?'

'He did. We couldn't stop him talking. He said he couldn't bear the thought of being bankrupted. He said if the divorce didn't bankrupt him then the maintenance payments, including the care costs would. We need your cooperation ma'am.'

'Yes of course.'

The questioning continued. One of Freya's first thoughts was that she might be suspected of colluding with Simon. As the interview progressed, in a firm but sympathetic way, it became clear that they were in no way holding her to blame. She had made a point of always carrying her documentation with her, including proof of where she was staying. She would be allowed to remain free. They expected Simon to make a full formal confession, although they believed they already had sufficient evidence to put together a straightforward case. Freya dreaded the thought of facing Simon in court. At least it would be the last time she would see him.

'May I spend a few minutes alone with my father please?' said Freya. She was shown up to his room.

The room emptied of medical staff and police, leaving one nurse and a police officer, who stood in the corner and who apologetically explained that she could not leave a crime scene unattended. She added that for this reason Freya would not be allowed to kiss her father for a final time.

'I'm so sorry,' said the nurse, as she clasped Freya's hands.

Freya looked down at their interlocked fingers. She spoke: 'That's an unusual tattoo.'

*

Freya returned to England, still struggling with her thoughts and emotions. She was drained of energy from the events of recent weeks and months and needed time to be alone. She tried her best to rationalise all that had happened and to put everything into order so as to be able to get on with her life.

She ignored Alex's repeated attempts to contact her, refusing to answer his many calls and messages. He deserved an explanation, she knew that. A few days of solitude would help. She booked herself into a retreat in a monastery in Devon, where she walked alone between sessions of contemplation. Finally, she composed an email to Alex:

Dear Alex

I'm sorry it's taken so long…

…I've been such a fool! I fell into Dr Kristal's trap. I should have realised that there was a catch to his offer of enrolling dad in his process free of charge. It should have been obvious that his business model was to make a fortune from the rich and vain for something unproven. The whole concept was unlikely to yield results and, even if it did, would potentially preserve damaged brains in an eternal hell, with no recourse from the dead.

Dad was so fortunate; there's talk now that the state will ban the process completely: they've already imposed a moratorium on future trials – that's all they are.

Now that it's over, I want to share with you what I have learned about the human condition and what makes us human. Life is not about singular enjoyment of experiences, real or imagined. It's about the interaction with other human beings, with an independent existence, whose mind you can influence but not necessarily control. We are not a single person, independent of others. We function through the changes we give and receive from the people whose lives we cross, that develop us into a coherent and meaningful whole, capable of growth and goodness.

I am not angry with Simon; I am disappointed. We could have had such a wonderful relationship. I believe I worked as hard as I could at it. This is not to say that I could not have done more. In any relationship failure, both parties have some responsibility. I don't know whether what he did to my dad was criminal. The court will decide, the difficulty being that it could be argued that he was already legally dead. I am told that the most serious charge he could be convicted of is attempted murder or attempted assault. Even these may fail, as he was aware of dad's condition. To my mind, his real crime was to destroy my dreams. And now he has destroyed those of my father.

The irony is that he carried out the act that I had intended. It could easily have been me in prison. A police officer at the hospital told me that they suspected he was able to bypass security and gain access to dad's room with the help of an accomplice. She turned out to be the nurse with the tattoo I told you about. I recognised her from the photographs in the papers. Apparently, she was a member of a group objecting to the whole AI aspect of the process and infiltrated Dr Kristal's organisation.

As for the future, what will become of us as human beings? Will we live in a divided world, with half the population incorporeal, controlled by machines, or possibly worse, by individuals who may be irresponsible, manipulative people, working for their own ends or, worse still, spiteful torturers? Will there be tormented captive souls who have no hope of escape? Will the other half benefit from the thought processes of an enormous, growing number of captive brains, the thoughts of which can be controlled to work on tasks and problems, on the pretext that it is for the common good?

What is the purpose of keeping it all going? It's all we have, yet would we want it to stop, or would we prefer there to be nothing more than a void, populated largely by inanimate brains with no bodies or human interaction to give it meaning or to appreciate it?

What makes us human? It is other people and our relationships with them. If all this comes about, one day there will be a revolution. People will decide to return to the pre-cryonic days and rise up and destroy all of these preserved brains. A sub-class of the ruling humans will rebel against the machines and destroy them.

I may have been a fool, but some good has come out of this. Dad was terminally ill as a result of his fall and he was able to die as close as possible a natural death. He was a good man; if there is a heaven, he will have been welcomed at the gates. Perhaps this will confer some form of redemption on Simon and the nurse.

And dad is at peace now. Something within me tells me it is so. I feel I have been touched by his guardian angel.

I hope this helps to explain things and I apologise for the delay. I hope we might meet up again in a few weeks, when you too have had time to come to terms with it.

Love, Freya.

Freya pressed 'send'.

A knock at the door announced that her cab had arrived to start her journey home. The driver said nothing, as the car wound through the countryside.

Sitting in the back, Freya looked out at a solitary oak tree in a field.

'One of his favourite images.'

The upper branches were framed, dead, against the cerulean backdrop. The lower ones sprouted dense green foliage.

'He would have loved that, and taken comfort from it.'

THE WHITE GARDEN

I walk towards the entrance. There are words above the doorway.

Behold, I shew you a mystery; we shall not all sleep, but we shall all be changed.

I pass through the tunnel and into the light. A bright mist curls on the far side. For a moment I think I see its shape form an image of the Green Man. The illusion dissolves.

I am not conscious of my body; I think its movements. I can see my limbs moving, yet I feel nothing. I feel calm, at ease, with no sense of fear or danger.

It is a serene place, dream-like, yet I know it's real. Real, unlike anything I've known before. I am at a place where my arrival is expected, intended. I have never been here; I know it well.

There are many others here, some alone, some in groups, including a large group of children. My family are here, the ones that I love and who love me. They smile; some wave. They greet me in silence. Why are they here and how have they arrived before me? The light brightens. I now see them all clearly through the bright mist, all smiling, radiant, looking as if they have been airbrushed.

'Everyone comes here eventually, in their own time, each taking their own route.'

I am in God's waiting room, eavesdropping on his thoughts.

I hear the music again, the introduction to the In Paradisum movement of Fauré's requiem.

I no longer know what *is* or *was* real and what is a dream. I am not troubled by this; they are one and the same now.

Light…

I will go under the hill. I will submit.

I no longer know the boundary between dreams and reality: how much of what I think I remember is real and what is imagined. It doesn't matter any more. This is so unlike when I used to dream: imaginatively, creatively, but was afraid to let go of reality.

Although I am no longer aware of my body, I feel the security that comes with one hundred per cent confidence that someone else is supporting me, and that when the end comes it will be painless.

Thus only in a dream we are at one.

I don't know whether I have lived these things, or am being fed experiences from my own life, a previous life, or someone else's life: another life. Am I just an extension of a machine? A library or repository of thoughts, emotions and sensations that constantly changes form, like an amoeba?

I see a young boy, smiling at me and waving.

He has forgiven me.

I had but one debt to pay and it has been honoured. I have reached the end of my responsibility for the lives of others. I no longer need to worry about being a burden and a drain on my family. There is only the present, which I now know is the same as the future. I am assured of continuity.

I will accept and acknowledge.

I am in a new place. The past is forever behind me. There is only the present.

*There is no remembrance of former things; neither shall there be
any remembrance of things that are to come with those that
shall come after.*

ECCLESIASTES 1:11

ACKNOWLEDGEMENTS

I am indebted to several books and their authors for the factual and historical information I have called upon in the writing of Another Life.

Much of the science I learned from To Be a Machine by Mark O'Connell and Homo Deus: A Brief History of Tomorrow, by Yuval Noah Harari.

The history and origins of the Green Man are fascinating. Ronald Hutton's Pagan Britain is a comprehensive and entertaining read. Uprooted, by Nina Lyon offers a less formal, occasionally anecdotal account. The Green Man, by Kathleen Bastord, is concise in textual terms, but succinctly conveys much information that I found useful, in particular how the expressions on the images of the Green Man changed over the centuries. It contains a wealth of photographs from many locations.

The website **www.thecompanyofthegreenman.com** gathers, archives and provides freely-available information and images of the folklore associated with the Green Man and the traditional Jack-in-the-Green. It also provides a useful introduction to the history of the Green Man, together with an ever-growing gazetteer of recorded sightings of ornaments and monuments featuring the image.

The image of the Solomon's Knot came from reading *Medieval Graffiti*, by Matthew Champion, a fascinating account of the history of images recorded on walls of churches and other buildings by ordinary people, to bless their venture or to protect them from evil.

Film has provided several sources of inspiration. In a general sense, my imagination has been stimulated by the films of the great David Lynch. His ability to evoke a sense of menace and a fear that things are not as they seem, using everyday dialogue and with restraint and economy that leaves much to the reader's imagination. The students' film was inspired by the work of the Quay Brothers. I am grateful to my son for giving me the BFI DVD collection, Inner Sanctums: Quay Brothers: The collected animated films 1979-2013. I recommend this to everyone as an example of innovative creativity. Leon Carax's Holy Motors (2012) features a wealth of original, sometimes disturbing images, which again I found inspiring. To quote *The Guardian*'s review, 'Leos Carax's *Holy Motors* is weird and wonderful, rich and strange – barking mad'. Need I say more? David Rudkin's *Penda's Fen* was first transmitted by the BBC in 1974. It was unavailable for many years until the BFI released it on DVD in 2016. Set in the Malvern Hills, it features hidden pagan beliefs and evokes conflicting forces within England past and present.

And of course, I willingly acknowledge my debt to Frank Capra's evergreen *It's A Wonderful Life*, from 1946, without which *Another Life* would not have been written.

My special thanks go to Mel Thompson, a freelance writer on Philosophy, Religion and Ethics, for identifying some of the grosser errors in my drafts. I have the deepest admiration of his skills in conveying complex concepts to a general audience, and his ability to wear his knowledge lightly.

I have incorporated some real-life experiences, heavily disguised, and dreams, which are a major source of new material.

AUTHOR'S NOTE: THE WRITING OF ANOTHER LIFE

A few years ago, my 'The Invisible College' trilogy was published. It included a reference to the Green Man, whose strange face peered from the wall of a church, encircled by leaves, his image at the same time stern and smiling. The vicar describes his presence as representing a fertility symbol, common in churches and elsewhere. He explains that the ancestry of the Green Man dates back to ancient Egypt, or even further, to when the gods were feared and worshipped for their influence on the seasons and crop cycles.

Although the Green Man plays no further significant part in the trilogy, I continued to think about whether I could build a story around him. My initial research was centred on whether there was a connection with paganism, for which I found little evidence.

Around the same time, I had made notes about a character who believes he is a failure, that everything he touches goes wrong, despite his well-meaning efforts to the contrary. The key moment arrived with the idea of combining the two themes. My reading of the history of the Green Man had revealed that images of him had changed over the centuries, progressing from jovial, to merry, smiling, serene, worried, distressed, tormented and finally to resigned. This was allegedly due to changes in the political and social environments of the centuries. I was sceptical of the reasoning; it nevertheless suited my purpose that the changes in mood could mirror the mental state of my human protagonist.

And then there was the trigger, the catalyst that set in motion a train of events. I had indeed visited a 'hidden' village in the west of England thirty years ago, where I leaned on a wall and waved to a woman who noticed me absent-mindedly watching her, busying herself at an upstairs window of a stone cottage.

I now had a framework from which to build a story and Another Life was born. The mirroring of the story arc with the evolution of the Green Man lent itself to the episodic approach adopted in Part 2.

Dreams and imagined events and landscapes occur frequently. Oliver's ability to conjure up unknown images, landscapes, events and people is one that I share. It can be both terrifying and empowering, sometimes leaving me in a state of shock for hours after waking. More importantly, it is a source of material and is a blessing for which I am thankful.

Some of the incidents Oliver describes from his family life are variations on my own experiences, although none of Oliver's family is directly based on mine. I am grateful not to have lived through Oliver's troubles.

I am drawn to the idea of hidden locations: places that are 'off the map', where different rules apply, a theme I used in my The Invisible College trilogy. The setting for Another Life followed naturally, from the discovery that, to subdue the Welsh and border tribes, the Roman invaders recognised the need to assimilate their deep-rooted beliefs and traditions, integrating them into the Christianity to which they, the Romans, had been converted. The idea that pockets of local beliefs survive today, in which tightly-knit communities adhere to long-held beliefs and practise their peculiar ideology, added a defining element to the story. This is not as far-fetched as at first it seems. From time to time we are shocked by news reports of the tragic consequences of cults committing acts of control and violence, of which the outside world had previously been unaware.

Throughout Another Life, a major theme is the nebulous distinction between what is real and what is imagined. The world is becoming stranger and stranger. We must retain an open mind, while at the same time questioning everything that we are told about our past, present and future.

ABOUT THE AUTHOR

Owen W Knight is the author of The Invisible College Trilogy, an apocalyptic dystopian conspiracy tale for young adults and adults alike, described as '1984 Meets the Book of Revelation'. The trilogy comprises Book 1, They Do Things Differently Here, Book 2, Dust and Shadows, and Book 3, A Perilous Journey.

Owen was born in Southend-on-Sea at a time when children spent their days outdoors, creating imaginary worlds that formed the basis of their adventures and social interaction. He has used this experience to create a world based on documented myths, with elements of dystopia, mystery and science fiction, highlighting the use and abuse of power and the conflicts associated with maintaining ethical values.

Owen spent many years as a director of a software company and as a business and IT consultant. The experience provided him with a background of selling ideas, envisaging change, producing scenarios of differing outcomes and developing pragmatic solutions. All useful qualities to apply to creative fiction.

He is now pursuing his passion as a full-time writer, with new adult and young adult ideas in development. He is a keen photographer, whose travels have provided inspiration for researching different cultures and mythologies.

Owen lives in Essex, close to the countryside that inspired his trilogy. He regularly appears on local radio and at literary events, including the Essex Book Festival..

www.owenknight.co.uk
Twitter @OwenKnightUK

OTHER TITLES FROM BURTON MAYERS BOOKS:

October's Son

John Michaelson's haunting, biographical horror takes readers beneath the facade of vampirism and exposes the dangerous subculture operating under the guise of real vampires. Packed with first-hand accounts and commentary, Michaelson's descent into the unknown will come as a chilling revelation to those hoping for an orthodox vampire novel.

Published October 2015 – £9.99

ISBN: 978-0957338739

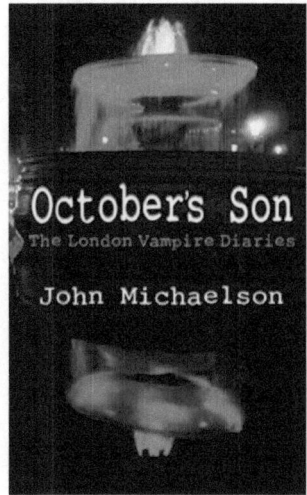

Complete Darkness

In the near future, we map the elusive 'dark matter' around us, only to find out that it is hell itself, and it is very real...

As the satanic President Razour attempts to bring forward Armageddon to prevent humanity repenting, the fate of us all rests in the hands of Cleric20, a hedonistic loner with a chequered past, and his robot sidekick, GiX.

An action-packed literary shock to the senses that mixes flights of comic fantasy with bouts of brutal violence.

Published October 2019 - £7.99

ISBN: 978-0957338777

NOTES: